Michael Hughes was born and raised in Lady, Northern Ireland, and now lives in London. He attended St Patrick's Grammar School, A..., and read English at Corpus Christi College, Oxford. He trained in theatre at the Jacques Lecoq School in Paris, and has worked for many years as an actor, under the profesional name Michael ... . He studied creative writing at Royal Holloway, and at London Metropolitan University, where he still taught. *The Countenance Divine* is his first novel.

Praise for *The Countenance Divine*

'*The Countenance Divine* is never less than superbly stimulating. It is a debut of high ambition that marks the arrival of a considerable talent'   *Guardian*

'An intriguing broth of a first novel . . . The author swoops between four centuries with considerable chutzpah . . . Hughes is thoroughly in control of his material'   *The Times*

'Sumptuous . . . A gloriously extravagant novel'   *Irish Examiner*

'A strange, witty and dazzlingly clever fable on art, ambition and morality'   Sarah Perry, *Guardian*

'One of the most exciting novels I've read in recent years. Michael Hughes writes like a brilliant cross between David Mitchell and Hilary Mantel . . . A powerful, gripping meditation on history, poetry and ...'   Toby Litt

The Countenance Divine

MICHAEL HUGHES

JOHN MURRAY

First published in Great Britain in 2016 by John Murray (Publishers)
An Hachette UK Company

First published in paperback in 2017

1

ISBN 978-1-47363-651-4
Ebook ISBN 978-1-47363-652-1

Typeset in Adobe Garamond by Palimpsest Book Production Ltd,
Falkirk, Stirlingshire

Printed and bound by Clays Ltd, St Ives plc

John Murray policy is to use papers that are natural, renewable and recyclable
products and made from wood grown in sustainable forests. The logging and
manufacturing processes are expected to conform to the environmental regulations of
the country of origin.

John Murray (Publishers)
Carmelite House
50 Victoria Embankment
London EC4Y 0DZ

www.johnmurray.co.uk

High matter thou enjoin'st me, O prime of Men —
Sad task and hard; for how shall I relate
To human sense the invisible exploits
Of warring Spirits? how, without remorse,
The ruin of so many, glorious once
And perfect while they stood? how, last, unfold
The secrets of another world, perhaps
Not lawful to reveal? Yet for thy good
This is dispensed; and what surmounts the reach
Of human sense I shall delineate so,
By likening spiritual to corporal forms,
As may express them best — though what if Earth
Be but the shadow of Heaven, and things therein
Each to other like more than on Earth is thought?

John Milton, *Paradise Lost*

Principal Characters

PART ONE

Beginning

Chapter One

01. One Sunday morning, at the end of the twentieth century, on Brick Lane market in London, a computer programmer called Chris Davison found an odd little thing. The old man who sold it, from a collection of other knick-knacks on a blanket spread on the ground, said it was a Practical Rebus. Chris didn't know what that meant, but he didn't want to admit it, so he nodded. 'Oh yes, I see,' said Chris.

Chris took the object in his hands. It was a kind of puzzle or toy made from hexagonal pieces of wood in a frame. Each piece had an image or a motif painted on it, but together they formed one overall design. The pieces could be interchanged, and every arrangement made a different pattern. He wondered if the person who made it had worked out every possible combination in advance, or if some of them were accidental.

It was a clever little thing. Chris liked it a lot. The wood was varnished and the paint had faded. It looked very old, though he knew you could never be certain. He paid the twenty pounds the old man asked. He was pretty sure that was far too much, but Chris felt sorry for him. His face was shiny and swollen, as though it had been burnt a long time ago. Chris tried not to make it obvious that he had noticed. He didn't want the man to feel bad.

On the walk home, Chris had a funny feeling that something awful was happening nearby. Every time he turned a corner, he kept expecting to find someone lying dead in the street. He had a very clear image of it in his head. He knew it must be from a film he'd seen, but he couldn't think which one.

He tried to ignore it. He had always felt safe in London, even though he did know people who had been mugged. This area was becoming fashionable, but there was still a lot of poverty. Chris was careful never to wear his Discman in the street, and not to carry his laptop unless he had to.

When he got home, Chris put the little wooden object on his desk by his computer. If he was stuck on something, or he wanted to take a break, he played with it. He arranged it in different configurations and tried to see something in each new pattern. He always did.

He wondered if he should bring it into work to show Lucy.

He decided not to.

Sometimes, when he looked at it for a long time, he had very strange thoughts. He had been alive for hundreds of years. The city was on fire, and he was hiding underground. He was making a tiny man out of clay. His hands were digging around inside a woman's belly. The world was about to end, and it was all his fault. They felt like things he could remember, but he had no idea where they came from.

Other times he just held the little thing, and thought about the people who might have owned it and played with it in the past. He wondered if they had ever tried to imagine someone else having it after them. Once in a while Chris pretended that he was this person, living long ago, and the modern world around him was just his fantasy of what the future might be like. He enjoyed that.

When he was younger, Chris used to do the same thing. He

would always try to imagine his life in the year two thousand. That was the beginning of the future. If only I could have a glimpse of myself then, he used to think, I would know who I'm going to be.

Now, it was only a few months away. It made him smile to remember how he once thought twenty-seven years old was far into adulthood. He had been certain that, by now, his life would have achieved its final form. In his young imagination, nineteen ninety-nine was the end point, the culmination of everything. Civilisation would have been perfected. Things would stop changing. History would be over.

These days, Chris never thought very much about the past. He didn't own any other old things. He hadn't taken anything with him when he first moved to London, and everything he had bought since was modern and new. When he thought about it, he realised the oldest thing in his flat was him.

He knew that wasn't completely true. He knew that the materials his stuff was made from, the metal or the wood, could be any age at all. Everything was made of something else.

But this little thing he had bought was different. It just seemed to be itself. Chris couldn't shake the feeling it had been meant for him. When he touched it, he felt a physical connection to an entire world that no longer existed.

02. As a child, Chris sometimes doubted that the past was real. He used to enjoy thinking that the world had come into existence when he was born, and it would end when he died.

If the family was on a long journey, he used to daydream that they were driving through a series of domes, each only a few miles in diameter. The domes were connected by tunnels. When it got foggy or cloudy, and he couldn't see very far into the distance, that was to hide the tunnel. When the weather cleared, and he could see further ahead, that meant they were inside a new dome. Everything he could see was everything that existed. This fake world was laid out entirely for his benefit, to accommodate his movements, which appeared spontaneous to him but were actually controlled from somewhere else.

Other days, the past felt very real, but very far away. He simply understood the vast distance from then to now. He would stare out the car window, looking for signs of modern life in the countryside, and imagine he was explaining this strange world to a visitor from another time. That was his favourite game.

He still did it now, once in a while. He imagined he was giving a presentation to a room full of notable people from history, great thinkers and writers and leaders, all transported to the present. They were hanging on his every word. It was a dazzling performance, illuminating what had otherwise seemed a confusing and hostile place, in clear and simple terms.

He especially liked to explain to them how computers worked. He had honed this speech on flights and Tube journeys, in reveries during dull meetings, while lying in bed at night. He thought it was a shame he couldn't actually give the lecture in public. He knew there were lots of people who didn't understand very much about modern technology. No one ever bothered to explain it, and no one ever asked. As long as it worked, and it made their lives easier, they really didn't care. It might just as well have been some kind of magic.

03. At primary school, Chris used to tell his friends he was an android. He remembered one day, when he couldn't have been more than six or seven. The teacher asked them, for their home-

work, to find out from their parents what time of day they were born. He put his hand up and asked what if you weren't born. He didn't remember anything after that, except a sensation of blushing.

Even when he grew out of that delusion, he held on to the fantasy. He hated the human parts of himself that got tired, and needed the toilet, and had to eat. It was such a waste of time. He sometimes thought he preferred machines to people. They were efficient, hard-working, reasonable and obedient. That was how Chris saw himself. That was how he tried to be.

He wished he could be a cyborg. He would keep his identity, but have it work within a perfect artificial body. He had always been convinced that, by now, this should be possible. He was genuinely disappointed it wasn't. He was still sure it would be, one day. He wished it would hurry up. He often got frustrated that he found so much of life so difficult. He had thought being an adult would be easier.

Sometimes Chris was afraid that everything could only get worse. He knew that any closed system left alone would eventually tend to decay. That was the essence of the second law of thermodynamics. Entropy increases. Just to keep things as they are, you have to constantly improve them. The only alternative is to sweep it all away and start again.

That was what Chris really wanted. He wished there was something he could do to make it happen. But he didn't know what. So instead of making things better, the best he could do was stop them from falling apart.

04. Chris's job was fixing the Millennium Bug. That was what most people called it, but in the industry it was known as the Year Two Thousand Problem.

The problem itself was very simple, and Chris enjoyed explaining it. Because the first computers had limited memory, a convention developed to identify years by using two-digit numbers, without a nineteen at the beginning, from double zero up to ninety-nine. By the time computers had enough memory for four digits, the convention had become a tradition, and no one questioned why it was done.

Decades later, most computers still didn't know any better. They thought time itself only ran for a hundred years.

When the next new century came, exactly at midnight, as ninety-nine ended and double zero began, those computers would think that, instead of moving one second into the future, they had gone a hundred years into the past. They would have reached the end of time. Everything would start again from the beginning.

05. Chris knew that computers didn't really think anything. They were just machines, which used fixed rules of logic to carry out calculations, faster and more reliably than we could.

But some of these calculations involved future events, and we'd forgotten to tell them that the future didn't stop at the end of nineteen ninety-nine. As far as the computers understood, everything to come after that had already taken place long ago.

Some of them would figure out this was wrong, and tell us. Others would simply stop working. Some would continue to function, but give out inaccurate information. Others would be entirely unaffected. The trouble was, there was no way to predict which, and not enough time to check all of them just in case. By the time we realised this was a serious problem, it was already too late.

A lot of people, especially in America, talked about The End

Of The World. Energy supplies would fail, planes would fall out of the sky, nuclear power stations would explode. The most anxious had sold their houses and moved to the middle of nowhere, with stockpiles of food and gold. A few of them were even looking forward to it. The corruptions of the modern world would be swept away. Life would be simple and pure again.

Chris thought this was over the top. There were power cuts all the time, computers crashed and systems failed. The world hadn't ended yet. And even if everything went wrong all at once, the collapse-of-civilisation scenario relied on the belief that people were stupid and selfish, or would run around in circles panicking.

Chris imagined most people would probably get on with their day as best they could, which would include starting to fix things. In a couple of weeks, most basics would be up and running. A few months later, you'd hardly know anything had happened.

And that was in the worst-case scenario. As far as he could tell, none of this was going to happen. Even if the panic had been justified to start with, there was so much work going into fixing essential systems that probably no one would notice anything at all. It would just be another new year.

06. Chris liked his job. It was hard work and the hours were long, but he was very good at it, and the pay was excellent. He had never imagined he would earn that sort of money at his age, especially for doing something he enjoyed. But he had never thought very much about what he would do for a living. He had imagined something would just come up. It didn't.

He had felt lost when he finished university. It was supposed to be the start of his life, but it felt like the end. He went travelling for a couple of months, because everyone he knew said he should, but he hated it. Other countries never felt completely real to him. Somewhere deep down, he couldn't shake the sense that it was all put on, like a film set, or a show organised for tourists.

He started to feel that way too when he was in other parts of England, even around where he grew up. The pretty little villages were too perfect, as though they'd been rebuilt in the style of some imaginary past. And the other cities, he thought, were just trying to be London and not even getting close.

He had loved London since he first arrived at university. It gave him everything he didn't have inside him. He felt like he couldn't manage anywhere else. London was the only thing he was absolutely sure about.

07. Chris had asked around. One of his university friends had an attic room going in her parents' place. They were moving abroad while they had the house done up, and they wanted someone to deal with the builders and keep an eye on the gardener.

He ended up staying for two years, even after the renovations were finished. He worked at a cinema for a while, selling tickets. Then he took a job with an agency that monitored the news. He had to read all the papers and watch news broadcasts, and highlight any mentions of a particular company or subject.

For a while, he became very interested in politics and current affairs. He thought he might like to be a journalist. But he didn't know how to get started, and he didn't know who to ask.

The agency closed down. Chris decided to sign on for a while. He thought it might be a good way to get some more training without paying for it.

They offered him a computer course, and he found he was

good at it. Chris had done Computer Science for a while when he was at school, but it didn't feel like a proper subject, and he thought the teacher didn't understand it very well. This time, it was different. He felt at home. It reminded him of why he'd always enjoyed Maths at school. He liked to work out the underlying principles for himself, and then use them to solve a new problem.

It was the same with computers. You followed the rules, and applied logic. Everything was under control.

08. When the course finished, Tammy and Al, who ran it, told Chris they were very impressed with his work. They said they were starting a business in Year Two Thousand compliance and asked would he like to be involved.

He said yes. And that was it. He had a job. He rented a flat in Shoreditch, and got the bus in and out to the office near St Paul's every day.

He was happy. This was who he was going to be.

09. When he first met them, Chris assumed Tammy and Al were a couple. Tammy explained to him one day that they had been for a bit, when they were students, but they'd decided they worked better as friends. She said she didn't believe in mixing business with pleasure. Chris agreed.

He didn't have a girlfriend. He lived alone, and he liked it that way. He couldn't imagine sharing with someone else.

He had the occasional fling with girls he met when he was out at the weekend, friends of people he knew from university, but it never lasted more than a week or two. Sometimes Chris didn't sleep with anyone for a couple of months. He didn't really mind. It meant his life was uncomplicated, and he wanted to keep it that way. He liked knowing what was going to happen tomorrow, and he liked that it was very much the same as what had happened today.

10. The business began to take off. After a few months, there was more work coming in than they could handle. Tammy hired Lucy, another programmer. She said she wanted a woman because she hated being in an office that was all men.

Al wasn't very happy. He said Lucy didn't bring an especially pleasant vibe to the working environment. He said her chief modes of expression were silence and sarcasm. Tammy said she was perfectly fine once you got used to her. Chris didn't know what to think.

11. Lucy was a sort of goth. She had dyed straight black hair. She always wore obvious make-up and she dressed entirely in black, with lots of silver jewellery. She had six or seven piercings in each ear. She had one in her nose, and one in her tongue, and she said she had one in her belly button, though Chris had never seen it. She told them one day that she had others in her nipples and in her clit, but Chris didn't know whether to believe that.

She never seemed especially happy or unhappy, but she had plenty of attitude. She hardly ever smiled, and when she laughed it was usually mockery. Nobody ever saw her eat, though after work she drank as much as anyone. During the day she seemed to live on cups of tea and cigarettes. She smoked Marlboros, the red ones, and she always left the packet out on her desk where people could see.

Al told Chris he knew her type. She was all mouth and no trousers. Tammy said she was extremely good at her job, and no one would care how she looked or behaved if she was a man. Chris thought that was probably true.

12. Chris tried his best to be friendly to Lucy. He was confused and upset that she wasn't friendly in return. He wasn't used to that.

Al told him not to take it personally. He was wasting his time. She was the same with everyone.

Chris didn't want to be everyone. He saw himself as a particularly kind person. It was important to him that he could get on with people. He hated the idea of anyone not liking him. As far as he knew, he had no enemies. He couldn't really imagine what having an enemy would be like. He was sure they could never think worse thoughts about him than he sometimes thought about himself.

He had always tried to be good. He couldn't understand why other people didn't. Everyone knew that's what you were supposed to do. He didn't automatically like every single person, but he tried not to judge them. And he found that if you were pleasant and patient, they would almost always be the same in return.

Lucy wasn't. She just stared at him, or ignored him completely.

13. Lucy wasn't the same with everyone. She and Al developed a sort of bantering relationship. He was always having a go, and she gave it right back, in her deadpan northern accent. Chris couldn't figure out if they were enjoying it, or if they actually hated each other. Sometimes he wondered if they weren't sure themselves.

'You know a lot of blokes think you're a dyke,' said Al one

day. 'I wish they did,' said Lucy. 'I don't,' said Al, 'because I'm broad-minded.' 'Christ,' said Lucy. 'I'd hate to meet somebody narrow-minded.' 'You would indeed,' said Al. 'Your problem is, you think the sort of people you hang about with are most people.' 'Believe me, I don't,' said Lucy. 'I hang about with the people I hang about with because I want to stay far away from most people.' 'Very wise,' said Al. 'The trouble with democracy, as Winston Churchill once said, is that most people are cunts.' 'I'm not sure Churchill said that,' said Tammy. 'Well he should have done,' said Al. 'Something we can agree on at last,' said Lucy. 'I'm not most people,' said Al. 'That's not what Winston Churchill thinks,' said Lucy.

14. Chris invented a private nickname for Lucy. He called her Dark Satanic Mills, because her surname was Mills, and because of how she dressed. It was a phrase from the hymn 'Jerusalem', which his dad used to make him sing when the rugby was on. Chris could still remember most of the words.

He never called her that out loud. He didn't even know what it meant. It just seemed to fit her, and it made her seem less scary when he was thinking about her.

He thought about her a lot. When he asked himself why, he decided she was a puzzle he hadn't solved yet. But he was convinced he could.

15. Chris made it his business to make friends with Lucy. He paid attention to what she talked about. He read reviews of the books and CDs she bought during lunch at Dillons and Our Price. He watched the films she mentioned, and then he mentioned them too.

She went on a lot about *The Matrix*, which she had gone to see three or four times. Chris thought she was a bit obsessed with it. When he went on the Web, he kept an eye on the various newsgroup theories about what it meant, so he could discuss them with her.

It wasn't completely forced, Chris told himself. Everything was interesting, if you got into it enough. And since he didn't have many interests of his own, he was happy to borrow someone else's.

Lucy seemed wary at first. But he could see she was glad to find there was someone at work who was into the same things.

They started to take cigarette breaks together, and go out to get lunch, though she always had some excuse not to eat anything. She made him a couple of tapes of music she liked, and lent him some videos.

16. One day Lucy brought in a book for Chris to borrow. It was a graphic novel about Jack the Ripper called *From Hell*. She said it had just come out, but it was already her new favourite thing.

She told Chris the title was the return address given on a famous letter sent at the time of the real killings, in eighteen eighty-eight. It was posted to a man called Lusk, who was investigating the murders, along with a jar containing half the kidney of one of the victims. The letter claimed to be from the killer, and it said he had eaten the other half.

'I'm not sure I understand the great fascination with serial killers,' said Chris. 'Good,' said Lucy. 'I don't either. It's those five poor women I care about. Nobody gives a fuck about them. A hundred years later, and everybody's still obsessed with the sick bastard who ripped them up and ate their guts. It freaks me out.'

'I don't know if he really ate their guts,' said Chris. 'It says so in the letter,' said Lucy. 'Right,' said Chris. 'I wonder if the killer actually wrote that, though.' 'If he didn't,' said Lucy, 'then some other sick bastard did, pretending to be him. If you ask me, that's worse.'

The graphic novel was full of outlandish conspiracy theories about why those particular women were killed on those particular days. There was lots of stuff Chris didn't understand about supernatural forces and the occult. It was the kind of thing he usually hated, but he found it quite engrossing. He told Lucy he liked it, and she said that was good news. He had passed the first test. Chris didn't like the sound of that, but he just smiled. Lucy didn't.

17. Al liked to joke that Chris and Lucy were an item. When she was out of the office, he would ask Chris if she had taken it up the arse yet. He said the piercings were a good sign.

Chris tried to ignore it. Tammy just laughed. She once told Chris she thought the truth was that Al quite fancied Lucy, but he didn't want to admit it.

Al always talked a lot about sex, but he said he didn't want a girlfriend. His problem was that he didn't like having anyone else in the bed at night. He could never get to sleep, he said. So most of the time these days, he kept things basic. He said his ideal Saturday night was a few drinks, a line or two, and then a blow job in his car.

'It's why I'll never get one with a cloth trim,' said Al one Monday morning. 'Maybe if I tie the knot. You ever see me driving a car with seats you can't wipe down, you'll know I'm a changed man.' 'Christ, you're sad,' said Lucy. 'You say so,' said Al, 'but girls go for me.' 'Some girls, maybe,' said Lucy. 'That's right, Lucy dear,' said Al. 'Some girls is all I'm interested in. Some girls is plenty for me. I'm not greedy. My great piece of good fortune is, the sort of girl I'm attracted to is the sort of girl who's attracted to me. It's the pursuit of the unattainable that leads to misery.' 'You'd better not try it on with me,' said Lucy. 'I'll show you misery all right.' 'I'd say so,' said Al. 'Oh get a room, you two,' said Tammy. Al winked at Lucy. 'In your dreams,' said Lucy. 'In my nightmares,' said Al.

Chris found it exhausting to listen to Lucy and Al compete over who would get the last word. It could go on all day. Sometimes he pretended he had to go out to see a client just to get away from them.

18. 'Once,' said Al another day, 'I got so fed up with all the chatting and listening and buying drinks, that I decided to just wait till the end of the night, and then pick one of the girls who was still on her own, and say, Fancy a fuck?' 'And how did that work out for you?' said Lucy. 'Please don't encourage him,' said Tammy. 'That's the funny thing,' said Al. 'Not all of them said yes, not by any means. But quite a number did. More than I would have expected. And when I worked it out after a few weeks, my hit rate was more or less the same.' 'Somewhere near zero,' said Lucy. 'Quite near,' said Al. 'As in, one. I only want one at a time, Lucy dear. Not into anything pervy.' 'Christ,' said Lucy. 'If a threesome is your idea of pervy, then you really need to get out more.' 'Simple pleasures,' said Al. 'I'm a simple bloke.' 'Simple's one word for it,' said Lucy.

19. 'I love ugly women,' said Al one evening, when they were all in the pub. 'They're so grateful.' 'The whole New Man thing just passed you by completely, didn't it, Al?' said Lucy. 'New Man is old news,' said Tammy. 'It's all about Mr Darcy now.' 'That's me,' said Al. 'Strong silent type.' 'I wish you were,' said Lucy. 'And how do these less attractive ladies show their gratitude?' said Tammy. 'In the time-honoured tradition,' said Al. 'Oh Christ,' said Lucy. 'I can't stand hearing any more about your bloody blow jobs. Do you never give these lasses a proper seeing-to?' 'Once in a while,' said Al. 'But only from behind.'

'You know what I think?' said Lucy to Tammy. 'I think he's actually a virgin. I think he's never had a shag in his life. I think he gets it all from reading *Loaded*.' 'If we were in America,' said Tammy to Al, 'I could have you dismissed for sexual harassment.' 'Steady on,' said Al. 'I've never tried it on with anyone at work.' 'For the stories, you fuckwit,' said Lucy. 'For talking filth all day long in front of the ladies.' 'What ladies?' said Al. 'I can't see any ladies in here.' 'Charming,' said Tammy. 'See, that's where Clinton ballsed it up,' said Al. 'Schoolboy error. Don't shit where you eat.'

'What do you think, Chris?' said Tammy. 'Sorry,' said Chris, 'I was miles away.' (This wasn't true, but he didn't want to have to take sides.) 'Wish I was,' said Lucy. 'Anyway,' said Al, 'I never fancy Americans. They've got no sense of humour.' 'A sense of humour is what a girl would need if she was going to cop off with you,' said Lucy. 'I definitely give them something to smile about,' said Al. 'What, a throatful of your jism?' said Lucy. 'Stop it or I'll vom,' said Tammy. 'I never heard you complain,' said Al. 'That's because you'd passed out,' said Tammy. 'Fair's fair,' said Al. 'I treat a girl properly. I always buy the drinks.' 'Mine's a Listerine,' said Lucy.

20. Even though they spent a lot of time together, Chris still had no idea if Lucy actually liked him. It bothered him a lot. He never knew where he was with her. If he said the wrong thing, she mightn't speak to him for the rest of the day. Then the next morning, it would all be forgotten.

All the same, Chris found he did like her. She was sharp, and thoughtful, and intense. She didn't make everything into a joke, like Al, or spend most of her time bitching about hopeless men, like Tammy.

21. When Lucy didn't come to work for a couple of days, Chris wondered if something was up. Tammy said she had called in sick, but Chris had a nagging feeling there was more to it than that. He was worried that something was going on, but she didn't want to say.

He was also concerned about her work. It had always been impeccable, but recently there'd been a few complaints from clients whose software she had worked on. Processes that already used dates beyond the end of the year were giving out strange results.

When he'd asked her to take another look, she blamed the clients not understanding their own systems. He wasn't convinced. He decided to recommend that Tammy take her off programming for a while, and put her onto certifying compliance. Tammy said they couldn't afford to lose a programmer. She asked Chris to keep an eye on things.

22. When Lucy stayed off the rest of the week, Chris began to get really concerned. He couldn't shake the idea that something bad had happened to her, and he was somehow responsible. When he played with his little wooden toy, he kept thinking about her throat being cut. He saw her guts being ripped out, over and over again. The street outside his flat was running with blood. The earth was crumbling, and the sky was on fire, and he was to blame.

Chris told himself to get a grip, and stop imagining things, and just check that Lucy was okay. He didn't have her phone number, so he sent an email from work that Friday. He was pretty sure she had a computer at home, and an Internet connection. To his surprise, she sent an email back a few minutes later. She asked him if he wanted to come to a gig that night, but not to tell Tammy.

He found he was happy she had asked. He said yes.

23. Chris hated the gig. It was very loud electronic punk. He couldn't make out a melody, and the bass was so heavy that the whole building shook. Lucy told him the vibrations were so strong at some of their gigs, it made people in the audience lose control of their bowels and shit themselves. She said that like it was cool, or funny.

Chris didn't think it was. It frightened him a bit. It worried him that anyone might think that was a good thing in any way whatsoever.

24. Afterwards they went to a bar. Lucy didn't seem ill at all. But she didn't mention anything about being off sick, so Chris didn't bring it up.

They drank vodka and smoked her cigarettes for a couple of hours. Chris didn't usually smoke very much, but he always did when he was with Lucy. It was only ten o'clock but they were already into her second packet of the evening. She didn't seem to mind. She said he could buy her more later on. It looked like she wanted it to be a long night.

Lucy talked for a while about the gig, but Chris couldn't think of anything to say without letting her know he had hated it. He started to talk about work instead. He'd been thinking a lot about their job, and he had a few theories he wanted to share with her.

Very often these days, Chris told her, he got frustrated with the software he was working on. There was a basic structure that had been put in place maybe a decade before, with all sorts of bits and pieces added on around it. It was like a garden shed that had grown into a whole shanty-town. It would be so much simpler, he thought, to scrap all the messy old software and design a completely new system. But the problem was, as long as it worked pretty well most of the time, people were happy to leave things how they were.

Now that everything might actually stop working, real action was finally being taken. But instead of starting from scratch, they were asking him to tack on yet another extra bit, a jerry-built chunk of code that would trick the system into behaving. It would do the job for now, but sooner or later the whole lot would have to be fixed properly.

'And sometimes,' said Chris, 'I actually think it might have been better to completely ignore the problem, and let everything go wrong. Sometimes at work I get this wicked urge to do nothing, and just pretend I'm fixing it. I want to leave things exactly as they are and see if the sky really will fall in. And if it does, then we could start all over again, and we'd finally have a chance to get it right.'

'You're talking shite,' said Lucy. 'It doesn't matter where you start, there'll always be things that need fixing and new stuff to be added on. You can never get anything perfect. It always falls apart in the end.' 'That doesn't mean it's better to just muddle along,' said Chris. 'The old systems that have grown up organically will have to be replaced some day. So why wait for them to go wrong? Why not do it now?'

'Are you saying anything new is automatically better?' said Lucy. 'Obviously it is,' said Chris, 'otherwise we would still use the old ones.' 'People do still use the old ones,' said Lucy. 'It's only you who's saying they shouldn't.' 'It's very simple,' said Chris. 'If we actually want things to get better, instead of just not falling apart, there's no other way. We have to get rid of everything we have already, and start again.' 'That's bollocks,' said Lucy. 'That's what caused the Nazis and Pol Pot.'

'But don't you think we should even try to improve things?' said Chris. 'Why bother?' said Lucy. 'It never works.' 'So basically it all just keeps getting worse,' said Chris. 'Fucking right,' said Lucy. 'And there's nothing anybody can do about it. That's what life is.' 'If I thought that, I'd kill myself,' said Chris. 'The future's got to be better than the past, otherwise what's the point?' 'There is no point,' said Lucy. 'The best it'll ever be was a long, long time ago. And it's not coming back. But fine, whatever. I couldn't give a monkey's. We're all going to die anyway.'

'I don't believe you really think that,' said Chris. 'Don't you ever get anxious about the huge responsibility of what we're doing at work?' 'That's the best part,' said Lucy. 'I love the sense of power. It's like having your finger on the nuclear button. Gives me a right bonk-on. But I don't waste my time worrying about fucking things up. I'm only doing this stupid job for the money, so I can get on with my other stuff.'

Chris was annoyed by that, but he wasn't sure why. He didn't ask what her other stuff was, though he could tell she was dying to tell him. He asked if she wanted another drink. She ignored that. She said she needed a regular income just now because she was working on something very big. She said she wasn't supposed to talk about it to just anybody. Chris said that was fine, she didn't have to. Lucy said he wasn't just anybody. Chris wondered if that meant she liked him. He still couldn't stand the thought that she didn't like him. He asked her what her other stuff was.

She was an artist, she said. That was the only thing she was serious about. Chris was surprised. She'd never said anything about it before. He asked what sort of art she did. She said she worked with a collective, and they were getting a major project ready for the end of the year. It was going to be fucking amazing. Maybe he could even come and take part, on New Year's Eve, if he didn't have other plans.

25. Chris didn't have other plans. He had vaguely imagined he'd be at a cool party somewhere, if he wasn't working, but he didn't really know those kinds of people. Maybe Lucy's project would be that, he thought. On the other hand, he didn't want to tie himself down so far in advance. It was still only September. He told her he would probably be with his family, but if not, he would definitely keep it in mind.

This wasn't true. That was the one place he knew he definitely wouldn't be. About a year before, his sister Jenny had broken up with her husband Brian and moved back to where they grew up, so their mum could help with the children. Brian had been a sort-of friend of Chris's, which was how Jenny had met him, and she'd been funny with Chris ever since the break-up. She acted like it was somehow his fault, even though Chris hadn't been in touch with Brian since, out of loyalty to her.

Since then Chris hadn't been to visit, even at Christmas. He always said he was too busy, which was only sometimes true. He still phoned most Sunday evenings, but he just half-listened to his mum talking about people he'd been to school with, while he watched TV with the sound down low. He never asked how they all were or what they were doing, and they never asked him about his life. He preferred it that way. That was the thing about living in London instead of back there. No one was watching.

26. Lucy asked Chris if he thought the Year Two Thousand Problem really did mean the end of the world. He said he didn't. She told Chris she had to listen to that stuff all the time from her ex-boyfriend, who was working on the project too. He was obsessed with the old poet William Blake, who wrote 'Jerusalem' and 'Tyger Tyger', about two hundred years ago.

She asked Chris if he knew those poems. Chris said he did. He wondered if Lucy had somehow found out about his private nickname for her, and she was saying all this just to wind him up. He felt like he was blushing. He hoped she couldn't tell.

Lucy told him William Blake believed that Jesus had come to England when he was a baby, and that London was the New Jerusalem. This was the final paradise God would set up on earth, once the Devil had been defeated at the end of time. It was in the Bible, she said, in the Book of Revelation. The poem 'Jerusalem' talked as if this had already happened long ago, but somehow we had lost it, and we had to fight to get it back.

She told Chris that poem wasn't really called 'Jerusalem'. It was a bit taken from the beginning of a longer poem Blake wrote called *Milton*, about the old blind poet who wrote *Paradise Lost* coming back from the dead to talk to him. Her ex always said Blake was a kind of prophet, and saw things that no one else could.

Chris told her he didn't believe in anything supernatural. Life was complicated enough already. Lucy said it wasn't like that. There was another way of looking at the world, where everything was connected, including the past and the future. Prophets were just people who were good at reading the signs. And there were a lot of prophecies about the world ending this year. Chris said he would be amazed if there was anything specific. Those things were always so vague, you could read anything you liked into them.

'What about Nostradamus?' said Lucy. 'He predicted the end of the world for this year. There'll be a world war in nineteen ninety-nine that's going to wipe out civilisation.' 'When did he say that?' said Chris. 'In fifteen fifty-five,' said Lucy. 'That's the whole point. It always happens when the numbers line up. And this year is the last one. The air will turn to fire and consume the face of the earth. I'm telling you, there's going to be a bloody great war.' 'No there isn't,' said Chris. 'Look at the news. Even if another world war was going to happen some day, it couldn't be as soon as before the end of the year. We'd see it coming.'

'What if somebody just ups and bombs the Houses of Parliament?' said Lucy. 'Who?' said Chris. 'I don't know,' said Lucy. 'Some gang of nutters.' 'That's different,' said Chris. 'You can't go to war against a gang of nutters. Only a country. And no country is going to be stupid enough to launch a surprise attack on a nuclear power.' 'They might do,' said Lucy. 'It would be complete suicide,' said Chris. 'Some people are happy to die if the cause is worth it,' said Lucy. 'What kind of cause?' said Chris. 'They might just think we need a rude awakening,' said Lucy. 'And I think we probably do.'

'You mean you want someone to blow up the Houses of Parliament?' said Chris. 'Why not?' said Lucy. 'Some fucking thing. Don't you miss real stuff going on in the world? Proper news. Not just Bill Clinton shoving his cigar up some fat little tart's twat-hole. There's evenings I get embarrassed for Peter Sissons. Honestly, I'm so bored of everybody feeling smug and safe. We need teaching a lesson.' 'What lesson do we need teaching?' said Chris. 'Pride before a fall,' said Lucy. 'Nothing lasts forever.'

'You almost sound as if you'd quite like to see civilisation collapse,' said Chris. 'Fucking right,' said Lucy. 'I used to fantasise about a nuclear war. I really wanted it to happen. Playing out in the ruins, like my grandad talks about. Having to make everything over again, out of old junk. Totally *Mad Max.*' 'So that's what you think is going to happen after New Year?' said Chris. 'Just wait,' said Lucy. 'And you'll not see it coming. Nobody will. We're fixing the clocks, so everybody can sleep cosy in their little beds. They won't know a thing about it. Tick, tock, and it's all gone. Just like nothing was ever there in the first place.' 'That's a bit depressing,' said Chris. 'Don't be a baby,' said Lucy. 'History's over, mate. Everything's happened already. Nothing's real any more. The future's shit.'

27. Lucy asked Chris if he fancied meeting the other people she worked with in the art collective. There was a house party, she said, and some of them would be going.

He didn't want to go home yet, so he said okay. He couldn't

tell any more whether Lucy actually believed the stuff she was saying, or if it was just part of her art project, but he was enjoying himself all the same. He had been trying not to drink too much, but he thought it was probably too late now, and he might as well make a night of it. He didn't like drinking too much, but once wouldn't be the end of the world.

They had to run to get the last Tube.

28. By the time they got to the party, most of the people Lucy knew had already left. She told Chris some of them were quite a bit older, and had families. That surprised him. He had imagined they were all like Lucy.

He wondered if he was underestimating her. She might actually be a talented artist. He wasn't sure he would know the difference.

Lucy introduced him to one young guy called Oliver, who was in charge of the stuff she was working on. He was tall, and slim, and very polite. Chris liked him.

Chris asked how many people were involved. Oliver said he wasn't sure exactly. What he and Lucy were working on was only one element of the overall thing. Chris asked what sort of thing it was. Oliver looked at Lucy, and then looked back at Chris.

Lucy said it was top secret. If they gave away too much in advance, it would spoil the surprise. Chris asked how they expected anyone to turn up, if they didn't give some idea. Oliver laughed, and said that was exactly what he'd been thinking.

He said they still had different views on how it should work in the end, but he could best describe it as a vision of London, past, present and future. There were a few significant moments in history they were especially interested in, one from each of the previous three centuries. He'd been doing a lot of research, and he'd found out some interesting things. It was just a question of how to bring it all together. But when they did, he said, it would really be something special.

Oliver asked Chris if he might like to be part of it. Chris said he didn't know very much about history. Oliver said he probably knew more than he realised. He asked Chris if he had heard of Jack the Ripper, and William Blake, and John Milton. Chris said he had, but he didn't really know a lot about them.

Oliver said John Milton was a blind poet in the seventeenth century who wrote an epic poem called *Paradise Lost*, which told the story of Adam and Eve, and described the war in heaven between God and the Devil. He said that even though Milton was a devout Christian, most people thought he had made Satan a more interesting character than God. William Blake said that Milton was of the Devil's party without knowing it.

'Blake was another poet,' said Oliver, 'a bit more than a century later. His work was pretty much ignored during his lifetime, but today it's seen as very significant. He was an artist as well, and some critics now think he was one of the most important England ever produced. Many of his greatest works were inspired by visions he had. Some people thought he was mad, but others said he was a true genius.'

'What about Jack the Ripper?' said Chris. 'That's the big question,' said Oliver. 'Nobody knows anything about him, except that he was the person who did what he did. But of course there are various theories as to who and why, some more plausible than others.' 'And what do you think?' said Chris. 'I think someone, somewhere probably knows the truth,' said Oliver. 'But it's almost certainly less interesting than the mystery.'

Chris thought it all sounded quite good. He asked if he could bring a few friends along too. Oliver said they didn't want lots of people. It would be invitation-only. Some of it was already underway, and more would be up and running soon, but the whole thing would only come together at the end, on New Year's Eve itself. There was still a lot of work to do. They weren't really supposed to discuss it at all at this stage, he said. He would have to give Lucy a scolding. Lucy told him he could fuck right off. Oliver laughed, and said in fact he better had, but it had been nice to meet Chris. He had heard a lot about him from Lucy.

That surprised Chris. He looked to check if Lucy had heard, but she was talking to someone else now. He said goodbye to Oliver. He said he hoped he'd see him again some time. Oliver said he thought that was highly likely.

After Oliver left, Chris asked Lucy if she wanted to stay. She did, so he said he would too. He told her he was enjoying himself, though he wasn't sure if he still was. He had liked Oliver very much, but something about their conversation made him feel embarrassed and awkward, as if he wasn't quite good enough.

29. The house was really packed, and the music was very loud, so Chris and Lucy went out to the garden. Some people were talking about computers, and Chris said that was what they worked in. He explained they were fixing the Millennium Bug. One girl said not to fix it, she wanted to see what the end of the world would be like. 'I know what it'll be like,' said Lucy. 'I'll be dressed in leather, sat on the back of a motorbike, shooting at stupid twats like you.'

A bloke in a suit said computers were bullshit anyway. The Internet wasn't going to catch on. He could see the point of it for porn, but it wasn't much good at anything else. There was no way to make money off of it. Chris said what about advertising. The bloke said that didn't add up, and it never would, unless everyone carried a little computer in their pocket and they were surfing the Net all day long. Lucy said that would probably happen before long. The bloke said it wouldn't be in their lifetime.

Lucy said she wasn't going to listen to anybody who said surfing the Net. No one actually called it that. The bloke in the suit said lots of people did. Lucy said he meant the Web, not the Net. Net just made her think of fish. The bloke said Web made him think of spiders. Which was about right, he said, with all the creepy shit there was on there.

They started talking about Web pages and groups for people with odd sexual fetishes. Lucy said she found it quite moving that there were all these people out there who used to think they were the only one with a particular thing. Now they could find other people to talk to, and realise they weren't freaks. The bloke said they definitely were freaks. He was quite drunk, and he looked like he wanted a row.

The others said it was getting too cold, and went inside. Lucy said she wasn't cold, and Chris said he wasn't either, though that wasn't true. Nobody spoke for a couple of minutes. Then the drunk bloke said he was going inside as well. He could tell when he wasn't wanted. 'Fish,' said Lucy. 'Spiders,' said the bloke. He went.

'They're both things to catch you in,' said Lucy. 'What are?' said Chris. 'Nets and webs,' said Lucy. 'The difference is, the fish gets caught in the net, but the spider's in control of the web.' 'What about the poor fly?' said Chris. 'Well exactly,' said Lucy. She told him she was lucky, because her kind of porn wasn't even porn. Piercings were what turned her on, her own and other people's. Chris was startled that she was happy to admit this kind of thing so easily. But he just nodded and pretended it was a completely normal subject to talk about.

Lucy said the biggest rush she ever had was getting a new piercing. Finding out somebody she fancied had piercings made her fancy him even more. She said she hardly ever fancied women, unless they had lots of piercings, and then she almost always did. There were loads of piercings groups on the Web, and that was where she went when she was feeling horny, to look at the pictures. There were Web pages for men who liked pierced women, and she had a right laugh going on the message boards and teasing them. She thought most of them probably assumed she was a man too, pretending to be a woman, but that just added to the fun. She liked having a place where she could flirt as much as she wanted, but she was always in control. She enjoyed being the spider and not the fly for a change.

Chris wasn't sure what he was supposed to say to that. He didn't say anything. They were both quiet for a while. Lucy said she didn't know why she'd told him that stuff. She had never talked to anybody about it before, even her ex-boyfriend. But she felt like Chris was somebody she could say anything to. She hoped he didn't mind.

Chris said it was fine. He said most people probably had some kind of private thing they'd never told anyone, even though he had no idea if that was true. But then he wished he hadn't said anything, because Lucy got very curious. She asked him if that meant he had a deep dark secret of his own. She said it was always the quiet ones.

Chris could tell Lucy really wanted him to tell her something.

He thought he probably should. He had never heard her sound so excited, and he didn't want to let her down. But he couldn't think of anything to say, so he just sort of laughed.

Lucy wouldn't let it go. She said whatever it was, it was nothing to be ashamed about and she swore she'd never tell anybody. Unless it was young children, she said, and then she'd call the police. He said it wasn't that sort of thing. She said even if it was young children, it was okay as long as he didn't do anything about it and tried to get help. He said again that it wasn't anything like that. She said that was fine, but he had to tell her now otherwise she would think he was lying, and it really was children.

Someone had switched off the kitchen light, and it was very dark in the garden. Chris couldn't even see Lucy's face except for the glow around her nose and mouth every time she took a drag of her cigarette. He had thought of something now, but he didn't know if he wanted to tell her or not. He'd never told anyone before. He had no idea why it had suddenly come into his head. It wasn't something he ever thought about these days. He wasn't ashamed of it, but he certainly didn't want people to find out. He was sure there was a difference.

But Chris wondered if this was her way of trying to be friendly. If he confided in Lucy, he thought, that would make her feel that he trusted her. Then she might decide she liked him. It still worried him that he had no real idea what she thought of him. He couldn't stand not knowing.

So he told her.

Lucy didn't say anything. She wasn't excited any more. Chris thought she seemed a bit upset. He said he didn't mean to piss her off. She said she wasn't pissed off, she was just thinking about stuff. Chris told her to forget he'd said anything. It was just him being random. He wished now he had made something up instead.

She said it wasn't as random as all that. She had friends who had much weirder secrets. When he asked her for an example, she told him he should mind his own fucking business. She said she had to go for a piss, and would he go out and buy more cigarettes.

30. It took a long time, because Chris had to find a cash machine first. When he got back to the party, he couldn't find Lucy. He asked the bloke from the garden before, and he said she'd gone home. Chris told himself he didn't mind very much. In a way, he was relieved. He got talking to a few interesting people.

But she hadn't. When Chris went into the bedroom later to get his coat from the bed, he found her curled up asleep there. He tried to get his coat without waking her, but it didn't work.

She asked him for a cigarette and they both sat there smoking, not saying anything. When they finished, she lay back down on the bed and he did too. They started dry-humping. It was gentle at first, but soon they were really grinding. He thought she had started it, but he wasn't completely sure.

He tried to open her trousers. She pushed him away gently. She stood up, and then sat down again and said she felt a bit woozy. She asked him to call her a taxi to Whitechapel. He said they could share one since they were both going in the same direction. Neither of them said anything for a while.

31. Lucy started to talk about being off sick from work. She hadn't been ill at all, she said. She had been feeling very low.

She didn't speak to anybody. She couldn't get out of bed. She didn't see the point. Nothing was real.

But she ought to be able to snap herself out of it, and get on with things. She was a spoilt lazy brat, like her teacher wrote on her homework once when he thought she'd copied it but she hadn't. She was a selfish, scheming little bitch who made everybody's life a misery, like her mam said that time she lied about where she was going for the night and stayed over at her friend Paula's house. She was a worthless slut and a mental case, like her ex-boyfriend used to tell her every single fucking day. She should have been aborted and flushed down the bog.

All these voices were inside her head, she said, and they were taking over from her own voice. She didn't know what her own voice was any more. It was like a disease in her brain.

She kept seeing things that weren't there. One time it was a tiny little midget with no eyes. Another time it was a bloke cooking her guts in a pan. There was a shiny metal face telling her she was made of clay. She would be walking along the street, and everything around her was on fire.

She knew she was a psycho freak and a total nutjob. Everybody knew. He, Chris, was only being nice to her because he wanted to fuck her. And then when she let him, he would laugh about it with Tammy and Al.

Chris didn't know what to say to that. He tried to light a cigarette but his lighter wouldn't work. He wanted to ask to borrow hers, but he didn't want that to be the next thing he said. He hoped she might just pass it over to him, but she didn't.

Lucy said she felt a bit sick and she needed to get home. She said not to worry about her, she was always going off on one like that and she would be fine. Chris said he wasn't worried. She said she knew that, but just in case he was. He went out to the phone in the hall and called a cab.

32. As soon as they left the house and the fresh air hit her, Lucy seemed very pissed. In the cab, she could hardly keep her eyes open. She said she was going to be sick and the driver said she had to get out. She stumbled on the kerb and said she'd hurt her ankle. Chris got out to help her. She asked the driver to wait while she found a bin or something, but he drove off. She found a bin and stood over it for a few minutes, but she didn't vomit.

She told Chris they weren't far from where she lived, and would he walk her back. He didn't want to, but he couldn't think of a way to say no. Because she was so drunk and vague, and because she was hobbling on her sore ankle, it took nearly an hour.

He kept feeling like they were being watched. Once or twice he convinced himself a man in a mask was following them. He had a very clear image of it in his mind. But when he looked round, no one was there.

Chris had to unlock Lucy's door and help her inside, and guide her into the bedroom. She lay down on the bed and fell asleep straight away. Chris wasn't sure whether to go home, or sleep on her sofa. He went to make tea.

While the kettle was boiling he had a quick look around. Lucy's place wasn't what he had expected. It was an ordinary council flat, with pink wallpaper and chintzy furniture. Everything smelt of smoke, and there were full ashtrays in every room. The curtains in the living room were drawn, and there were piles of tabloid newspapers and women's magazines on the floor. There was a Nintendo plugged into the TV, and a big stack of videos against the wall, almost to the ceiling. The only books he could see were poems and engravings by William Blake. He had a look, but he couldn't make much sense of them.

In one of the kitchen cupboards he found a large jar full of fluid, with a long piece of strange stuff floating in it. It looked like meat, or some kind of offal, but it was grey and flaky. He couldn't see it very well because the liquid was cloudy and full of tiny bits. It was like something from an old medical museum.

There was a collection of handwritten letters with it. They looked very old too. He read the first one. It was only a few lines long, and badly spelled. It was written to someone called Lusk, and the return address on it was 'From hell'. It talked about eating half of a kidney taken from a woman.

Chris remembered the graphic novel Lucy gave him about Jack the Ripper, and the historical figures Oliver mentioned. He imagined all this was part of their art project. He decided it was exactly the sort of stuff someone like Lucy would have in her kitchen cupboard, but it still made him feel queasy. The things looked pretty convincing.

He tried not to imagine cutting Lucy open. That was her kidney in the jar.

He felt a bit dizzy. He wondered if he should go home.

33. Chris checked on Lucy. She was coughing a lot in her sleep. He was worried about her choking on her own vomit during the night, so he decided to stay. He put some cushions from the sofa on the floor by her bed. He didn't sleep at all. He just smoked cigarettes and watched her. He thought about a lot of things.

She felt very significant to him. It was like he had always known her, and he always would. He had the same feeling again, that something really awful was going to happen to her, and it would be his fault. He had to make sure she was all right. He had to protect her. He had never felt like that about anyone before. He didn't like it one bit.

He knew there was still time. He knew he should go home right now, and not be there in the morning. He knew that if he didn't, he would look back to this moment some time in the future, and very much wish he had.

He didn't.

Chapter Two

From hell
Mr Lusk
Sor

I send you half the Kidne I took from one women prasarved it for you tother piece I fried and ate it was very nise. I may send you the bloody knif that took it out if you only wate a whil longer.

signed
Catch me when you can Mishter Lusk.

From hell
Sor Charles Warren boss of police
Sor

I heard you been diggin in Jerusalem one time well what did you find. Not what you thought I bet. I was ther and now Im here. Englands green and pleasant land. And up to my old tricks.

Tis funny how women is differnt down below. When you go diggin ha ha. Youd think theyd all be the same but ther not

39

some has big fat Kidnes and lovely red guts and some has stinkin black horrible stuff in them. Funny how you dont know to look at them.

Ile send you another word soon General Warren sor and sometimes I hope your peelers catch me so we can talk like men. I think you know what I mean o yes you do. Ile tell you where to meet me and lets cut a women together I know youd like that. What man woudnt. The best part is scrapin out the hipbone it makes a squeal with my knif against her bone. Sometimes I have to stop it gets too much and my blood gets hot. Im in hell but are you Sor Charles well you soon will be. One more to go then youll know all. Jest wait.

Till then keep diggin my friend you never know what youll turn up.

signed
Come and play Sor Charles I know you want to.

From hell
Your majesty Queen Vic
Mam

When I come for you Ile put my hand on your throat and squeeze. Ile be standin behind you and Ile pull back your head jest a few inches with one hand, with tother hand Ile take my knif and stab it in your neck under your ear the left one and pull its a good sharp knif and it wont go too hard with you.

You wont scream cos Ile cut rite through your windpipe you wont know a thing and they call me a monster and a beast and all the rest if only they knew what I could do but I dont. Ile near clean take your head off but Ile set you down on the ground nise and gentle. Maybe in your chamber or by the river at Westminister. O no no you say people mite see but I dont mind they can watch. I think everyone would like to see that.

Then o your majesty forgive me but here it comes. Ile rise up your skirts and your underskirts and Ile find what Im lookin for. You got one too though I bet no one thinks of it. Yes you do youre jest a women unless youre not and Ile soon find out. In the knif goes. Again and again. Then time to cut you open. I know jest where to slice. Up and round and under. Deep. Ile get my hands bloody but no matter. Dip them in and take what I want. Cut it out one two and Im all done. Dont worry youre dead already so you wont feel nothin. Once youre dead its all jest meat and its jest meat anyway guts and gristle so what odds. When I do you theyll know Im no joke. Like some say.

signed
Youll know me by my fingers round your neck so jest wait.

From hell
The honourable Prime Minster Lord Salsbury
Sor

Sometimes I wish I mite get caught. Do you think I thought Id get away with it no way never. I thought everybody would know twas me. I thought youd have me on the rope by now. I never thought you cared so little nor your peelers was so dim.

But we planned it good my master and me. I see his face everywhere I go. He tells me all. The first five was easy jest practisin one every year wring ther necks and drop them in the Thames. But now six seven eight nine I cant believe I done so many these few weeks. Leavin them to be found cut up an ripped. And still they scratch ther heads. I even sent her Kidne number nine to Mr Lusk but no they aint caught me. Now jest one more to go.

Why dont everybody jest kill and wash ther hands in whoors blood cos no one stops you. Only a fool kills his wife or his mammy no no jest some drunken whoor and its easy. Ther all askin how does he do it so no one sees. Well of course they see but no one says a thing. I have a crowd round me when I does it they all pay me a sovren to watch and I know theyll say nothin for who wants it knowd they like to watch women gettin cut up. Twenty or thirty every time they clap and cheer. Its free trade if they want to pay and Im hurtin no one what harm.

O Im hurtin the women you may say but not so much as you are. They die every day and no one gives two damns of hunger and awful disease and you think o the undasarvin poor sarves them rite dont you. Yes you do. Well when I does it real quick and no pain and has my fun then you say awful awful. Well its not awful or if it is then hang yourself afore me cos you kill more nor me.

Do you ever wonder what if we turned on you Prime Minster well I do. I see you in the gutter with your neck on the block and whoors dancin in your parlour and drawrin

room. I see your head on a stick. Not for what you done but
what you never done. When you look down at Whitechapel
what do you think sometimes I wonder. It takes a dozen men
in the mornin jest to get you dressed and on your feet. When
you take a box of matches do you ever think of the match
girls well I bet you do now ha ha. But what about them
women gluin the matchboxes in her room all day hunderds of
them just to get a few pence for her roof and bread for her
childern maybe even none for her self. Them rooms is black
and filthy and I mean black theres wet mucky slime all down
the walls and no lite maybe a windo with no glass jest a bit of
rag in it to keep out the wind and the landlords charges them
sixpense a week repares on top for havin that rag. And who
dares blame them. Theres no other way of makin money but
take it out of somebody elses mouth thats jest the truth. Alls
fair in free trade so why have a damn goverment jest let the
banks and bosses run all.

What can one man do you may say. Well I hope I ansered
that question. One man can make the hole town shit ther
britches. One man if hes smart like I am can turn the black
hair white of the hole cuntry. With just one knif I can get
you all where it hurts yes even you Prime Minster and all
that you are. Under your skin like I gets under ther skin the
whoors. O some day I want to hear one of you scream. Ile
cut you rite in the open in Peccadilly and no one will stop
me theyll clap and cheer.

And sometimes I wish I might get caught. For then youll
know. Lucky for you I aint been. You think its bad now well
this aint the worst there could be nor near it. My master told
me all. His gold face loves me and I fear him for it. Youll fear

him too. Jest wait till if they get me. Then the real badness comes. Then all hell is loose. Jest wait.

O if that day comes youll wish you done yourself in when you had the chance. Youll scream and scream till you lose your wits. You and all the others every one. But not me no no Ile laugh and laugh. You think Im a crazy man but Im no crazyer nor you. Youre more crazyer nor me. And if you knew all then youd thank me youd giv me a gold cup and a medal well done lad well done. Lets swap jobs Prime Minster and see who does better you nor me ha ha.

signed
My master is here I must ready my knif and off to work bye bye.

Chapter Three

The Life to Come

The year is seventeen and ninety. The season is Eastertide.

Will Blake is in his workshop, printing his *Songs*.

He loves the clean order he imposes here, good habits from his long apprenticeship. But the method is his own invention.

Simplicity is all the ancient genius, as Mr Basire taught him. How my master was mocked in his day, thinks Will. How I am in mine.

He stoops at the copper plate, wipes the ink from its tiny crevices. He loves the smallness of the work, the patient devotion to each little task.

He hears Catherine above, dressing the bed. The rhythm of her feet always comforts him. Sometimes she lilts while she works, fragments of his own songs.

Not today.

He has engravings to finish: hard, long work, which takes care and attention, but none of his soul. He neglects it. And she knows. She says nothing, but in her silence is the rebuke he dreads.

Money comes in these days, more than they ever had, but he saves none; when there is excess, he takes time to engrave his own designs. There is wisdom in excess, he knows. And foolishness in caution.

He fears his own light dying. He would rather starve and beg. She would not.

He reaches for a clean rag, to shine the plate, ready to begin. Then:

He feels the old tug in his chest. A hot, gnawing chatter in his toe.

A vision is brewing.

He wishes it gone; then burns with guilt for the ingratitude.

Will sighs, holds his brow. He must pause, and let it come. The last thing he needs, but next time will be worse, he knows, if he resists.

He folds off his apron, dips the rag in oil and wipes smears of pigment from his hands. He stacks the sheets, with a blotter and a board between each. He carefully lifts the bitten plate, stows it with the others. He kneels there a moment, savouring their craft; his own. Neat curls of letter and line: the mirror-writing he has laboured to perfect. He could sit down now and write out the half of Genesis in this contrary mode. A Bible of Hell.

He opens the window, and lets the city in. The horse-smells, the echoing melodies of men and women crying their trades and stock. His nursery song, his lovely mind-clatter. It feeds his soul.

Once in a while he has wished he was born a country boy, soothed by the blue air and the grand sky and the sweep and roll of green. But an empty vista makes him itchy; and it stoppers his vision. In childhood he saw angels in trees, treading among mowers, throngs of them filling a field. But these days: nothing but long grass and empty air. The imaginary world he loves to inhabit is flamed into being only by the racket and anger of London. Pure energy. Eternal delight.

He sits, receives the noise and smoke and rush. He breathes.

He feels the twitch in his eye, the quiver in his chest. A shudder breaks through him.

He wishes again it could be otherwise. If he could banish this gift, he should do it. They are only glimpses now, in these days of toil and care, but each one wears him thin. At this moment, he wants to be a dull simple soul, with eyes sewn shut.

The edge of his sight tingles and sparkles. The passing street begins to flake and peel. The world beyond imposes. A rainbow descends.

Then:

A transfigured countenance, blind-eyed, inches from his. A whispered smile, blessing his days. This is more than a glimpse, he knows. This is the golden face of God.

Purple song thrumbling, a rich heavy chord like a hundred orchestras tuning their fiddles. And it throbs into a single chanting voice, *basso profundo*. He sees the words rise up around him, solid as a stone circle:

'*And did these feet in ancient time walk upon Englands mountains green.*'

His eyes fill. Will's fingers rise to touch his own hair, to make sure he is still flesh; that life is here; that now is real.

'*And was the holy Lamb of God on Englands pleasant pastures seen!*'

A green flower opens, a soft pink taste fills his mouth.

'*And did the Countenance Divine shine forth upon our clouded hills?*'

A sweet flame greets him, his twinkling skin is liquid with its grace.

'*And was Jerusalem builded here among these dark Satanic Mills?*'

Will weeps. He remembers. It is the sacred song of his first true vision, that showed him the life to come. Thirteen summers ago, seventeen and seventy-seven. That glorious year, which ever now shall be. An ancient bard returns. Revelation is near.

This shining face shall unfold his secret destiny.

It is the beginning of the end. The world awaits a prophet.

He is ready.

An Example to Us All

Will is at dinner, with Joseph Johnson and his gang.

Radical men, talking shop. He knows they invite him for colour, to liven the dull chatter with his bursts of fancy and his flair for contraries.

He does not mind.

As they use him, he uses them. Models for his verse, possible patrons, ways to take the temperature of the times. There are good friends among them, bright stars from whom he may learn. And others who might learn from him, for the greater good to come. Every inch is the first of a mile.

Johnson tugs his sleeve, seats a foppish fellow beside.

'This is Mr Cock. His grandfather kept company with Milton.'

'As I do myself,' says Will. 'I shall mention you to him when next we speak.'

Knowing eyes meet. He keeps his smile simple. They may think him touched, but he will not be a traitor to the life he knows.

Though the truth is, he has seen John Milton's spirit, but never spoke with it. He feels the poet shuns his company. And it pains him.

They are discussing the yoke of marriage.

Johnson stabs at the air with his fork.

'If Godwin were here, he would tell you.'

Fuseli flaps his hand, bats away their absent friend.

'Godwin, pooh. That man is too far even for me. Marriage may be an evil, but a necessary one. If not, we are rutting beasts.'

His foppish neighbour leans in to speak.

'Mr Blake, are you a married man?'

'I am so blessed. Eight years since.'

'And you still find her pleasant, and beautiful?'

'As I ever did. We two are in perfect sympathy. She is my right hand, my true disciple. There is no boulder she would not heave from my path, and no burden I would not happily take from her shoulders onto my own.'

Johnson wipes his mouth, one finger raised.

'But she would not permit you take in a concubine?'

'My every desire is hers. She is not my jailer, nor I her judge.'

'A rare creature. You're a fortunate man.'

Fuseli shakes his head, snorts a laugh.

'Come, Blake. Deal plainly. Your good wife is too pure in heart. She should never consent to such a travesty.'

'We are one heart, and one mind. I will tell you. When I first met my wife I knew her not, though her spirit knew mine, and it much affected her.'

'Ah.'

All quiet now, to listen.

'I was staying in the country at Battersea, to cure an ill heart from lovesickness, for another maid had much abused me. But this young Katie Boucher saw me and fainted away. This was a sign. Later I saw her again with others, and told her of my heartbreak. She said she pitied me, which made me love her, and I told her so. She said she loved me too, and all in a moment my eyes were opened and my spirit knew hers. We married the next year, and now she is my Catherine Blake. I have never been apart from her one day since, and I hope I never shall. Her precious love is my horizon.'

'You are an example to us all, Mr Blake.'

'I know that, Mr Johnson.'

He smiles, and they laugh uneasily. As he likes it.

Fuseli, though, laughs outright.

'Your soul is beyond mine, Blake. You have a gift.'

The company is ready for another subject, but the fop at his side wants more.

'Tell us, Mr Blake, how it is to see a spirit.'

'As it is to see a man. Different every time.'

'Have you always been so gifted?'

'As a child I saw God the Father at the window, and another time Seth son of Adam called to me from a seashell. I often saw spirits in the flowers but thought nothing of it, for I supposed that all men did, since the poets spoke of them so readily, and all men held poetry to be the greatest truth, after scripture, which also spoke of visions and spirits. But I was young then and I knew not how rare was this chance. I thought all life might be conversing with angels and singing their praise.'

'And now you know better. You have put away childish things.'

'Not at all. I mean, rare for the general man. I did not know I was so particular. And it puzzles me still why this is so.'

'Did you not ask your angel?'

'Not then. I saw angels often, but I never spoke with one till I was twenty years old, seventeen and seventy-seven. That sacred year opened my life to me. I live still within its eternal bounds. I am the figure one, followed by the three sevens: my Catherine, my master Milton, and my angel, whom I first knew on that holy day, walking in Dulwich. I will tell you. I passed an aged man who stopped and asked the way. He told me he was going to Dovercourt, and asked was this his road. I said it was, but he had a long journey ahead.

'All at once he was a lady, clad in a rainbow. She glided over me, and blessed me, and asked me to sing. I did so, and the melody was as beautiful as I ever heard. I keep it locked in my heart still. Then she blessed me again and said she would return when the time of revelation was near, and an ancient bard would rise from the grave to guide me.'

'Had you taken much gin, Mr Blake?'

'None at all. I was full to the brim with energy and delight, and I rushed to my rooms to draw out the words and pictures I could see.

'But the instant my pencil met the sheet, the vision crumbled into sand, my finger trembled and what I drew was no better than a child might scrawl.

'In a fury I burnt the sheets, but after I dearly wished I had them still, since for all their rudeness they must surely be closer to pure vision than the poor Grecian forms I have tried to sketch since. I thought my fame might rest on sharing this blessed sight, since all men say they desire to know the world beyond, but memory danced ever just out of view, and though I still discerned a shadow of what I saw, I had it in my eye no longer.

'Little did I know in those innocent days that all men bar

a very few are liars and clay-heads who care for nothing save gold and brute force. I too care for gold and for force when I think it needed, but also and more I care for beauty and liberty and energy and life. I do not seek to squeeze the life from others, but to water what seeds of life I find, and to use my own modest arts to give colour and form to the visionary place I am blessed to inhabit, for I tell you, this angel has finally returned these last days, and I know my destiny is now upon me. I only await a sign of rebirth, the promised visitation by an ancient bard to show me the way ahead. The golden face of God has told me so.'

And he smiles.

The food is cold.

Lips are pursed, noses pinched.

Fuseli folds his napkin, refolds it.

'Forgive Mr Blake. He is something of an enthusiast, in all matters. His heart is larger than all his other faculties together.'

'A wonder you can manage in the world, Mr Blake.'

'The wonder, sir, is that the world can manage me.'

The Harness of Marriage

She weeps; he smiles.

'I resign myself to the harness of marriage,' says Will, 'because it regulates this vegetative world, and frees me to inhabit the spiritual. But I lose too. I lose the freedom to act from energy and desire. If I wish to enfold myself in another love, you ought to permit me.'

'I ought to permit a pettifog,' says Catherine. 'You're lucky I don't knock your head off with the broom-shaft.'

'But I know how much you cling to my soul. Sometimes I fancy that I have died, and you are broken. I console myself that were I taken from you, nothing would subdue your pain. I see you yelling with grief, shunning all words and arms of pity, hopeless and mad with despair.'

'You are funny, Will. This is just what I see of you, were I to be taken. For you know you will miss me somewhat more than I will miss you.'

'What's that?' he says, and his mind is black.

'Who sweeps your floor, and cleans your brushes, and buys your food, and wipes your glass, and washes your linen, and keeps your silver, and counts your coppers, and minds your shop, and runs your errands, and warms your bed? And for this, I have the pleasure to share the life of a Great Man? Aye, and I do, Will, I truly do. But I'll wager I'd find another, sooner than you should. Paupers shan't be choosers, they do say.'

'Do not forget that I am your Will,' says he, playful, mean.

'I do not,' says she. 'But I still have my own.'

A Child of Light

Climbing to bed, Will passes his angel on the stair. He does not turn to look, but he knows the messenger is waiting. He is a child of light, and Will asks the reason for his visit.

'I am come to discover why men are content to live in shackles,' says he.

'I can tell you!' cries Will, and brings the golden man to his workshop. He asks if he might draw him and the angel assents. Will finds he draws a finer line than he ever has before. As he draws, the celestial visitor speaks.

'I have toured the hills and vales of Heaven, and I find only grace and joy. Yet the men of the vegetative world are slow and dull, and flee from the light.'

Will takes him to a prison, and the angel weeps to see men in chains. Will takes him to a brothel, and he weeps to see women in bondage. Will takes him to a church, and he weeps to see children in fear. Will takes him to the field of war, and he weeps to see men in arms, drunk with hate. Across the ocean the angel sends his thundering scroll, roaring upon the air to awake the slumbering spirit of man.

'You fool,' says Will. 'Man shall not awake until his own energies rouse him. Reason cannot liberate desire. Desire must overwhelm reason.'

The angel's face glooms and the light is drawn from the place, every lamp and candle burns black as night, the moon shrinks to a shadow and the stars peep upon us.

'You dare to call me fool, who is a child of light?' says he.

'I do!' cries Will. 'For until the men of clay have defeated the children of light, there can be no liberty. The Devil, called Satan, shall enter our souls, and the struggle shall take place behind our eyes, and in our bowels. When Satan is the victor, our redemption may begin. If Satan was defeated, there is no struggle. Without struggle, there is no redemption.'

'Christ died and rose again to redeem you,' says the angel. 'If you are not redeemed by his sacrifice, did he make it in vain?'

'Christ did not rise again,' says Will. 'He became the serpent, and returned to the Garden to tempt the woman, to give his brutish end a purpose and a meaning.'

'All this is but your fancy,' says the angel.

'And all the other is but yours,' says Will.

The Shadow of the Future

Proverbs of the World to Come

Trust your enemies. Suspect your friends.

Kill a man, and another is born. Kill a woman, and thousands never live.

Love is nothing without fear.

What the law condemns, the heart desires.

Satan is light. God is darkness.

Every word is true while it is spoken.

Memory is the shadow of the future.

Never speak your true name aloud.

Your mother has wished you dead a hundred times.

Let those who deserve it die in agony.

The sinner shall be saved before the virtuous.

Peace lies one way, wisdom another.

Delft and Drapes

The boy counts out the money, Catherine smiling at his side. Will tips the lad a copper, he grins and skips away.

'Poison to me, to see money make a child smile.'

'It is not the coin, Will, but what it may buy him. Bread, or beer, or a toy.'

'Aye, aye.'

He is not in the mood for it. Her sophistry is wearing him thin. This is his penance, he knows: she wants new delft, drapes for the good room. He wants space to ponder his precious visitation, shape it into song, new-create the shift of times he lives in. When men two centuries hence think of this place and these years, they will think of Blake, he knows that. His angel has told him.

But he sees too his work perish in fire. A cleansing flame which takes the precious and the rubbish alike. He has so much, and only a little time. His hand must turn the wood he fells himself, not another man's.

It is not his own fame he covets. It is the soul of Albion, and the light it may give to the world. An axe for the neck of the king, that is what they once said his verse should be. Was it Flaxman who said it? Or Stothard? In those days, they spoke with one voice. A scourge of the wealthy, bane to the slaver.

He hears his own youthful words:

'The Last Age is upon us, but it is we who must build its New Jerusalem. Trees grow, vegetative life blooms whether we will or no, but a city must be made by men. Brick by brick, stone by shining stone.'

And he is at this holy work, as Moses was, as Isaiah, as Jesus, as Milton. If he does not add his leaf to the Great Book of Life, then the generation to come will see a different road ahead. He must invade the soul of every unborn man who has eyes to read, and ears to listen. That is where he builds: in the heart of the child; fathers of the future, who carve out the caves of our young imagination.

'You are still unhappy with me, Will.'

He snaps back to earth. London; his little shop.

'Not you, my Catherine. This petty, pinching way of life.'

'We are not pinching in these days, my love. We have plenty.'

'Plenty is never enough. Feed a man to bursting, and next time he is hungry for twice as much. But a small bag is easily filled.'

'Were you happier at Green Street, when the cupboard was bare? When we could not sleep for hunger? When I made a meal from the leavings of others?'

'I never knew you did so.'

'I never told you.'

He thinks.

'I was not happy, and nor were you. But happy be damned, I say. I was honest in those days, for I would not take gold to engrave another man's vision. It is dead work.'

'Some of those are worthy visions.'

'Worthy soothes the weak of spirit. We need fire. Do you not see the times? The American States have thrown us off. Now France itself is up against its king. An ancient bard shall rise again, and the Bastille of our spirit will be next to shudder and fall. These are the days we have been promised.'

'You are a prophet, of course. We must allow your humours.'

'You well know I have never said so.'

'But you suffer others to say so.'

He bites his tongue. She means to needle him.

'I thought we had done with Swedenborg,' she says.

'Swedenborg is not my master.'

'But you hold with his gifts.'

'Swedenborg named the year of my birth as the New Age. That is a fact. I am now come nigh on thirty-three years old. That is another fact. And I see what I must be. This is no time for delft and drapes!'

'And tomorrow we rest.'

He hears the sulk in her voice.

'Yes. Tomorrow, and for eternity.'

'It is always tomorrow, Will. May we not live a little in today?'

'Yesterday, today and tomorrow, we may rest! Why, all I wish is to rest! Leisure to live and read and listen and see! Not to slave at a plate and a rolling press, so you may fancy yourself a lady of court in a silk gown!'

Her cheek flares with a blush, as though he has slapped it, and he feels worse than if he had.

'I am sorry, Will. I did not know I pained you so.'

His anger slips off him like melting snow.

He takes her hands.

'Oh my Catherine, it is not you. I pain myself. I have so much to tell, so many visions, and I laze them away, or work them down to dross at the press. They fade. They crumble. But you are my most precious vision. You are the child in my heart. I need no other love. Yours is my only food and my every breath. If not for you, I should be lost.'

'Just words, Will.'

'More. You fill me. You bless my days. Your gentle hands hold my very soul together.'

She looks for a flicker of deceit in his eyes, and finds none. Her head droops to his chest, his arms enfold her.

'Oh Catherine! Catherine!'

Small Men

Will counts their coin: six, seven, eight, nine. It is not enough.

He knows where his business lies: in the salons of the town. And he knows who can gain him access.

He sees the man at his usual place, hails him.

'Johnson! Mr Joseph Johnson!'

'Ah, Mr Blake. My pleasure to see you.'

'And mine to be seen.'

'But I am pressed, I may not tarry.'

'A moment only. Half a moment.'

'You look for employment, I know, but I have nothing just now.'

'Aye, but you take on other men. Lesser men. I don't ask you to put out my verses, just a few weeks of copying.'

'I have nothing for you, Mr Blake. I wish I had.'

'Do you hear of any going elsewhere? I am in a pickle at home.'

'There are men in your pickle with infants to feed, Mr Blake. Is that yet your happy situation?'

'Ah, no. We two remain two.'

'Then I suggest you sell what you may of your own work. You have your admirers, I know.'

'Time is the thing, Johnson. If I am to stay in this fretful city I need to buy me time.'

'Perhaps you ought to up stakes, and travel. Bristol, or Dublin, or Philadelphia. You might find the Western soul has a greater taste for your fancies. In the meantime, join us for dinner. This evening is sure to spark into flame if you grace us with your presence.'

'Come, Johnson. I work fast. Browne will disappoint you. He

takes on too much. His work will be faddish and fussy. You know I can do a good clean job, by the date, and in advance.'

Johnson lowers his gaze, troubles a cobble with his toe.

'Have I ever let you down, Mr Johnson?'

'Oh, my dear Mr Blake. How may I answer without offence?'

In a fury, Will stalks the town. He takes in an exhibition; the stuff is offensive to him.

But he sketches it, trying to ape the fashion, to hone his skills in the taste of the age. It wastes his powers, he knows, but he cannot live without bread and London both. Nor without Catherine. A cunning man, said Johnson once, he will never starve. Blake could not afford a serving-girl to pay, so he married one.

It made Will mad. They did not see what he saw. No one did.

Yet is this not pride? He sinks in his own funk. What if his work is indeed mere noise and fancy? What if the taste of the age is true, and his defective? If no man alive or to live ever thinks him inspired? Might he not throw his heart into engraving proper, and make a decent living for his little family? There is no shame in honest labour, he knows. To live by sweat is our first inheritance.

He should burn his notebook, free himself from the weight of his own unworked designs. It disgusts him to imagine it, but he does. Out of love, or fear, he cannot tell. His brain is full of mud and steam.

He cannot think when hungry. Still time to dine with Johnson.

*

After, they move to the tavern below. Johnson's crooked little room is too small, and the men want port and tobacco. Will dislikes the loss of time, but he comes.

They are discussing the caprice of posterity. Will looks around the table. 'We are such small men,' he says. 'Those of the past age, we shall never see again. My master Milton was the last of them. Who in the centuries to come will quiver at the name of Paine, or Godwin? Will any wish a statue to Joseph Priestley, or Mary Wollstonecraft? I think not.'

The company enjoys this. They agree, though there are blushes.

'None sees his own life as great, Blake. Unless you do yourself. I am sure Milton thought of no monument.'

'Then you know nothing of the man, or his works. He spent his very sight to build his own monument, a vision we may all enter. Wren did the same with St Paul's, though I abominate his style. Milton's Hell is more real to me than my own Poland Street.'

'And his Heaven?'

'Oh, it is a deadly thing, a mere rubbing from a Grecian temple. But it is there, in every particular. He finished what he began, the true mark of an artist. You style yourselves Sons of Liberty, but you grub around in policy when you could hone your greater gifts, shine a light for all time.'

'And will the age to come see a monument to Blake?'

'I do my best to leave them one. I can do no other. I will tell you. As a child, all my pleasure was reading and drawing. The one was as food to my imagination, the other its purest expression. Later I came to attempt poetry, but I found it a dull thing without colour and line to enliven it. And I knew how much my dear friend Mr Johnson would ask for the privilege of putting out my poems. But if I could make and sell the book myself, then every penny was mine to keep. So I spent the last of our money on the first stuff for my new engraving method. I see no dishonesty in this. A printer may write his own verse, which costs nothing, and print it up for sale. Why then should not a poet become printer? My father did not pay a man to tell him what tint and size of hose to stock. He did this himself from knowing the business. And I know mine. I need no hireling work. I am content if my only monument shall be the simple little songs I leave behind.'

Johnson smiles; patient, indulgent.

'But your master surely deserves more, Blake. And I may tell you, I have just such a scheme hatching, with Fuseli and Cowper. A public gallery of painted subjects from *Paradise Lost*, just as they lately presented the works of our dear Shakespeare. Milton merits no less, for there is not a single statue to him in England, that I know of.'

Cunderley interrupts.

'Aye, but there is,' he says, 'or shall be. Something is afoot. I had a letter tapping me for a pretty sum, to do just such a thing.'

He is not one of their party. They barely know him, only from the tavern.

'Oh-ho. More is afoot than a statue. Has none of you heard the goings-on beyond, with the grave of the poet?'

A voice from the side, thick-tongued with brandy. They turn. An idling gent with a scarred, mottled face, among a small group at the corner, listening in. Always a shudder to feel spied upon. He fixes eyes on Will, a hard and shining gaze.

'Aye. All the talk in the street is of the bones of the poet, hawked around the town. Tooth for a shilling, hair for sixpence.'

'What's that?' says Will.

He is disturbed. The bones of a poet are sacred things. They retain the power of his pen, the shadow of the sinews which brought his precious words from brain to paper.

'They've dug up old Johnny Milton, goes the word around. It's sixpence for a peek at his rotten old skellington.'

The tavern crowd hushes, gathers in to hear the tale: delivery boys who need an excuse, pipe-smoking layabouts always ready for the next diversion, a skulking parson in search of something to condemn.

Will leans in to see the teller, now quizzing a heckler.

'Say again, son?'

'I said, who's Johnny Milton when he's at home?'

He snorts, dismisses the man, leaving another to explain. Beneath him.

'Fool. He means Mr John Milton, who wrote the great poem of *Paradise Lost*, a tale of the Devil rising up against God and being thrown down into Hell, whence he crawls out again to tempt the first man, and from there springs all our misery. Any fool knows that poem.'

'Aye,' says another. 'Of man's first disobedience and the fruit, of that forbidden tree whose mortal taste. My old dad made me learn off damn near the whole thing. I could tell you chunks of it from now till midnight. Don't half go on.'

The teller takes back the tale: 'Well, now, the story is, my lads' – (and they hush) – 'the story is, they were doing some works inside in the church where he lies. St Giles, beyond in Cripple-Gate. By the old wall. That's the one. And with the notion abroad to put up a statue, the dispute started up as to where the grave really is. Not marked at all, you see. There's a dozen or more come in near every day and ask to see the place, it seems – but depending on who they find to ask, they might be shown a different spot. So the warden decided to settle the matter, and instructed them to dig where the parish book says, and see if they can find a coffin.'

'No stone or plate to mark it,' goes the murmur. Something *off* about that.

Another man butts in: 'Well, he was a regicide, or as near as. You don't go building a monument to one as chopped off the head of the King.'

'Fool. Don't you hear they're taking a collection to do just that?'

The doubter hawks and spits heavily. They see he means business. Silence. 'As well worth it, if you ask me, to dig him up to hang and quarter the bones, or break his wreckage on a turning wheel as the Frenchies do – aye, and spike his rotten old head on the bridge. Show them what's what. There's some in this country now as wish they were Frenchmen, I'll warrant. But there'll be no rising up against the King on this side of the Channel, if the ordinary God-fearing Englishman gets his way.'

The man looks towards Will, and other eyes follow: he is known as a radical. He smiles his prettiest, gentlest smile.

The parson, lingering at a distance, speaks. 'I know Mr Milton would not have agreed, sir. But of course, as a freeborn Englishman under the King, he would have firmly upheld your native right to differ. I wonder would you trouble yourself to defend his voice so hard.' And he takes his leave. And that shuts the doubter up. Though they all get the feeling: *for now*.

The teller smirks, ready to pick up: 'Good sport, boys, all good sport. But hark at my tale: they dig and they dig and they dig, and then they come upon this coffin. Made of lead, it is, and not inscribed at all. Nobody was expected to disturb it before the Last Trumpet, I daresay. So that settles it. They put him back and mark the spot and that's the end of it.

'Aye, only it never is, boys, is it? That night the diggers and the wardens get a load on in the alehouse, and they run to daring each other to see if it truly is the man himself. And they get the idea to open up the coffin in the morning. Still stinking of ale. They ain't slept a wink. Up it comes, and they break the top open, and there he is.

'Well. Wait now till I tell you.

'They say he looked perfect as soon as they pulled back the lid, wrapped up in the winding-sheet, like he hadn't rotted one jot.'

Nods at that. Will says: 'It is well known a saint will not decay. Old kings themselves have been dug up and found incorrupt. In my apprentice days I myself was present when the tomb of Edward the First was opened in the Abbey, and his skin was dark, but clear as a baby's. His hair as golden. The winding sheet stainless. I saw the light of God stream from the ends of his fingers and toes. This resurrection of the poet is a sign for our times. The Good Old Cause is alive and well.'

'Not so fast, Mr Blake. The instant they touched old Johnny, he all broke up into a heap of dust and bits, amid the rotten crumbly cloth.

'The word gets about and the crowds start coming to see the old fellow. The grave-digging lass takes sixpence a time from those as wish to gawk.' ('A lass!' Shakes of head and tuts at that.) 'And the workmen take the price of a pot to let you inside. Some climb over the wall. It's a kind of Bedlam. And by the end of it, why half the poor man is gone. His hair is snipped, his teeth tapped out with stones, his arm-bone twisted out, even his rib-bones broke off and lifted.'

Something Less than Perfect

Next day, the town is alive with it.

Will hears the talk at the pump: 'Milton's teeth are sold over the whole town. An hundred at least. Such a craze of them, for I never yet knew a man with an hundred teeth. Unless his were Dutch choppers made to bite off the Pope's niblick. A set of wooden falsies as I've heard some men do wear.'

A customer in the shop declares: 'I been for a look myself. And there's his skull, still with a fine head of long hair, tied back and all it is. Large as life and twice as ugly. They knocked out his teeth with a stone, and clipped off locks of his hair, and kept them for theirselves. But I got mine. Look here, that's one there. That there tooth. A Jew pedlar offered me four shillings for it. The same one, maybe, chewed the end of the quill that wrote his great poems, as it's said. Though he was blind all his life, they say too.'

The doubter from the night before is there, listening at the door. Unsmiling. Something about him gives Will the shivers. 'No, not all his life. It's well known God struck him blind as a punishment for his works against the King.'

'Aye well, if it's so then he has been punished by God and it's not for you nor I to punish him further. Leave him be, I say.'

'No, no, I'm for digging him out and mixing up his bones

for him, so that when the Last Day comes he'll have the Devil's own job to get his self back together to enjoy his paradise, or else it'll double his sufferings in the Hell he deserves. He can burn on a fiery lake with his arms sticking out of his arse, for all I care. His balls in place of eyes, that's my eternity for him. Too good for him. Teach him and his King-killers a lesson. And a good warning against any more as gets the same idea, Frenchman or no.'

'Don't be daft, who's going to get the same idea after the kingdom has come? To revolt against the final kingdom of God? Don't be daft, I say. The lion is to lie down with the lamb, remember. All shall be perfected.'

Now another chips in. 'Well Satan got the same idea when he was the angel Lucifer. He rebelled, and all was surely just as perfect before the Creation, as it will be when the kingdom comes.'

'No such thing. It will be far better. For what good would there be in having a kingdom to come, if it wasn't better than what came before? Why bother with the whole thing?'

'Are you saying the Heaven that Satan fell from was something less than perfect? That won't wash. For that gives Satan an excuse, you see, and then it's God who is to blame.'

'But God knows all, so he saw the rebellion and the rest, the moment he created Lucifer. The whole thing is the fault of God, if you like. All must be as he wishes. How could it be otherwise?'

'Perfect is perfect, I'm saying. There's no such thing as more perfect. A thing either is or it isn't.'

Will smiles.

'Perhaps the God of Creation is not the Father God, but a lesser. A prideful artisan, unsure of his own powers.'

'Be careful, Mr Blake. You would rewrite the Bible.'

'I would, sir. Have patience, and you may buy it from my little shop, engraved and coloured by my own hands.'

'The Bible tells our sin, and states our laws. Would you confound our laws?'

Will is done with them: 'None of this is Gospel, my friends. The Gospel is forgiveness of sins, and an end to laws.'

A snort. 'Oh, a radical, is you? Don't let no soldier hear you say so, is all my advice. England ain't no France, and never shall be.'

The men peer at each other, a wink is exchanged, a finger waggled at the temple. They sidle out, to continue the disputation in the street.

Will shivers in the August sun.

An ancient bard is risen. The visitation he was promised.

He sees his angel descend in the street, alight by the pump, chant a verse he cannot quite hear. Smooth-faced, humble-bowed. The beautiful golden visage is a smile that melts his heart. It holds a globe of glass, with a tiny human shape inside.

A blossom of light. Another life.

His destiny.

A Good Sixpence

Will queues up. It is dark now. Only a handful of others, but still he waits his turn.

The smell itself is rotten. A kind of evil black sticky sludge in the bottom of the lead casket. A tinderbox is held by the young crone hunched by the hole, a round metal tin on the bottom of a candle-stand. He admires the device. 'One of the new sort, ain't you seen them?' How poor could she be if she can buy the latest tins and lights, he wonders. But he passes over a sixpence.

She strikes the tinder, lights the rag. Touches it to the candle. The gloom is swept aside: *And there was light.*

Like a fair-day display. A house of horrors. In the flicker of the candle you see just his tiny skull leering at you, the dark caves of the eyes, and the gappy fearful grin; but the whole hideous bony mess of him, all the dust that was his brain and heart, is become slime and grease that turns your stomach. A few ribs and arm-bones tangled up in the rags of the winding sheet. Mush and fragments. A void.

Tears prick his eyes at the shabby state of the whole scene.

'Why, where is he?'

'All gone, sir. The gentlemen as came to see him took him all away, part by part. He's scattered over the four corners of London by now.'

'Can you tell me who took what?'

'I seen nothing, sir.'

'My dear lady, I must recover the pieces. Our end is near, but Milton must rise before the trumpet, to dictate his lost works.'

He takes in her even gaze. Women have a way of showing nothing.

'Oh sir, I know none of them. Not one.'

He sighs, and passes another coin. These crones are all the same. Silver loosens the tongue. Silver and gin. But he pities her, for it is the hirelings of Church and Empire have made her so.

She finds a smile for him. 'Oh, yes, I remember now. Mr Ellis the player. Have you seen him, sir? He gives a gorgeous Romeo.

He came, he said, to pay his respects, for his company are to play a drama writ by Mr Milton. But I saw him smuggle away a rib wrapped in paper under his coat, like a man running from the butcher with a cheap cut. I said nothing, for he'd paid me a good sixpence the same as the others, and then a shilling on top. I'm a poor woman with a sickly child and you wouldn't have me starve, would you, sir?'

'I would not!' he cries. And he hands over what silver he has. Jangles out too the few copper tokens from the bottom of his purse, the little local coins which everyone uses these days, when silver is scarce. Putney, Hackney, Middlesex. One, he sees, has a motto against slavery. Perhaps he can have his own struck. He must remember to ask at the copper mill on Walthamstow Lane, when next he visits.

Milton's Rib

Will visits the new Pantheon the very next day, and sees a fine *Midsummer Night's Dream*. Mr Ellis kindly agrees to speak with him after, still in his costume as Puck. Will is delighted by the little horns he wears.

Will idly enquires after his future plans, keeping his own powder dry.

'Well, now. I have lately taken on the Royalty Theatre, at Wellclose Square in Whitechapel. It was built for Palmer, you know, not five years gone. The great tragedian of Drury-Lane, yet the only tragedy played there was his own, for without a license, he could give nothing but common pantomimes. The miser West-End denies the sacred muse of drama to its starving eastern neighbour. You surely heard the scandal? Palmer saw it as such, and defied their petty warrants. But, no! Drury-Lane had him closed down, the dreadful business ruined him quite, and he lies in the gaol today. Still, music and pageant are permitted, and I shall present a non-pareil for our opening: the grand tragedy of *The State of Innocence and the Fall of Man*, that is, Mr Milton's *Paradise Lost*, as rendered into a dramatic opera by Mr Dryden, and improved if I might say so, by being put into decent couplets – for the original, as you may know, sir, had no rhyme at all, to its very great detriment in my humble opinion, and for all its great virtues apart.

'Our senior player is a fellow called Gavron, and this player's father knew Dryden. He once showed him the pages of his drama, which is printed and sold in all the bookshops, but never yet was played. And Gavron there is to play Adam, naturally. A little old, sir? Ah, but the stage works its own magic. And as Adam was created a full-grown adult, well – we are not told at what age. Our first father was ageless, surely.'

Will flicks over the pages of their drama.

It begins with a speech of Lucifer:

Is this the Seat our Conqueror has given?
And this the Climate we must change for Heaven?
These Regions and this Realm my Wars have got;
This Mournful Empire is the Loser's Lot.

In spite of the hollow ding-dong clanging of the verse, Will Blake sees the power of the enterprise: to put a vision before the people, an image of Hell and Satan. It might awaken something.

Mr Ellis shows him their designs for the angels, which Will merrily tells him do not resemble those with whom he has conversed himself.

Ellis begins to understand.

He tells Will that he himself is to play the angel Raphael, but Will tells him to claim the role of Lucifer, far the better part. They argue back and forth.

Then Will gets to the point.

'But I hear you are a resurrectionist too, in your spare time.'

Ellis is silent. A rarity, Will imagines.

'I confess I have my informants, Mr Ellis. You will not deny it.'

'Now, now. Judge not, my dear young sir. The tale is this, and you may decide then if I have done wrong. When I heard they had as you might say disinterred Mr Milton, and in such a disgraceful manner, I determined to have a look, to see if I could regulate matters in any way, and to insist on his prompt and correct reburial, for you must know we players command some respect and even I daresay some authority among the lower orders of society, unsought though it is. And of course I could not resist to pay my respects to the poet himself. Though I must say he was not much to look at, since the worms have paid their visit. A very Yorick! Well, well – the fate of us all.

'And then as I beheld him, it struck me – as we are performing his epic, might I not, as it were, borrow his own rib to stand in for that of Adam?

'Now, of course, I foresee your objection: the scene in question, the creation of Eve, does not appear in Mr Milton's poem nor in Mr Dryden's opera. But we soon invent it, you see. In dumb-show. Raphael, the angel of the Lord, reaches within – would that be it? He takes the rib, and – Assist me, Mr Blake, you know your scripture, I am sure, you seem to me a plain honest Dissenter, and for all my virtues I am no theologian. The angel would take the rib from Adam's breast, and coat it in clay? Is that the case? The form is moulded from the earth, and the angel breathes in a spirit to give it life. And from that is born our mother Eve. Now – how to achieve such an effect?'

It is Will's turn to be silent.

'Well, we will attempt it. We may attempt all, I think. But the poetry of it! You shall not dispute that! What prouder fate could there be for Mr Milton's earthly remains than to illustrate and illuminate the most important story ever told, and which of all great stories he himself chose to retell? Might as well use the skull of Shakespeare to play Hamlet at the grave, you see? Yorick again! The poetry of it, sir! The public may never know – though we have ways of whispering out such a tale, and if we happen to sell a few extra seats on the account, that is all to the good, and to the greater glory of the man, not to say of the Lord God Almighty himself.

'But the difference to the player! Ah, the resonance one may feel, in handling a thing sacred and authentic in place of some plaster fabrication. And I believe the public can distinguish. The first ever performance of this great epic! I could not let it rest. So I took the rib – I admit it! Yes! I will fetch it for you! You may see for yourself. But my motives, I swear, were sound. Holy, even.'

Will Blake holds the bone in his hand. Trembles.

It feels uncannily like a pen. Parabolic, sleek and brittle. He feels a wicked urge to snap and crumble it, return it to the dust from whence it came.

Milton's rib, slender and smooth: the actual physical fabric of the man. Not his spectacles, or his library, or even his pen.

Him.

Without whom, none of his works would be. Those lines! Which feel to be carved from stone! Immutable! Yet were it not for the fleshy human life, energy bounded by reason, of which this bone is a part, then not a single word of it.

Will is elated, and troubled too. He will sell what he can, mortgage his plate and his business and even his clothes so he might possess this relic for his own holy purpose. Keep it from the profane use of men like Ellis.

'How much?'

Ellis sees the need in the young man's eyes. He doesn't like to take advantage. Still . . .

'A difficult position you put me in. I wouldn't care to part with it. You ask me to give it up? No, sir. I swear. For ten pounds I would not. What's that? Twenty, though – Ha ha! Well, you see. For twenty pounds, a man may do many things. This is a unique item, I dare avouch. But if you can find the money, you may have it. I ask you just one favour: to return it, as a loan, for our use in this great drama. One night only, and I swear it is yours to keep forever after. Then we shall both be happy men.'

His New Apprentice

Will scours the town, seeking more relics of his master. To possess the very matter of the man is not enough; he must absorb a true essence of his character, to guide the hand that will compose

Will's own great epic poem. The subject shall be Milton himself: the ancient bard reborn to tell us of a hidden world beyond, and the endless life to come.

Following a trail of hints and half-heard rumours, Will seeks out an aged bookman in the shadow of St Paul's, a keeper of curios from the century past. The gent shrinks when he sees Will approach, but dares a broken smile when he hears of his quest. He produces a little pocket notebook in the old style, written up in a decent hand, the ink still strong and black. Will turns the book in his hands, and the dealer raises his palms, as though to wash his hands of the affair. 'Contained herein is a rare account of John Milton's later days, composed in three parts by one who knew him well, a certain Tom Allgood, and of this Allgood's wandering adventures among the Ranters and Quakers of Cromwell's time, and then of the Great Conflagration which consumed the ancient London of our grandfathers, with much other strange matter too. I had it from the estate of a great-nephew of the same Allgood, who sadly left this world as rich as he entered it. His wife thought it might be worth a few shekels, and I took pity upon the lady. Little did I know. I have not studied the whole, but a brief perusal reveals many wonders, and many terrors too. A remarkable document, that never yet was printed and sold, and perhaps ought never to be, since I doubt it is fit for the common eye, and might best be kept close under lock and key till our descendants have the stomach or the wisdom for the mysteries it attests. To say the truth, I wish I had never laid my eyes upon it, and you will do me a favour if you carry it hence. It may be I cast away a fortune, but time is more precious to me than money in these days, I am sad to say. My years are short and my business is bottomless. Take it, take it with my blessing and my compliments. If there is any worth therein, I should rather see it patiently studied for scholarly profit than hoarded for the golden sort.'

Will reads.

Sixteen and sixty-six. London's reckoning. The beginning of the end.

He weeps for the fall of honest Allgood. This poor man's grief is his own.

He weeps for his master, betrayed and bereft. His song shall rise again.

He weeps for the heavenly host, for his own angel. They have always known.

Seventeen and seventy-seven, as it ever shall be. Now the poet's grave is opened, his bones are risen. We discover our future in the ash of the past. Will is the sacred messenger who must take a single rib, and form another flesh to bear it. Milton shall walk among us once more, to guide his new apprentice.

Chapter Four

The first Part of my History, by Thomas Allgood

i.   In the year of our Lord sixteen hundred and sixty-six:
Now that I, *Thomas Allgood*, face my death, though barely half my
allotted span expired, it is my solemn duty and privilege to set down
a full account of the wild and terrible events which have so knotted
my fate, and that of my master *John Milton*; and if I doubt any man
shall have occasion ever to read this *Last Testament*, or that any would
believe it true if he should, so perhaps for the best; yet for my own
self, the very act of forming the strangest happenings into simple
words makes solid and lasting what might otherwise blow clean away
like smoke from this last *Great Fire*, which I fear is the blind author
of my sudden end, no less than it is heavenly vengeance upon our
grand fallen city of *London*; but if any man chance to read, and dare
to believe, even in a distant age yet to come, let you know the hand
of mine which writes these lines to be as firm and lively as that hand
of yours which turns these pages; for never till I writ myself did I
feel the simple awful truth: that any word a man ever read, whether
Scripture or song, law or libel, was put there by the human touch
of one particular soul, just as full and quick to his own self in his
day, as you are to your self in yours: he laughs as you do, and weeps
as you do, and fears his *Final Judgement* as you do; know but this,
and all shall be well between us.

   And so to my tale.

ii. Throughout my wretched life entire, time and time and time again I see it plain: that all my sin breeds from fear, and all my fear from shame, and all my shame from hiding my most secret self far from the light of Grace in deepest inky shadows; so I unfold my very soul now and lay it out here upon this paper in every little particular, ragged and rotten though it be; for I know too that there is scant worth in a history without faith that the teller is a straight honest dealer who holds back no measure of Truth; therefore to begin in the very beginning let it be known that I was born at *Farrowsworth* in the Country of *Norfolk*, the youngest of three and the only lad, and though it come as a great shock to some who have pretended themselves my intimates, yet I confess I was raised in what we called the *Holy Roman Church*; and though we practised our Faith so-called in deepest secrecy, as any *Catholick* in those days must needs, yet if many in the place professed in braggadocio to hate all Papists, still they knew well of our family's private devotion to the *Old Faith* so-called, and none saw fit to censure us; for in the most backward parts of our land we may find the greatest display of honest Christian English virtues, of which *toleration* is one of the highest.

As an instance: I heard the tale of an old Papist woman, the last in the place, who was refused burial in the churchyard, and her Puritan neighbours took her remains and buried it there under cover of night, against the express instruction of the magistrate.

But to my history: I was possessed of a quick mind and a love of learning from an early age, and there being no school near by which might suit, my father, an honest and prosperous yeoman, sent me at the age of seven years to Mr. *Piper* of *Norwich*, for instruction in the Latin tongue, at no little cost, and despite of scorn from those of our neighbours who valued only what could be weighed in the hand, and who thought my father aspired above his station; for though I was his only son, his Faith so-called was such that he bore no vanity for the family name or property, but intended me for *Doway* in the *Spanish Netherlands*, where the best part of the recusant *Catholicks* from our great universities at *Oxford* and *Cambridge* were fled, there to be trained up for a priest, and to return in secret to *England* to await that time he was sure would come when the Popish rite should return to favour in our land, which he never tired to say, though he chose well his hearers.

But his wish was not long mine, for as my learning grew from seed to bud to blossom, so too did my hunger increase to learn more, and I passed from the restful shade of the pagan Romans to careful study of the source of all wisdom, the true bright sun-light of Scripture, which glorious lamp I am sorry to say is nigh unknown among Papists who yet call themselves followers of *Christ*, for though my father ever had a Latin Vulgate in our house and knew the rudiments of that ancient tongue, yet I never saw him turn a leaf or heard him cite a text, as though the mere presence of the printed words under his roof might somehow guide our steps; so that now when I opened this *Holy Book*, I was outright shocked to read that Scripture spoke out in the very boldest terms against every corruption I saw in priestly Churches so-called but especially the Roman, indeed I saw plain that much of the speech of *Christ Jesus* himself might have been the very words of *Luther* or of *Calvin* who my father so often condemned as intemperate hereticks; and this perplexed my spirit, so that I did not sleep many a night through from dusk to daylight one wink, but lay abed in great fear of my soul that for want of true Faith it might burn in Hell, which under-ground place I thought to be a dark local cave with a great smith's furnace, and the *Devil* a mighty black fist which thrust the unholy sinners deep into the coals till we burned red or white, then beat us flat with a clanging hammer for all Eternity; so that after many sweating nights of fearful wrestling within, I determined to attempt a prayer after my own form, which I knew to be the way of some Puritans;

and lo! as I ventured to speak my soul, all in a moment I felt my heart yawn open and easeful breath sigh out: I was flooded with a warm soothing balm and golden tears ran down my cheeks: my very being and essence reached wide to the great light of God to let him enter;

but still I barred the way, for to my shame I was not yet ready to receive his Grace, thinking instead only of the great hurt I might cause to my father and full of lively fears of his imagined wrath, which overpowered my weak spirit; and with a quaking heart I vowed instead to keep up our secret practice of the Papist rite, which was then only one time a month or less, when a priest could be found and persuaded to attend us; for though it pained me to see him give over his hard-earned gold to a Romish hypo-crite who pretended to speak for God himself, still the father on Earth stood yet in my view of the *Father in Heaven*, and cast a great shadow in whose chill I dwelt for months nay and years together, all the while in the wider world I feigned being the *Protestant* I truly was, to hide the *Catholick* Faith which I now feigned for my good father's sake.

I speak of those years when the Wars grew hot between the

Presbyterian Church and the *Episcopal,* that is the Bishops, which led to that famous fight between *Parliament* and *King,* whose history every Englishman knows too well; and in those wild days, preachers and verse-pedlars and chapbook men of every sect and of none passed through our little town in their way from *London* to *Norwich* and back again, and I confess I listened to every sort of crack-headed creed and claim with too-tender ears; and in *Norwich* itself where I dwelt now during term-time with Mr. *Piper,* who was himself an honest Dissenter, great disputations often struck up between *Quakers* or *Ranters* and the Puritan sort, and then the common folk forgot their foot-ball, their riots and their May-polls and took places to watch, as it were a sports-day, even gaming on which preacher should first be trumped, and pack up and flee, jeered and pelted on his backside with crusts and dung: I do truly believe the madness of those times has been too soon forgot in our *Restored* and *Civilised* age, and that today if the people saw a procession of naked *Quakers,* or an ass-mounted *Donkey Haughty* who proclaimed his Messiah-ship, it would cause such terror and panick as those hereticks might find their *One True Way* led only to a gallows or a madhouse; but in those wild days, though many schismaticks received a spell in gaol as the sole reward for their heterodoxy, only a few suffered any worse, and many of the hottest *Ranters* were soonest to cool, and find their way back to a decent simple life, with their good name restored by their neighbours; for few indeed will cast a stone when so many have dwelt under glass.

It happened my father was in *London* for the beheading of the King, which deed he thought a wicked shame on the English nation; but though he could not reach the square to watch, so numerous was the crowd, he often told how he heard the darkest silence as the blade fell, and then the great heavy moan of thousands; and he never knew a more solemn procession than the mute multitudes leaving that place: He saw then that the people would not long stand to be King-less, for such was his wisdom; and since his death I have often wept that I might not ask his counsel on my many troubles, and that a childish fear of his wrath kept me so long from his society.

iii. But to my history: Brick by brick I continued to build my own house of Faith (in my heart I mean, for I am sure I am no mason), and I surrendered now to the truth that my father's Faith so-called was in grave error and I could not continue in its practice even as a sham, precious as he was to me, and as it was to him, for he was a proud and principled man, as rigid in his beliefs as he was generous and loving to his family; but still it pained me greatly when I thought to twist such a needle of disappointment into his heart, and for all I meditated on the verse of *Luke* that I must hate my father to be a true disciple, yet the bonds of blood were strong and their straits weakened my spirit still; so I found reason after reason in my own heart to conceal my soul, even receiving the Holy Communion which he believed (as I too once had, for I knew no better) to be the physical body and blood of *Christ Jesus* there present (though in no manner which I ever could explain and I have never yet met any who could, except to say that it is a great mystery, which answer is supposed to close all mouths); but though I consoled myself that even *Christ* himself, as we are told, submitted to his earthly father's will until the age of thirty years, and found peace in so doing, yet in the end I am sure I am no *Christ* and my impatient conscience cried out against such hypocrisie: I found excuse upon excuse to miss the Mass he took great pains, and no little danger, to bring to our house each month, once feigning a fever and putting my sisters to much fuss and trouble in nursing me; but in the end, a man knows his son, and when my dear father asked me to sit and speak with him one summer morn, such a call to simple conversation was rare enough that I knew his intent straight away; but when he asked me to explain my absence, still I found my tongue tied, from fear of his wrath; but after some long moments of his awful silence, I wept bitterly, so that at once he surely read my secret heart, and told me so.

And I have known as much for many months already, said he. Have you lost your religion, or what is it? This greatly injured my youthful pride, that I had suffered needlessly in my vain effort to keep him in ignorance; or else it told of something petty in him to deny his son could possess any knowledge he did not, when he must admit that my learning was far in advance of his, which fact was all his earnest desire this many years; but still I held my silence.

You must know that your soul is beyond your own grasp, said he. If you are baptised a *Catholick* then a true *Catholick* you remain until death, for a man's Faith is a matter of inheritance and not of free choice. This grieved me too, but I kept my temper, though there was great churning and folding in my head and stomach both.

Before I speak more, said I, I wish to declare that this has naught to do with you and I as father and son. I must tell you that I love and respect you very much.

Well, said he, never mind about that. What I must tell you, my boy, is that I am most bitterly disappointed in you. Most bitterly disappointed. And these words truly stung me, for I had never before spoke aloud of my love for him, and now I wished I had not, which is a very poor thing indeed to feel.

If I reject your manner of worship, said I, it is not that I reject you, is all my meaning. Many a time since then I have wished I could have spoke straight out of my own grave disappointment in him that day, but the truth is that such a thing did not seem possible then, and scarcely does yet, were he among the living, though he was not in those days many years older than I am now; but a father is a father for all that, and it must be I inherit some shadow of his own father, as he did of the fathers before him, as we all do of every father back to simple sinful *Adam*, whose exile we suffer still, whose precious seed held the tainted homunculus of every man that ever shall live, like a multitude of nested poppets; and if the total of that throng could ever be computed to the ultimate soul, the very *End of Time* itself would surely be revealed to all.

I blame you not, said he. You are young, and still a fool, for all your learning. I only blame myself for allowing you to be taught outside my purview, and I curse that dog *Piper* who has led you to this, though I expect you will deny it.

I will, said I, and if you think so then you are much mistaken.

You mean to say you thought thus while you lived under my roof, said he.

I do, said I.

I will not believe that, said he, and you can say nothing to convince me otherwise.

I am the master of my own mind, said I.

Indeed you are no such thing, said he, and you shall never be the master of mine neither. I know what I know.

I fervently defended Mr. *Piper* though there was indeed some truth in what my father said; but while there was no wrath or squabble as I had feared, a black gloom descended on him for the following days; and though he offered his confessor to counsel me, in truth I knew Scripture better than that little man did, for all we passed a pleasant hour in discussing it, after which he told my father the fault was his own and he should leave his son to find his own path; which my father took very ill, for he imagined there was no *Roman Catholick Church* save that which he alone understood in every particular, be this but an image formed and nurtured in his own heart to suit the pattern of his own conscience; and in that respect I dare declare he was as likely a good *Protestant* as any, though he never knew it.

We did not speak more of the matter; though in the days to come he could not look upon my face without the most pitiful tears would come to his eyes, and when we were left alone together in horrible silence I felt such shame and anger, be it nothing more than self-pity, that in youthful heat I determined I could no longer suffer his presence; so I packed a bag with what few books and stuff I possessed and found a ride to *Norwich*, where that same Mr. *Piper*, on hearing the sorry history, agreed to take me on to teach the basics of the Latin tongue to his younger boys, in exchange for bread and bed, till I should find for myself a more permanent station in life; but still I do remember well how the feeling struck me hard, in the dark shivering hour I sneaked away from my father's house: that I never before knew what it truly means to have *a heavy heart*, and now I always should.

iv. If I have learned nothing else from my long hard years, I know this: that life is made from temporary measures which creep their way into permanence; for in the end I passed some three or four years with Mr. *Piper* and later took pupils in my own lodgings; and though I have pride enough to credit those who say I gave a sound and careful education, all the while I haunted the booksellers to increase my own learning, and in life and in prayer sought by degrees the way to discover the true light of *Christ* in my own heart.

This led me on my *Great Wandering* through the Churches: first the *Presbyterian* with Mr. *Piper*, then in great power in *London* which as I heard was busy with good *Protestants* fleeing heinous Papish massacre in *Ireland*; but the cruelty and pride I saw in some of its ministers, including Mr. *Piper*'s son who called himself *Elijah* though his name was plain *John*, and was no older than me but was pleased to jibe and barrack me for that I was more of a son to his father than he was (which if true was hardly a fault of mine), this cruelty of word and deed, I say, repelled me and pushed me out toward the *Baptists* and their practice of dipping grown men and women, and then I travelled the country a great while dipping and preaching too in some fashion though poorly, before I found the *Independents*; and then truly I felt the Spirit come upon me and a pure manner of preaching rise up inside me, for I disputed in those days with *Ranters* and *Anti-nomians* of every stripe, all crying that the *End of Days* was upon us, for each gave it out that he alone held the key to the terrible vision of *John's Apocalypse*, which told of our fated judgement: some who held all goods in common and stole enough to eat, saying this was the Lord's bounty; and some who said that there was no way to be free from sin but to commit every sin with joy in full view of all, save murder; and some further who said that judgement was long past and we lived again in Eden and saw it as no sin to lie with two women abed together and preached it out so, and indeed lay together as man and wife in the open fields like beasts (as it was said, for I never saw such), and took their hats off to no man, which mean offence was the cause of more strife than any other, though I never yet found the Gospel verse where *Christ* sends the penitent sinner away to return with his head uncovered.

Indeed the wildest of these *Ranters* held there was no *Christ* or God at all and Scripture was no more truth than the tales of giants and fairies we tell to children, and a man may do as he pleases for he will die just the same and with no Heaven and no Hell it is all one how we live; and one such prophet so-called I even heard say that the day will dawn when all *England* shall hold such a doctrine, and men and women alike shall drink and game and fornicate how they please, and any talk of miracles and angels will be a laughing-stock; and yet when I look at some lately in the Court and City and see their comportment I wonder if he was not a true seer, and perhaps the greater wonder is that God did not sooner blast us with a *Final Vengeance*, as he once did Sodom.

Some further pretended themselves as *Christ* himself reborn; and one of the strangest sights I ever did see was two such who each encountered other in the market square and set to disputing, which turned hot, till with violence the one attacked his fellow, who said this made it sure the man was no *Christ* at all; but still he beat at the first in return, till the two wrestled in the straw and the dung, and only ceased when the constable offered to settle the matter by crucifying both to see which rose from the dead, at which they quieted themselves and at length agreed there was nowhere in Scripture it was denied that *Christ* may not come again in two persons together.

v. Now in those days I first met that terrible man whose fate was destined to be so tangled in mine, though I knew it not then: This was *Henry Cock*, who I heard tell led a house of wild *Ranters* at *Jewin-street* in *London*, and he journeyed abroad one week of every month to preach it out that *Christ Jesus* was the Son of God but that he *Cock* was the Father of God and so Grand-father to *Christ Jesus*, and all Scripture and Religion was a product of his own imaginary, for there was no such stuff before he was born and none would remain after he died, and further, that all Jews must be returned presently to *England*, so they might teach him the true *Cabala* that with such skill he should ascend himself with all his followers to Heaven and send down the angels to live upon the Earth and the devils up from below to serve them, with *Christ Jesus* upon the throne of *England* and *Henry Cock* upon the throne of Heaven, and the angels and saints should pray to him and his followers in their station above to grant favours or to curse their enemies; and many came to hear him preach for he was a hard shining sort of man, though hardly older than I was myself, and was said to have twelve wives, which some wags held was enough to drive any man from his wits; but still some sober good gentlemen of my acquaintance took up with him and made report that he was a considerable prophet, if not all he claimed.

I saw him only two times or three in those days, but on each occasion a dark fear struck my soul, for there was some hot fiery essence in his voice and looks that froze my blood and made my very hair stand; though when I saw plain how drunk was the rabble on no more than his words, I knew what great glory his gifts could attain him if he put them to godly use; but I declare I did not find any trace of the Spirit in that man, and indeed the last time I saw him (in those days) I dared swear he could sense my poor opinion of him, for though we had never spoke a word, he clasped his eyes upon me in the crowd and cast me such a look of venomous hatred that I never wish to see again in another, and this made me sure to shun his society; till he rose in my way a second time, of which more shortly.

For all that, it was a time of great confusion in my soul, for I never forgot the great truth that *Christ Jesus* was turned out by his own people and seemed as a great joke and puzzle to his days and times; yet though my modesty kept me from their close society, some others of my circle took up with Sectaries and spoke with great feeling of the visitation of the Spirit to be found in such ways; but still I held my ground: *If all behaved so, who would bake the bread?* was a great word at that time, and I never heard true answer, except that our first father *Adam* knew no bread and lived upon the fruits of nature; but yet *England* is no *Eden* and the stubborn soil must have our sweat to bring forth food, for so Scripture tells us, till the *New Jerusalem* come; which if it hath come already, as some in those days did preach out, then I dare to declare it was not worth the waiting.

vi. But to my history: These same days saw the *Restoration* of the King, and in fear of the harsh judgement then visited upon Dissenters in some parts, I followed Mr. *Piper* and his fellows and found my path bent at last towards *London*, where again I found employment as a tutor to children; yet the *London* I found was none of the *Shining City* of my imagination, but a thronging stinking hulking gasping grasping place of crowding houses and miry streets and lanes forested around dank dirty streams of filth, and such shoving and pulling in the roadways as I felt at first that every man I passed wished to pick a fight, and near I came to oblige many; and often I reflected on how little a man may know of the world in spite of all his learning, for I had long thought *Norwich* a pale small place compared with the *London* I dreamed, but now I saw there was little enough between them for grand houses and finery, and much in the favour of *Norwich* for civility; still I felt a warmth in my breast that these were the same stones our *Shakespear* and *Spenser* walked, and the same wood and plaster their blessed hands might have picked and slapped, and if any place on Earth was an eternal place, this great city was such, as it ever was and ever shall be, and nothing save the vengeance of God himself might remove it.

I met a man born and bred who said he had never left *London* and did not know if such a thing was possible, for he believed it extended to cover the whole face of the Earth; so I assured him it did not and invited him to climb a spire with me for a penny where we both saw the reach of it, and though I was much impressed with the size he was astonished it was so small, and said he wished the day might come when *London* would encompass our land entire, for he did not think it right that *England*'s green country should stand empty if it might give work and shelter to God's children.

Mr. *Piper* invited me to dine with his friend Mr. *Ellwood*, and Mr. *Ellwood* at the time had employment reading to a blind old man of his acquaintance, a certain *John Milton* whose name I had often heard spoke, for he was well noised around as a fine poet and a great scholar, and a rare bird among *Cromwell*'s fellows for that he had the wit, or the plain luck, to escape the heavy fist of the *Restoration*; though if his tongue and pen were valued high in the old *Protectorate* (as Mr. *Ellwood* told me), still in those strange past days he was suspected by some close men of unsound doctrine, for which reason, along with the dimming of his eyes, he was kept from the centre of things; but Mr. *Ellwood*, as honest and cheerful a friend as I ever found, spoke of him in high terms as a great and godly man, at whose knee he learned much wisdom and good sense; and when Mr. *Ellwood* was taken away to the gaol for the practice of his *Quaker Faith*, which suffering that good man endured too often, he wrote and bade me take his place as Mr. *Milton*'s helper, which blessing I was happy to accept.

In those days I knew not Mr. *Milton*, and I had seen him only one time, when Mr. *Ellwood* pointed him out to me, for we chanced to pass the house just as he stepped into the street; and among the fashion of the day his unshorn locks and plain grey coat indeed marked him out as an old shabby relic of the topsy-turvy times past; but I delighted to see that he flinched not from what slings and arrows might be his due: He stood with head dipped a little, and then it jerked and turned from side to side like to some long thin bird taking the air, before he raised his hand and spoke to the sky.

If you are going to do the deed, said *Milton*, do it now and get it done. I'll give you the count of five, and if yet I stand after, I'll ask you have the courtesy to confess your cowardice and let me alone to take my walk in peace, and you may come back on the morrow and prove your nerve then.

As he counted aloud some folk in the street stopped their comings and goings to enjoy the spectacle, and one or two to laugh and jeer, at which Mr. *Milton* paid no heed; but I dare declare some other few were proud to have such a man among them as a token of the old *Commonwealth*, for they hushed when he appeared, and whispered to their children who it was; though in his blind cries to an invisible enemy he only made me think – may God forgive me! – of *Cain*, wandering in the land of *Nod*, untouched because untouchable; though I said not so to Mr. *Ellwood*, whose cheeks were damp at the sight.

vii.　But good news are ever tempered with bad, and I had notice then of my father's death, which greatly grieved me, and also that I was come into the property; so I returned to *Farrowsworth* to arrange the matter, in great regret that I could not take up Mr. *Ellwood*'s kind offer, though he had Mr. *Milton* write a letter to say in what great regard I was held by his friend, and how his hand should remain open as long as I had need of help, for which I was grateful; yet my business in *Farrowsworth* stretched out four more years, fighting a suit with cousins who claimed the legacy for themselves, which bound me up in continual travel between that place and *Norwich*, and which ordeal in the end ate up every penny of this legacy and more besides, through ill advice and my own simplicity in such matters, and also poisoned my family against my presence among them; till for a second time I felt myself obliged to remove from my own kin and country, though now with a heavy penalty on my head for that I owed such large sums as I could never repay; so when I heard news of the late plague in *London* and saw the great fear all had now of any traveller from that place, in desperate haste I packed myself up once more and journeyed in the contrary direction to most, that is, towards the blighted city, where I hoped no creditor would follow, and where I sought Mr. *Milton* to make good on his offer;

but again my luck had curdled, for I found him removed to the country himself in flight of the pestilence; yet when I saw the ragged hungry state of some poor wretches who remained, my heart was touched, and I took a vacant pulpit to preach repentance; and there I stayed, upon what meagre charity my little congregation could muster, until the pulpit was reclaimed, for its proper occupant was not as I was told deceased, and mightily unhappy to find me there; so he had me in gaol, and though I stayed no more than two weeks, yet when I came out my fortunes turned a sharp corner; for my suit at law had finally come to nothing, and worse than nothing, for my creditors declared upon me; and now I reduced more rapidly than I could believe, in mere weeks living by rags and crusts, shunned by all I knew and with no road back to Norwich for that the plague still raged there, which had taken one sister of mine, and the husband of the other, who suffered now in great poverty, and wrote often beseeching money to feed her infant; at which I was glad my father was not living, for it would have near finished him to hear word his son was fallen in such straits as he could not keep his own kin; so for pennies I took whatever dirty work I could: I swept muck and stuck pigs, buried the dead and ferried the living, dug clay and washed coins, chewed his meat for an old toothless judge, ever fearful and hopeful in equal measure that some of my acquaintance should find me out and see to what I was come; but none did, save the son of Mr. *Piper*, my old enemy, now thrown off his *Presbyterian* cloak and emerged a merry Royalist rake and Courtier, who to my great surprise took pity on me after his own fashion when I told him all my history, and offered a position as his manservant, which my stubborn pride would not allow me to take, knowing too how ill he used his servants;

still I threw myself upon his mercy and asked for any more help he could, at which he said he would speak with one he knew but it would be no work for a gentleman, and though I gladly accepted his offer, yet I waited and no favour came; so I slipped ever deeper into my *Wilderness of Spirit*, which bitter fate I felt sure I must deserve; and to my shame I took black pleasure in my own despoiling, for I disgusted my own self, and it gave me some small satisfaction to see how equally disgusted were all others I encountered.

I thought myself like to die a pauper, out of coin and not a friend in the world, which I hated my own poor sorry life so much in those dark days that I truly did wish it some nights, for my spirit was weak; and in the end I made ready to throw myself on my *Heavenly Father*'s final mercy, at his great cathedral, the heart of our capital city, the nearest thing I knew to the very house of God, there to lay my heart upon his altar and let him heal or trample it as he wished, for I was all done.

viii. So I came to the ancient church of St. *Paul* at the heart of the great tumble of *London*, and I wondered that such a beggarly wretch could find his way to the very bosom of God and the holiest altar of the true Christian world, and then how unworthy I was of that wide open generous Spirit which barred none; and I racked and dredged my soul in that place to know what I must do; and since I found no answer within, so I made ready to call for answer from without; but my heart was a great barren silence, the very breath lay flat in my throat, and the only words I discovered at last were those after the Romish fashion of my father, the old Latin prayers I learnt at his knee and which I still muttered over from habit when I feared for my life or my sanity; and now, when I set my heart to dig out my troubles, I found no other root to them but the moment I rejected his manner of Faith and all my misfortunes bled from that single wound; and now his wrathful ghost had conspired with some vengeful angel to thwart me quite, and deliver me up to a final repentance; so in my despair and weariness of spirit I felt I must surrender to his will at last, for all else I knew to do had failed utterly, and I felt the land itself was tearing me open: as *England* had bled and fought against its very self so I had toddled in its shadow like a mimicking infant; and now the *Restored King* was returned upon the throne it was time for me – aye, like my very land! – to abandon my wandering and return myself to the bosom of the eternal family where I began; so as once I shut my heart to the *Spirit of God* when the essence of *Christ* first swept upon my soul, now I pushed in a blunt knife to prise my heart out from its godly shell, to have it bound once more by the gilded chains of the *Popish Faith*, for I felt my spirit feeble even unto death and a suit of Roman armour the only fit gear for whatever battle lay ahead.

But as I knelt to make the prayer – and may God forgive me! – it was halted on my tongue by a voice that came to me, and spoke my name, *Allgood, Allgood*; and in my weak and silly state I took it to be the voice of *the Lord God* himself for I knew many who said they heard the words of God spoke to them aloud in times of trouble, and though I often fervently wished for such a visitation none ever came upon me; so I said, Yes Lord; but the voice said, I am no Lord, but a man as you are; and I turned to look but a firm hand pushed my head fro.

Seek not to know my face, said he, lest that knowledge be one day to your peril, and a dagger-blade pressed in at my side and

I sat silent then for I feared my life; and in that moment I knew I had not touched the bottom of my despair since the wish to live and to thrive now rose up strong in me; but the visage I saw there, though no more than a glimpse, placed a chill in my heart, for it was no face of flesh but a crude blank shining mask of bright golden metal beneath a hood, such as a man may wear who has evil scars or burns to the face, smooth like a sea-shell, simply slitted at the mouth and eyes, a vision of terrible simple perfection and I see it still in frightful dreams.

I fear you mistake me for another, said I, and my mind was in great confusion.

You are *Thomas Allgood*, said he.

Aye, said I, but many have that name.

Not so many, said he. And I confess I have had you watched, for longer than you would credit. There is work for you if you wish it. Young *Piper* it was who told me of your need. I will fill your debts and leave you well off besides. Do you wish employment or not?

He spoke something like a Frenchman, though I had not then known many, but with no flaw in his English.

I do sir, said I, and in a low voice for that we were still in the great church, though many fine busy men walked around and spoke aloud, surveying as I thought for works to the roof, pointing aloft and raising papers and glasses to stare, for the whole structure without and within was clung with wooden scaffold, like monstrous dead ivy.

Then listen as I tell you, said he. Have you ever heard tell of old *John Milton*?

And though it was not my nature, a cold fear of mortal danger to Mr. *Ellwood*'s good friend bade me speak a lie.

I have not, said I, and who is this man?

He laughed at this.

Good, good, said he. Well, so. This *Milton* I speak of is an aged Puritan of *Cromwell*'s party, known to all as the *Blind Divorcer* for that he scribbled his eyes out, as it is said, and wrote a long defence of the practice of divorce when his own wife proved faithless, so that his name was some times become a bye-word for policy made to suit the maker. He is lately returned to *London*, and is said to be at work these days upon some great work of poetry, a national epic on a religious theme. He badly wants a man to be his eyes, for the last he had, in the country beyond, distempered him quite. But you shall instead be mine, and mine alone.

Why me? said I.

You need money, said he, and I need a man in the *Milton* house.

Aye, but why me? said I once more.

There are many who might enter his household, said he, but would not take my money. And those who would take my money, I could not place into his house, not even as a pot-boy, to scour the stains of black regicide dung from his stinking shit-bowl. O, he is watched close when abroad, and it is peculiarly easy to watch a blind man, but the inside of the house remains his own. You shall keep close eye upon who comes and goes to visit him. It is an open chance to hear their words. I want to know who he admits, who he refuses, what is said, how long they stay, what is spoke about them after they leave.

But what wrong has he done? said I.

Not what he has done, said he, but what he may do. There are some abroad in these days who wish to see nothing less than the *End Times* fall upon us, and they plan a wild destruction to cleanse our *London* of all its sin. I wish to know is *Milton* party to it. If he is not, then those *Doomsday Men* are sure to seek him out, for he is a beacon to those who yet wish *England* to be rid of its King for good and all, with *Christ Returned* instead upon the throne. This was his own life's work in years gone by, and he might have been tried and executed with his fellows in the regicide camp, but that he had friends at court. Yet that itself was blow to his great vanity, for he had rather been martyred than believe he did not merit their punishment. But the time is ripe for a new rising up, and *Milton* would be a great and dangerous asset to their cause. His rhetorical powers are not dimmed, though his private self is a deep mystery. Watch him close. I want his every thought upon such plans and plots as are put before him. I want to know where his true heart lies.

I liked not this scheme, but I had no better, and if this was God's way for me then I dared not question.

I will do it, said I.

I know you will, said he. And what is more, I say that you do know of *Milton* from long ago, which is some of the reason I have sought you out. I was afraid then, but he said, O I am glad to see you lie, as it gives me surety you may be trusted; and though I followed not this reasoning, the man seemed content and withdrew his dagger so I questioned him no further, except to ask what name I should call him, which he said it was *Stephen Pedlow*, though he spoke it in such a way as made me believe it was not his name at all.

On the morrow his servant sought me out with coins and a letter, which explained that the bearer had no tongue, for he cut it out himself at the bidding of his master, who wished he should tell nothing even upon the rack, just as it was for my safety and not his own that I might not see his master's face; and this paper instructed me to present myself at Mr. *Milton*'s house the evening to come, with my credentials and bonafides, where I should find myself well received.

So it was I made the acquaintance of *John Milton*.

ix.　O – in my innocence I thought the worst behind, and the way to come a steady uphill climb towards solace and peace; but had I known then one tenth part of what was to follow, I should have thrown paper and coins both to the depths of the *Thames* and fled the city, nay, the very land, sooner than meddle myself in such dark doings, and lead my self and my master, and the ancient godly city of *London* itself, to such a strange and terrible fate!

PART TWO

Middle

Chapter Five

34. When he saw it was light outside, Chris got up and made tea. He opened the curtains, and waited for Lucy to wake up. When she did, she went out to the loo. She didn't say anything. She didn't look at Chris. She walked straight past him as if he wasn't there.

Lucy didn't close the door. Chris thought he should put on a CD or the radio. He didn't want Lucy to think he might be able to hear, and get embarrassed. But he knew that if he did, then she would know for sure that he could hear, or at least that he was thinking about it. Then they would both get embarrassed. So he didn't. He just stood by the bed and looked at the floor.

When Lucy was finished, she came into the bedroom and got under the duvet again. She went back to sleep, or pretended to. After a while, Chris went into the living room and looked through some of the women's magazines. About an hour later he heard Lucy calling from her room. She was asking him for a cup of tea. She said the one he had made was cold.

He made another, and one for himself.

35. Every morning when she woke up, Lucy told Chris, the sheets were soaked in blood. Her stomach had been cut open. Some days she found one of her kidneys in a jar. Some days her insides were laid out on the bed beside her. Some days there was nothing at all where her middle should be. And then she would get out of bed, and everything was back to normal.

And some days, Lucy said, things got so intense that she really did want to die. It would be such a fucking relief, she said, just to shut her head down, to stop it forever. There were times when she honestly felt like that wasn't as bad as her having to feel what she was feeling.

Chris told her she had to get things in perspective. She said she wasn't thick, she did know it was a seriously awful thing, especially for the people who had to deal with it afterwards. If all you were going to be was a memory, you didn't want to be a shitty one if you could help it. But at the same time, she knew it would cheer some people up. Chris asked her what that was supposed to mean.

'I know for a fact there are people who'd be happy to hear I was dead,' said Lucy. 'No one would be happy to hear that,' said Chris. 'I know you wouldn't,' said Lucy, 'because you're nice. But there are people, Chris. There really, really are.' 'I don't believe that,' said Chris.

'Aren't there people you'd be happy to hear were dead?' said Lucy. 'I can think of loads.' 'Maybe dictators,' said Chris. 'Milosevic, or whoever.' 'Right,' said Lucy. 'And why?' 'Because they cause other people so much suffering,' said Chris. 'Well, so do I,' said Lucy. 'And most people have a limit where they switch off their sympathy if you push them too far. There are a few people who've reached that limit with me. And just the fact of me continuing to be in the world makes them unhappy.'

'Even if that was true,' said Chris, 'that's not most people.' 'No, that's right,' said Lucy. 'Most people just don't give a fuck.

Even those two in the office. They'd say it was terrible, but they wouldn't actually feel anything. In six months or a year you'd have to remind them who I even was.' 'That's bullshit,' said Chris. 'It's not,' said Lucy. 'It's the truth. But don't you see? That's fine. That's the way I want it. I'm fed up of getting involved in people's lives. That's why I'm such a cow most of the time. I just want to stay out of the way. I want people to leave me alone. I know who I am, and it's not anything good. And then you have to come along and act all nice to me, and now I'm really confused.'

She started crying. Chris thought he should probably hold her, but he was worried she might think he was exploiting the situation to make a move, so he didn't. He stayed where he was, and made a kind of mmm noise in his throat every so often. He hoped that would tell her he was sympathetic and not just sitting there indifferent or embarrassed. He waited for her to finish crying. It felt like ages, but it was probably only two or three minutes.

36. Chris helped Lucy to tidy up the flat. They emptied all the ashtrays and put all the newspapers and magazines and crumpled tissues and wine bottles and vodka bottles into a black bin bag, and he brought it out to the big grey bin by the lift. The place looked nicer already, and Lucy said she felt better.

She asked Chris if he'd like to borrow one of her William Blake books. He didn't want to seem rude, so he said yes. It was called *The Marriage of Heaven and Hell*. She told him it would blow his mind. He said he was looking forward to that. She said she was too.

He left.

37. When Chris got back to his flat, a man in a mask was standing opposite the front door. The mask was made of smooth reflective metal, and the man was wearing a kind of cloak with a hood. It looked freaky. The man waved to him. Chris pretended he hadn't noticed. He went inside.

Chris was convinced he'd seen the outfit somewhere before. It must be a promotion for something, Chris thought. It was some weird publicity stunt. He was pretty sure he'd noticed these figures in other places, standing around, or following people. He told himself there must be dozens or hundreds of these men walking around the city, and there was nothing special about this one.

He could tell the man was still in the street. He peeked out the window, and saw him standing there, looking up. Chris wondered if he should go down and ask him what he wanted. He decided not to. Whatever it was, he didn't want to get involved. It was probably none of his business. He had enough to worry about.

He lay in bed, and tried not to think about it.

38. Chris slept for a few hours. When he got up, he looked outside again. The man was gone. He sent Lucy an email to check if she was feeling okay. She sent one back and said she was, and she'd see him at work on Monday. She said she wouldn't tell anybody about what had happened, and she very much hoped he wouldn't either.

She also said that his secret was safe with her. She didn't say it like it was blackmail, but he wondered if that was what she meant. He couldn't remember why he had told her. It had seemed so important at the time.

He sent another saying if she ever felt suicidal again, she should call him, and he would come over. Lucy replied. He'd got it all wrong, she said. She was never going to top herself. Sometimes she felt like she deserved to die, but the whole point was that somebody else would do it. She wanted to be killed. Some days, she got completely obsessed with the idea. She was absolutely certain it was going to happen. She could feel it coming. It was just a matter of when, and how, and who.

Chris wished he hadn't read that one. He deleted it from his inbox, and then deleted it from his trash. He decided that if she ever mentioned it, he would pretend he had never received it.

He was pretty sure she would know that was a lie. She'd be able to check. But he also knew she wouldn't say anything. No one ever did.

* * *

Red Clay

Milton's rib is his. In hock up to his neck, but he has it.

From a bankrupt sale in the street Will finds a hinged case for a pair of duelling pistols, lined with rotten velvet. He replaces the old fabric with new stuff, a pillowed lining for the bone. It nestles. As though it may grow. A cradle.

He sets to make himself a fine companion, a second Eve. He shall mould a whole man around this single remnant. A risen bard, a prophet for the Last Days. He will use the red clay of his own New Jerusalem: the City of God.

Scraping mud from the holy Thames in a pewter bucket, he fills a barrel in the cellar. Twenty-four visits, it takes. Under dark, with a lantern on a pole. He would be lifted by a watchman, but that they must mistake him for one of their own.

Smears the rib with this mud, and lets it dry.

Waits.

He returns, and sees the gleaming finish. Fancies it a first layer of skin.

He touches it, gentle.

It crumbles. Falls away. Like its own dried flesh, shed a second time.

A dead thing.

So, he starts again.

He cleans down the bone, burnishes the curved surface in gentle strokes, with a steel ball wrapped in felt, dipped in oil.

He scrapes and spreads the Thames mud on his plates and boards, stands each over a heated pan. He grinds the dried clay to fine powder, mills it down to brown flour; he fancies it the colour of skin.

This task is the longest: three full weeks before he is happy with its softness. Till he can breathe it like smoke.

As he grinds, this mill becomes his life. In every grain he sees a bygone age: this one a fleck of Shakespeare's ink, that one a fragment of feather from the crown of King Lud himself. The matter of London past. So we must all be ground down, Will thinks, by Satan's mill.

He sees the dust of the tablets Moses smashed, cinders from the burnt offerings of Priam and Hector. Since the river washes in from the channel, and the channel from the sea, and the sea from the wide ocean, there might be any and all traces herein. All things remain, all things return. And every atom one of the thoughts of God, fallen away from its origin. He can return this stuff to its divine source, for he knows the hidden words.

At last, clay as delicate as pigment. He mixes it with water, till it pours like cream. Strains it through two sheets of muslin, leaving a heavy lardy glob. Spreads this again on the backs of his copper plates, warms it over hot water, till it stiffens.

Then: glue. He was told the ancient secret. Will mixes it with the clay, to make a strong thick paste.

He paints this mud-pigment on with a sable brush. It takes him an hour to cover all the rib. When it is dry, he starts again, another layer.

After a week, it is clear this process will take the rest of his life, and several more beyond, to give the solid depth of human scale.

There must be another way.

Flesh of My Flesh

And the Lord God caused a deep sleep to fall upon Adam, and he slept: and he took one of his ribs, and closed up the flesh instead thereof; And the rib, which the Lord God had taken from man, made he a woman, and brought her unto the man. And Adam said, This is now bone of my bones, and flesh of my flesh: she shall be called Woman, because she was taken out of Man. Therefore shall a man leave his father and his mother, and shall cleave unto his wife: and they shall be one flesh. And they were both naked, the man and his wife, and were not ashamed.

'Oh Catherine! Catherine!' cries Will.

And he reads the verses again, tracing his finger along the words.

They are naked, in their chamber. Stretched out on their backs upon the counterpane. The late sunlight scatters its gold across their skin.

'To be unclothed,' says he, 'and to be unashamed!'

'Yes, Will,' says she.

'And that, you know, is why you have one more rib than I, my dear. You have even pairs, and I have one less.'

She smiles. 'I think you do not,' says she.

'I'll wager I do, for the Bible says it. Would you make Moses a liar?' And he reaches over, strokes with his fingers the firm ripples beneath her breasts.

And she giggles.

'Shall I count them for you, my dear?' says he.

He tickles, and she shrieks. High and wild, flushing her skin.

He cannot resist when he hears that sound. Like a child. The unaffected voice of simple joy.

'Oh Catherine! Catherine!'

He climbs upon her, and they make one flesh.

'My emanation,' says he. 'The nakedness of woman is the work of God.'

The Sacred Carpenter

Will is coating a warm copper plate. His daily work.

He rubs on a bar of wax; it leaves the film he will grave into. He takes care to cover every corner equally. He draws a feather over it, to cool and smooth the wax.

The Sacred Carpenter stands at his shoulder, as he has before.

'Joseph!' cries Will.

'My old friend,' says Joseph.

'You came to me once, in my hour of need, and told me of the ancient way: carpenter's glue to mix pigment. Dilute it down and blend with the coloured powder, on a piece of smooth marble.'

Joseph smiles. 'You remembered.'

'I did,' says Will. 'Now I must know: your glorious son once baked some pigeons from clay, when he was a child. I was told this by an angel. But it was the Sabbath, and the priest rebuked him, so he gave the birds life and let them fly away.'

'It was I myself rebuked him,' says Joseph. 'All energy must be bounded by reason.'

'Another time for that,' says Will. 'But what is the word he spoke to give them life?'

'It is the word written upon your heart,' says Joseph, 'and I shall say no more on the matter.'

'Thanks, Joseph.'

'It was the least of the mischief wrought by my son. He greyed my beard and lined my brow.'

'He does the same to many a learned bishop in these days. Ah, Joseph. Your boy Jesus is a friend to the poor, a comfort to the afflicted.'

'And at times, an affliction to the comfortable. I was among their number.'

'Why, so he should be!'

Will is alone. He puzzles it out.

'Oh Catherine! Catherine!'

'Yes, Will.'

'You know my heart better than any living.'

'I hope I do, Will.'

'What word, then, is writ upon it?'

'I have seen it there,' says she, 'but you know I have not all my letters.'

'I forgot!' cries Will. 'Can you draw it out for me?'

'It looks like tongues of fire dancing.'

He holds the paper. They are Hebrew letters, and he knows not the script.

He must proceed from his own invention, as he ever has.

* * *

From hell
Mary Ann Nichols
Number six
Mam

I been thinkin about you lots. I never killed no one before youre the only one. Thats a lie I killed five but they were good as dead already and then seven eight nine the real ones

after you. But Ile never do it again I promis. Thats a lie too
I got one more to do the last and then its over and done
with for good and all I promis. Cross my heart and hope to
die.

O I never knew I could be so sad. Youre like my mammy I
think I dont know I never knew her poor mammy she never
knew me neither.

O Im sorry Mary Ann. Im sorry mammy.

I cant tell you why I done it. I mean I know why but I cant
tell. Tis a secret. I never felt bad while I was doin it only after.
My master says that is repentanse and I will be forgiven but I
dont think so. I woudnt if I was God. Not if he knew what
we was up to. And he knows all.

You never knew what I done on you Mary Ann so Ile tel
you now. I was watchin you for days and days. Followin you
round and back again. Your bed in Flowrey Dean where you
sleep when the sun is up. I waited outside till you came again.
I was imaginin you sleepin like a farey princess. Blooms round
you and monks sayin prayers for you. Rabbits and lams snug-
glin up with you. Birds tweetin round your head. You dreamin
dreams of ships and treasure. Handsom prince come and take
you to his castle. Amen.

When you came out at dusk I followed you. Seen you in
the gin shop and talkin to sailers and men. Seen you whisper
them. Seen you take them up the yard and do bad things.
Your skirts up round your shoulders. Seen you callin men
your darlin when you never seen them before. I seen you
walkin back to Flowrey Dean when you coudnt hardly walk.
Like a cork on the river this way and that. I seen you fall
down and heard men laughin and seen you laughin too. That

was the worst part you laughin too. You should be sad and Im sad for you.

I was waitin for the next man. A real gent not like the others. I been told for sure the time has come do it now. This man and this women he said one day all will look to this moment unless you stop it. But I mean for no one never to know about this he said. I wated years for to do nothin but slay this women when the rite time came. And it was you he said and I was excited. So so excited. All them years and here it comes.

Maybe you thought that way when you got married. Cos I know you did. Maybe when you had your babbies. You was excited. After waitin for years. And then you got sad maybe. Where are they now your babbies I wonder and that makes me sad. But maybe you never knew nor cared where they were but still I feel sad for the babbies. Why did you take to the gin I wonder. Not cos youre a bad women I bet but cos youre not. The world is a bad place and that makes you sad. I know all about that one.

So what I done is. I seen you at your dinner in the Fryin Pan. I watched you through the windo. Takin your gin and laughin. Then I seen you walkin out. And I knew the next man was him. Nothin for an hour maybe more. I seen you tryin but no luck. I was gettin cold twas a cold nite. Youre whisperin men but they all say no. Youre callin them names. Fat old fool and worse. I can see you now when I close my eyes your in your ulster with them big buttons. Your pretty round face and I think Id like to cosy you and be warm. Nothin bad but jest huggin me like Im your babby. And Im thinkin this and I seen this chap very nise a real gent. Clean

and walkin straight up like a soldier. And you give him the
smile and he smiles back. And I seen you whisper him and he
laughs and then youre down yon passage. I followed you
down and you never seen me cos no one never sees me. Im
like a shadow youd never know Im there. I can do allsorts.
But I seen you. Hup your skirts and over a barrel and hes on
you. O o o he says and then done. And hes cryin then and I
dont know why. Dont worry you says that was real good. I
never knew a women before he says well I dont believe that
you says. He looks happy then and you gave him a cuddle
and he walks on.

Well thats my time is come. I dont even think it I jest know
and I done what I had to. Youre on the ground afore you
know it. My hand on your neck pushin real hard so you cant
scream and then my good hand tother one has the blade out
and in your neck. First time werent good I struck your bone
so I does it again. This one is good and I pulls it and your
neck is cut real good. Then to kill your guts and I pulls up
your skirts till I seen your skin your flesh. In at the top of
your tummy and I cuts down sawin and sawin to your hips till
when I know your guts is cut up good.

I dont know why but I gets the wobbles then I thinks I hear
somebody comin but there aint nobody. I aint thinkin I done a
bad thing not then but jest that its time to git. But I aint done
yet not properly but I cant tarry so I goes one two with the
blade in your cunt excuse me Mary Ann but thats what it is
and then youre done good. I walks away then I know jest
where to go and I climbs in this slaughterplase I know about
and I washes in the barrel. Tis all bloody in there and I
know if Im seen Im jest a slaughterboy washin which is what

I am. And I think nothin Im happy only hopin I done it rite. And will he be content I cant tell who but thats what Im thinkin.

But now o Mary Ann Im sorry. Sorry sorry sorry. I wish Id not done it. Youre dead and its a bad bad thing I know. And no one else done it jest me. My master made me but he didnt he jest said to do it and thats not the same Im the one what done it. I done it no one else. If you were alive now Id let you slice me for to show you Im sorry but you cant cos I done you proper and o I feel sad I feel like doin it to myself slicin myself but I wont Im scared and that makes me sad too. Jest I promise never to do it again. Except that one time more. And then its finished. If youre in heaven or nearly then pray for us all when its done. Not long now.

signed
If your ghost rises to haunt me then sarvs me rite.

* * *

The next Part of my History, by Thomas Allgood

i.   In the year of our Lord sixteen hundred and sixty-six:

I remember little of the hours that followed, save that I sweated and fretted but found no way out of my hole, so when next evening came I started off for the house I knew was Mr. *Milton*'s, though I was warned off by a ferryman I spoke with to ask the way:

Only trouble follows that man *Milton*, said he. If you choose to become his disciple then do it with your eyes open.

I knew too that *Bunhill-fields* hard by was lately stuffed with the bodies of those who succumbed to the awful pestilence the last year gone, but when I saw the ground of the fields was thick with fresh lime heaped like drifted snow, I judged it safe; then I raised my lanthorn and hailed a figure who stood hard by and asked was this the very house; which I knew rightly it was, but though I saw imperfectly through the dusky air yet this man's bearing struck me as sneaking and sinister, and I wished to make an estimation of his character and to show he put no fear in me, if that was any of his intent; so when he gave me no answer but stared back insolent, I stepped up near him with raised fist, at which he did not flinch;

and then I noted well his own limp arms, too thin for life, and dark as it was I saw in place of his face was a simple *Death's-head* with white empty gaze, and he stood in the very sewer-ditch so deep that the stink must be near up to his knees; and I knew now it was a risen plague-corpse come to chide me or drag me to Hell for my evil intent to betray Mr. *Milton*, so I shut my eyes and prayed to the Lord God that if I lived this night I should walk away from this sneaking whispering employ and find poor honest work; but I thought then of my sister and her starving child and the foreign agents all said were at work in our land, and I told myself I must if I could be of any service to retain the liberty of *England*, and that Mr. *Milton* had surely at some time engaged upon under-ground work for the greater safety of the people, and if I could one day confess all the truth he might understand better than most, and know that I surely held no ill-will against his person but thought only of that slippery fish the *Common Good*, which ever swam but never yet took hook.

I dared to open my eyes and the vision of hellish fright before me made not to move, and I waited more, but yet it moved not; and now the silence and stillness which had put such fear in me before made me wish to laugh somewhat, so I dared further to step in and draw my lanthorn up nigh to his face;

and a second time I saw I was deceived, for when I reached the thing it was nothing but an eldritch scar-croe, whose head was a lumpy mottled turnip with two peeled eggs for the terrible blank eyes mounted upon a long staff, wrapped in a grey worsted coat with an old Puritan collar all stuffed with filthy straw and a great gross parsnip poking through the skirts for an over-sized member; all which I understood to make a satyrick tribute to Mr. *Milton*; but still this ghostly encounter affected me, and I wondered would I be wise to take this as a kind of portent, that I should turn back upon my way, for it left me with a new sense of Mr. *Milton*, a thin strict cane-like sense, a rigid, frigid, rattling, chained sort of a man, which vision took over my imaginary and I wholly forgot the flesh-and-blood being I would see.

But the door opened then, and I was commanded to enter if I had business; which I did, and I was presented to Mr. *Milton* at last, in the same habit as I remembered, sat in his chair in a strange careless attitude, with one leg flung over the arm and his empty gaze upon the ceiling.

What delayed you in the street? said he. I heard you approach the house some minutes gone.

I had sworn I would tell him no lie, so I judged I should

inform him straight, and asked did he not know of the effigy at his door.

He did not, and when I told him of its form he laughed and expressed his gratitude, though he wondered aloud how long it had been stationed there and how many of his trusted servants and friends so-called, to say nothing of his own wife and daughters, had winked to tell him.

A pair of eyes is what I need, said he. Eyes that will not deceive. I want to know what is, not what you fancy I should like.

I know nothing of your tastes, sir, said I, so even should I wish it, I could not spin the ball to suit them.

I presented the letter Mr. *Ellwood* had supplied, which was read to him by his wife; after which he dismissed her, and asked me what it was that brought me to him; and all the while we spoke he played upon his organ, his habit of an evening as I was to find, so that we must needs converse with voices raised above the music, and if he did cease without warning, I was often caught in a sudden shout, which never failed to raise his mirth.

Fear of my life, and the love of my God and my country, said I, and if I stinted the truth then it was surely no lie, so my promise was fast.

And what do you seek from me? said he.

Only to serve you as you think best, said I.

You'll do, lad, said he. You'll serve a turn. But the work will be trying, and I am a hard master. This great journey is almost ended, and I need no stumbling at the crown of the hill.

I confess I have no feeling for poetry, said I.

All the better, said he. I have had some in here I suspect of trying to improve my verse. I require accuracy, not invention. I pay you to be my eyes alone. On your own clock and coin you may be your own.

We took our first walk that evening; and though I felt not inclined to speak, he much encouraged me to dispute with him, which kept his mental powers quick and fertile, he said, now his flesh and bones were shrivelled and dry; though as I held him I felt stiffer than he, for his legs were lean and strong, for all that his hands were crippled with chalk-stones.

I thank the good Lord I have not sight, said he, for if I could see to write, it would torment my soul that I may not hold a pen without bodily pain.

You play at your organ, said I.

In that case, said he, the results of the exertion provide the balm.

Should it not with writing? said I.

Composition is no comfort, said he, but only effort. It is my readers who shall enjoy the balm, which I labour to provide in my numbers.

It is wonderful, said I, that you find the strength for such an undertaking.

It is from fear, said he, the terror I should leave no trace. The sun may rise and fall, and it greens the flora and warms our blood; but without a lens, it will not burn. I wish to set this land aflame, that it may burn still after I depart.

For fame, then, said I.

Aye, said he, for fame. The ancients and the prophets saw fit to leave us a record of their deeds and sayings. Without their example, we should be pagan savages still, culling infants to appease the goblins of nature. And how many others whose record is lost, or who saw no call to write their wisdom? It may be only chance has given us *Plato* and *Hermes*, *Homer* and *Vergil*. Not all who reach for fame may grasp it, but no man shall who has not striven toward that goal. I am not satisfied to teach those few hundreds I have known, when I may speak to thousands of thousands yet unborn.

And is not this a kind of vanity? said I.

To know the quality of my own mind is not vanity, said he. Pride, perhaps. But I never saw the value in humility for its own sake.

Ellwood is a humble man, said I.

With good reason, said he. I have read his verse. God gives man uniquely the virtue of self-knowledge. I will not be a hypocrite to my own gifts. My flesh gives me humility enough; if my spirit may soar, then it shall.

On our return to the house we passed that crooked effigy at its door, and I wondered in silence that a man so aged and infirm should be so hated and feared; and in a manner I grew accustomed to, but never found less than strange, he seemed to hear the whir and click of my head, and asked upon what large thought I was brooding; and when I spoke my mind, I thought Mr. *Milton* was something flattered at the notion that he should inspire such passion in his enemies still;

and then my heart was struck hard with pity for him, so that all of a sudden I was flush with *Heavenly Grace*: I resolved all at once to make a clean breast of it and instantly throw myself upon his mercy, and in a rush of heat I told him I had a bitter confession to make, and a great pardon to beg; and with much solemnity he commanded me to speak my mind without delay;

yet to my shame I did delay, for the truth is I found no pity nor mercy in his manner, and I feared the bite and savagery I sensed in his tongue, for he had that quiet bullying way of those who make you seek their good opinion at all costs, and in every case he made his disapproval so plain and clear, and hang what the other may think;

so once again my cowardice overtook my good character, and with a whirling mind and a stammering tongue I told him instead the long tale of my Papist history, with a firm assurance that Mr. *Ellwood* had no knowledge of this matter when he put me forward; but though I found Mr. *Milton*'s blunt manner of question led me to confess many details I had never before spoke aloud, he did not berate me.

A man, said he, has no choice in his nativity. Your tale is very near my own father's history. Papists have ever been the scapegoats of the English mob, and I fear they ever will be. But count back the years, and every jack of them is born from *Catholick* stock. Blame the shepherd and not the sheep.

I was not flattered to be considered such as a sheep, yet I kept my counsel, and we passed indoors; but all that night my head swelled full of dark fears that Mr. *Milton* should sniff out my treachery still and cry me yet as a Royalist spy, which my starving conscience told me plain was a sign I must deal straight with him and confess to all at first light, which proof of my good character might persuade him to fill my pockets in gratitude;

but such stuff belongs in tales of Romance, for I knew full well my only hopes to thrive rested on a fast tongue and straight dealing with my first employer Mr. *Pedlow*, to whom I owed such loyalty as I could muster; so I kept my counsel, and banished all lively thoughts of discovery and punishment as best I could, for all that I feared they lurked and festered still in shady corners of my heart, and would creep out in the murky nights ahead to gnaw at my peace once more.

Chapter Six

From hell
Annie Chapmen
Number seven
Mam

Heres what happened. My master said Im to follow the same
gent where he goes and comes. I watches him all week. He
goes and comes to his club and for to see his mammy I
think she is. Hes quiet and kind. I likes him. Always tips his
hat for a lady and gives a penny for an urchin. Never goes
to no whoors but I know hes the man I seen with Mary
Ann Im sure of it. The whole week I watches him. But I
dont get tired. I does what Im told and I does it rite. I dont
forget who looks after me. And I dont mind. I likes the big
grey stone buildins round the bank and watchin all the gents
comin and goin. All the messenger boys runnin and horses
clip cloppin tis better nor the circus. Lads with barrows
sellin herrin and nuts and cigars and hokey pokey men and
barrel organs and bootblacks and fotografmen and sweepers
and swags and sandwichmen for canned this and patent
tother.

Then one night he goes walkin down Whitechapel. Long
long walks but he dont mind. He walks and I walks. Rite
down Shorditch and in them narrow streets. He goes in and

out of music halls and respectable public houses and then
down he goes the back roads when it gets dark. Still I follows
him. Each one cheaper and darker nor the last. And I hear
children shoutin here comes a Hottentot and all laughin like
we do when we see a toff. Runnin after him and makin mock
of how he walks. He dont mind.

Then its proper dark and hes in this one nasty public
house. Ther lookin after him cos they know hes money and
cos they don want no peelers in ther. But hes keepin quiet
and cool jest watchin all. And Im watchin him. Tis late dark
now and hes gettin up and goin. Out in the road and I thinks
I know what hes after. Hes got that look about him and that
hot little eye like some men get when its time. Women come
to him but he says no no thank you no. Like he knows jest
what he wants.

Then you came up. Im sorry Annie but I didnt like you.
Youre big and whoorish and drunken. Im thinkin o I hope he
goes with her cos I woudnt mind doin her after. Im sorry
Annie but thats what I thought. But whatever he wanted I
dont know but you were it.

You know what happened then. You took him down that
alley and through the gate and down yon steps and done
him in the yard. I was hidin watchin all and I seen. O youre
dirty I thought. Youre a dirty women youre not like my
mammy. Youre not like no princess. Youre like the wicked
old queen or the forest hag. What you done. O my Annie.
O o my.

After he was cryin again and you laughed. Away out of
here youre a child you says I dont want no virgin mens
muck in me. O he ran and ran. I didnt follow him though.

I knew whats next. I comes out and I says I was watchin
you. O you dirty boy says you. Yes I says and you want a
real man now I suppose. For a consideration says you. Heres
my money I says and shows you. Will you I says I will says
you. You seen some people then and you says come in here
the same place if you dont mind. I dont mind I says and in
we goes. Down the passage and the swing door and the
three steps and into the yard. Afore you knew what youre
on the ground. Ive my hand on your throat and youre
gaspin and your fat face is gettin red and fatter nor it is
already. When you stop movin I cuts your neck. Rite hard I
done it I near broke through your backbone I think. Could
have took your head clean off and carried it home but I had
no bag big enough ha ha.

Then tis time and time to do it rite. My master said I want
to know tis done and done proper. Rite I says youre goin to
know. I sees its quiet and all is asleep and Ive got time. So I
takes my time.

Cuts you in the belly. O here it comes. Slice slice slice
nice and clean. Ive got a real sharp blade I do. Open you
up and thers your guts. The wriggly wormy ones I takes
them out. I puts them up by your head so I dont tread nor
kneel in them and get myself messed up. You smell shitty in
ther but I dont mind. And boose I can smell that too.
Another bit of belly I cut off and put by your head on
tother side to make it neat. In I goes then. My fingers in
and pushin about in your guts. I takes my time. I know by
feel. Pushin and pushin. Its dark but Im used to it. Til I
finds it. The start of all pain. Slice cut slice and tis out.
Real small. I have it in a jar I brought with me. Like a little

skinned bird. Like a flower of meat. Like a bloody
monthrag.

Now I thinks of the peelers and I want to fox them. I takes
off your rings two of them and I looks to see what else.
Theres a comb and a bit of hanky and I puts them by your
feet for to finish the picture. Now you looks good. Better nor
before.

But I see lite in the sky and its time to go. No one comes
they dont care. No ones cryin for you Annie. Not one
sinner. O theres some with me standin round watchin but
ther the other sort. All them I writes to. Ther watchin and
sayin good boy good boy well done. I likes that. When I
finish they all clap ther hands like at the music hall and I
feels good. And tis over. I takes your thing back and shows
it to him my master I cant tell you what he is. He says well
done boy well done. Now that man will know there shant
be no one born of his seed. Now God shall suffer as we do.
His plan is spoiled. I dont like that but I says nothin. And
thats it.

So Im sorry I killed you but twas you that messed your life
not me. And when you know why I done it you wont mind
dyin. Tis worth it youll see. Poor women they all say poor
nothin. They talk all about the whoors but naught about the
men as keeps them in business. Amen.

signed
Theres wheels inside wheels he says my master I think hes rite.

* * *

39. When he was a child, around the age of ten or eleven, Chris had thought for a few months that he might be the Second Coming of Christ. He had learned at school that Jesus was supposed to return, and from films and books he picked up the idea it could happen soon, and in much the same way as before. He also knew that Jesus himself didn't know for sure he was the Messiah until he was older.

At that age, Chris always liked to be good at things, but he had never found the one thing he was best at overall. He felt very strongly that he was significant, and his life had to mean something important. Maybe his thing was to become the best possible person, he thought. That was what being Jesus meant. He could be the perfect human being, the standard by which everyone else was judged.

He was certain he shouldn't talk about this to anyone, because he knew what happened to Jesus before. And the same thing would probably happen to him in the end, but not until he was old enough to have followers, and it was time. He would bring on the end of the world, and defeat Satan in the final battle.

He wasn't sure if there was anything he could do to make sure it would be him. It seemed to be something that was either in you or it wasn't. He would just have to wait, and look for signs.

40. Sometimes Chris used to wonder if he was letting himself off the hook. He didn't always feel like the perfect human being. This might be only one of several potential futures for him, and it wouldn't happen unless he worked hard towards it.

That thought worried him a lot. The destiny of humanity

might depend on whether he could be bothered to make the effort to be the best possible version of himself. He might end up ruining the most wonderful thing just out of pure laziness.

He asked himself if it was really all that hard to be perfect.

No one else seemed to be even trying.

41. At that age, Chris liked to play with his penis in bed at night. He had done it for as long as he could remember. No one ever told him he shouldn't. He discovered that if he kept going for long enough, he would have a huge rush of pleasure all of a sudden. It was almost too much. It was as though, just for a few seconds, he wasn't there at all. Afterwards he felt exhausted, but very relaxed and happy.

One night some sticky fluid came out too. Chris was worried. He stopped playing with his penis. He thought something had burst, and he might have to go into hospital. But it wasn't sore, so he didn't tell anyone. He looked things up in the dictionary and the encyclopaedia, and in books he found in the library. After a while, he understood what had happened.

He started again. He discovered that if he thought about certain things, it felt better while he was doing it, and especially at the end. He was careful to catch what came out, so no one would know. He lay on his back, and opened his pyjama top, and spread a tissue on his tummy. Then after, he flushed the tissue down the loo. He did it every night, and some mornings too.

He was glad there was nothing wrong with him. But he also knew it meant he couldn't possibly be Jesus, or anything like it. He was just a sinful, corrupt, ordinary person. He would never be pure enough to be the ideal human.

In one way, it was a relief. But he was also disappointed. He had wanted it to be true.

42. This was the secret Chris had told Lucy at the party. He kept wondering what she thought. At first he couldn't decide if she'd found it a bit weird, or really pathetic. In the end he convinced himself she'd found it really pathetic. He felt that was unfair. He didn't get what she found so sexy about piercings, but it didn't mean he thought any less of her.

He really wished he hadn't told her now. He hoped she would forget all about it.

43. When Lucy came back to work, she didn't mention anything about having been off sick, or why. No else mentioned it either. It was very busy these days, so there was plenty else to talk about. Tammy and Al had taken on more programmers, who did most of the on-site projects. Chris hadn't even met some of them. He spent almost all his time in the office, implementing new systems that Lucy had designed. Tammy said she'd never met someone who could work as fast. She kept giving Lucy more and more to do.

When they were both in the office, Chris was sure Lucy was avoiding him. He thought it might be some sort of test. He knew that because of everything she'd told him, he was expected to stay being her friend. He wanted to be there for her, or he thought he did. He still spent quite a bit of time listening to music she liked, and watching films she talked about. He'd read the William Blake book she lent him three or four times. He didn't understand it, but he felt like if he kept trying, then he might begin to. Bits of it kept coming into his mind when he wasn't thinking about anything else.

But he didn't want to get too involved. He couldn't handle the thought of being responsible for someone else's emotions. Something might happen, and then he would be expected to fix it. He had no idea what to do in that kind of situation.

He started avoiding her too.

44. There were only a couple of months left until the end of the year, but more and more businesses were already reporting serious malfunctions. Most of them were reluctant to go public, in case it looked like they hadn't taken the whole thing seriously. But every time they fixed a problem, a whole set of new ones came up.

Al said it was the same old story. The more you put things together, the more they kept falling apart. He said he sometimes wondered if the world had long ago passed the point of total collapse, and they were the only ones holding it together.

Chris hated it when Al talked like that. It made him feel responsible for everything. Al said it was true. People like them were responsible for pretty much everything. Computers ran the world, and they were the ones who kept the computers going. If something happened to them, the whole world would go to pieces overnight.

45. Lucy called Chris one Sunday on his mobile phone, and asked him if he wouldn't mind coming round to her flat. He was at the office, trying to get on top of the backlog before new jobs started coming in the following week. She said she'd been sending him text messages, but he told her he never bothered opening those. They were always from the phone company telling him he could send text messages. She didn't laugh. She hung up.

Work had made him get a mobile phone so they could reach him at weekends when it was very busy. He'd have preferred a pager but Tammy said she didn't trust them.

Chris didn't think anyone else had the number. He didn't like people having his details without him knowing. But since Lucy was from work he thought maybe she'd been able to look it up. He decided he had better go round, in case something bad really had happened, and then he would feel awful that he hadn't.

When Chris got there, Lucy told him she had cut herself, on her arm. She already had it bandaged. She wouldn't go to the hospital or the doctor. She said she'd done it before and she knew she'd be okay. She always sterilised the razor. She said she tried not to do it very often, but there were times she just couldn't stop herself. She said things got so bad some days that she felt like it was what she deserved. She said she imagined it was somebody else cutting her. She liked to picture a person she knew, somebody kind and thoughtful and generous. That made it easier, she said.

Chris didn't say anything. He just nodded and listened.

46. That night, Chris had a sort of waking dream while he was lying in bed.

Lucy was beside him.

She was open. It was sticky.

Some of it was above her shoulder, still warm. It was like a snake. He could smell fried egg from inside it.

Her head was hanging back, wobbling.

The sheets were wet and red.

She wasn't quite dead. Something small was moving.

He closed his eyes.

When he opened them, she was gone.

47. Lucy showed the bandage to Chris again a few days later, when they were both having a cigarette in the office kitchen. She always wore long sleeves, even in hot weather, so no one in the office had seen it. She said the scars were already healing, but they would take a long time to fade, and him knowing they were there was kind of nice. It was like another secret they shared. She said she found it quite sexy.

Chris pretended he didn't hear that part. He didn't find anything sexy about pain or violence or domination. He knew he was supposed to. But the only time he'd been with a girl who wanted him to handcuff her and pretend to strangle her, he'd been rubbish at it. He was too worried about actually hurting her, or what it might mean if he started to enjoy it. She told him he was scared of living on the edge, and he agreed he was. He didn't see what was so great about the edge, he said. You could easily fall off. He hadn't seen her again.

48. A couple of weeks later, Lucy was off work again. Chris was annoyed. He felt like it was directed at him. When he sent her an email, she didn't reply.

Chris knew he should probably let Tammy know something was wrong, but he also knew that Lucy would hate that. Instead, he did Lucy's work as well as his own. He didn't sleep much.

When she hadn't come in for a whole week, Chris stayed at home on the Saturday morning and phoned her over and over again until she finally answered.

Lucy said she just knew he would keep calling. She needed

him to come round now and do it. He was the only one who could. He asked her what she was talking about. She said he understood exactly what she meant. She was fed up pretending. She told him she knew it wasn't time yet, but she couldn't wait any more. She wanted it over. She wanted it finished.

And if he didn't do it, she would tell them at work about his secret. They would all laugh at him. She would put it on the Web and everybody would know. It would be there forever. He could never get rid of it. He would have to be that person for the rest of his life.

Chris told her she could do what she wanted. There was no way he was going to so much as talk about anything like that. She said he didn't have to finish her off, just cut her open and then leave. There was a place she knew, where no one would see. They could light some candles and make it special. He might get into it, once he started.

Chris said he understood about fantasies, and that was fine, but some things were too dangerous to even think about doing in real life. She said if he didn't do it today, he would do it some time. She would make sure of that. He told her there was no possible way that could ever happen.

'If you won't do it, then I'll do it myself,' said Lucy. 'You have to stop this now,' said Chris. 'It's your choice,' said Lucy. 'You decide.'

She hung up.

Chris was very worried. He kept thinking that she might actually do something serious to herself, but he really didn't want to get involved again. He tried calling back but she wouldn't answer. He thought she might be trying to call him, so he waited for a bit. After about half an hour, he started to panic that he'd left it too late. He called an ambulance, and then got a taxi to her flat.

49. Lucy wasn't there. Her friend Oliver was.

Chris was happy to see him again. He was sure Oliver would know what to do.

Oliver told Chris that Lucy had phoned him too, and he'd come straight over. But Chris had probably saved her life by calling the ambulance, Oliver said. It had arrived just as he did. Lucy didn't answer the door, so they'd had to break it open. One of the neighbours helped. In the end they had to drill the lock off. The police arrived too, but by that stage they were already inside.

She had cut herself open, Oliver said, but they'd got her in time. He would check with the hospital later and make sure she was okay. They would probably keep her in for the rest of the week at least. Chris said he wanted to go and see her, but Oliver told him it was best he went home. He said Chris should try not to worry.

Oliver explained to Chris that Lucy was a very special person. She wasn't like everyone else. She had unusual beliefs about herself. She had particular knowledge of certain things in history. She had a collection of items which were extremely valuable.

Chris said he had seen some of them when he was at her flat. Oliver got very interested then, and wanted to know when Chris had been there. Chris said it was one weekend. He didn't say he had stayed over. He didn't want Oliver to think there was anything going on between him and Lucy. Then Oliver might decide that what had happened was somehow Chris's fault. He didn't want Oliver to think anything bad about him.

But Chris knew it was probably true. It was his fault. He was the one who had made all the effort to be her friend. She opened herself up to him, and he turned away.

He wasn't a kind person at all. He was a cunt.

50. Chris knew he should go and visit Lucy the next day, but he couldn't. He had to call in sick to work. He was physically shaking, for hours at a time. He had never felt worse.

He kept thinking something awful was going to happen if he turned his back. A few times when he looked out his window, he thought he saw a huge fire on the horizon, in the centre of London. He was sure he could smell it too. But when he looked hard, nothing was there.

He couldn't sleep. He constantly wanted to cry. He couldn't take any more. He wished he could go away and live in a hole somewhere. He hated everyone. He felt like everything was falling apart.

He especially hated Lucy, for making him feel like this. He wished he had never met her. When she phoned Chris the next day, he told her that. He was very angry, and he couldn't hide it. He didn't even see why he should.

Lucy said she was really sorry. She promised she would never do anything like that again. She'd been thinking about a lot of stuff, she said. There were going to be some big changes in her life. She also promised she would never ever tell anybody about his secret, no matter what.

'I need to tell you a secret too,' said Lucy. 'Please don't,' said Chris. 'I think you really are Jesus,' said Lucy. Chris sort of laughed, but he could tell she wasn't joking. She sounded a little scared of him.

What she must mean, he told himself, was someone who was only kind, and not at all cruel or selfish. That was certainly how he'd always liked to think of himself, at least towards other people, but he didn't want her to know that. It was embarrassing.

'I honestly don't think I am,' said Chris. 'Neither did Jesus,' said Lucy. 'At least, not at first.'

Lucy told Chris she shouldn't be alive, but thanks to him, she was. That meant he had created her, the new her that carried on. Whatever she was from now on, was because of him. The old Lucy Mills had died, and good riddance. 'Now I belong to you,' said Lucy.

* * *

Gold and Silver, Brass and Iron

Will clips copper from the ends of his plates.

He lays it in a crucible on a burning brazier, till it softens. He takes tongs and a hammer, taps each piece into the shape he wants: a tiny shallow curve, a miniature of the single precious original.

Now he solders one end of each piece to the bone, as ribs to a spine. Heats and bends these copper strands, curling them further, forged into a golden cage. Like some terrible headless insect; an Indian orchid.

Making life, he thinks. As the sun itself does. The great God of the pagan ancients: Sol.

I shall be his contrary, he thinks. This is the hammer of Los.

He feels the anvil of the ancients, the giant forms occluded from our sight.

A blue fluid threads in from the rib, reaching in sinews. A red sphere descends, conglobing. Fire and water. A howling form.

He completes the skeleton: gold and silver, brass and iron. A coin of gold at the head, silver for arms, brass the ilium, iron legs. It makes the statue of Daniel, that first great vision of our end.

Will presses on the clay, a sculptor of old. Thumbs it and smoothes it. Thickens the little skeleton. He lays out anatomy sketches from his Academy days, and works in reverse. Builds up muscle, stripping on a layer of flesh and skin.

It begins to take human contours, though tiny. One foot long.

Hairs from his own head are sinews and nerves. With his graving tools he carves out fingers and toes. He draws in every curl of the hair, as he has seen it: the noble inner Milton, not the hard forbidding phiz of the familiar portrait.

'You shall tell the future,' he says to it, as he works. 'You are the wonder of the age. I will prove the wisdom of Paracelsus.

'I am plagued with glimpses of the life beyond our sphere, but I have not yet the great final song I know is coming. I had it offered once, and it slipped my grasp. Seventeen and seventy-seven. Now I begin to discern that vision again. I must new-create my ancient muse. Milton reborn will tell me what lies beyond. He has dined with giants, the bards of ages. He sees all.'

The Natural State

Proverbs of the World to Come
Madness is the natural state of man.
The only true evil is self-love.
Your infant daughter shall one day be a whore.
God despises those who pray when they could act.
Poison the flesh to heal the spirit.
Every child is called, but we stop their ears.
He who dies a virgin had better never been born.
Only a fool asks why.
Taste every vice, and choose one for your own.
Christ asks the impossible, for no man yet forgave another.
Mourn the dead, and then forget them, as they have forgotten us.
At dawn, weep. At noon, drink. At dusk, destroy.

Homunculus

Will is ready. He places the finished homunculus in a glass jar. The curve of the rib-spine gives a curl to its back; it lies like a frozen embryo, in a glass womb.

Buries the bottle in dung in their yard. Every day he digs, opens it, drops in lavender seeds and earthworms for food, as Paracelsus instructs him.

He waits.

*

The forty days produce nothing.

His angel tells him: those days are gone. In the antediluvian age, this magic would work alone. Now, we must work it ourselves.

He writes out the Hebrew letters which Catherine spied upon his heart. He folds the paper, places it in the jar: he has heard the late Rabbi Falk did so, the Baal Shem of London, to create a clay golem to be his slave.

He waits.

He fancies it knocks on the glass one day with its baby hands. Will does not see it, but hears. He knows it is growing.

He finds he can manipulate the living clay. Remakes the body ever more as he wishes to see it. A strong, youthful, Grecian shape.

The little man shall grow and grow, till it is forty feet tall. Terrorise the city, trample it to dust. Stalk the world like the giants of old. Demand an end to monarchy and slavery. This itself could be the promised end.

He waits.

The thing is inert. It mocks his effort, his patience, his vision. Nothing but mud, metal and bone. A nice trinket; a foolish hollow toy.

One more attempt.

He looses some seed from within, spreads it on the head.

He waits.

The head turns a fraction, the small face opens.

Alive.

The little man rouses in the glass jar, rises and stretches.

Will's heart swells and shudders, frightened at his own power.

He has given back life to dead matter. Now he knows: there is no boundary to what he may attempt.

The thing gestures to its face. Again. And again.

Will waits for it to speak. It does not. He asks himself why.

He sees now: it cannot. He has carved the lips, but they remain sealed.

He gives it a full mouth. Wets the clay, cuts and slices, forms a tongue.

And it speaks. As from the back of its throat, a reedy monotone.

'Ah. Ah. Ooh.'

Will watches. It plays with its new capacity, finds the sound it seeks.

'Tha. Tha. Hoo. Hoo! Hoo!'

Will stands back, afraid it will spasm and shatter the glass.

'Ah! Ah! Ma! Yoo! Yoo!'

Will fears it is in pain, accusing him.

'Yoo Ma! Tha Ma! Hoo Ma! Ma!'

He listens, transfixed, unsure if they are words, or grunts which sound like.

'Ma-na. Ma-na. Tha. Tha-ta.'

It quietens, like a dog wearing itself out of a frenzy. He is sure now: this is English, spoken with purpose.

'A man. Tha. A man. Who. You. Who. You. Tha. Man. Who.'

Will comes to see it is a question.

'Who am I, gentle creature?' he asks.

It wriggles now like a swaddled baby, excited, as though it has understood.

'Who! Who! Man! Who!'

'My name is Will Blake, poet and engraver. I have made you, from some old pieces and stuff. Enough of that for now. But who are you, little man? Do you know?'

Its clay lips purse, the brow crinkles into a baby frown. He is frightened the thing is only a moronic slave, a brute mechanical.

'Ma. Ma.'

He understands he is to say more.

'You are made from the substance of a great man. Do you know your inheritance?'

'Loh. Loh. Lon. Don-Lon. Don-Lon.'

'Yes! London. This is London, and you are made from London too, that is true. But at your heart, or, rather, you have no heart, but at your centre, you are the blessed matter of a great poet. Well, perhaps that is too much. But do you know yourself in this guise?'

He finds it a suddenly depressing prospect, to have to teach a stunted shade of Milton who it is, to be responsible for this awkward man-thing.

'Jaw. Jaw. Jaw. Jaw-Mill. Jaw-Mill. Mill. Mill.'

Blake thinks he hears it.

'Mil-ton,' he says, feeling a fool. 'That's right! John Milton. Can you say that? Can you say Mil-ton?'

The thing shakes itself ferociously, in recognition, excitement.

'Mill-ta! Mill-ta! Jaw! Mill-ta!'

It sounds like a Chinaman, struggling with a simple English word. He might improve the mouth, he thinks. But what can he do for the mental powers?

He unstoppers the glass. He has heard it said they cannot live for long outside. But he sees the jar as a glass womb, and if the thing is ready, it must emerge. A second nativity.

He takes his little one on his knee. It wriggles in protest, clumsy and clinging, but he holds it tight. It does not cry, as an infant might. It makes a little clucking, from the back of its throat. Will can almost persuade himself it sounds contented.

* * *

ii.   I reported what I saw and heard to Mr. *Pedlow* each week, by way of a written account given his servant of all was spoke and done, and I had nothing in return but more coins as he promised, the greater part of which I sent to my sister; but while I greatly feared discovery of my double employ, I consoled myself that there was nothing secret or strange about Mr. *Milton* or his household, so no report of mine could do him harm; for while many foreign men did come to visit, their talk was of *Erasmus* and *Aristotle*, not of Dutch wars and Popish plots; and when aged scholars paid their respects, all their words were remembrances of departed friends, and regrets at youthful follies and passions; but still I watched Mr. *Milton* close and made careful note of his discourse, of his character, and of his daily habits, for so I was tasked and paid to do:

We began early, at dawn or before, and from his bed he would bid me read aloud the last verses I wrote out for his great epic on the *Fall of Man*, and he would chant along with me, for he worried and fretted over each word, and weighed the many rhythms and sounds it might convey, sometimes cloaking his own dark meanings within the sense of a line.

For those who would see it, and have eyes to, said he; and when the chalk-stones did not plague him so bad, he played upon his organ to loosen his faculties, great chiming rounds of *Monteverdi*; for the Italians pleased him best, and it tickled him greatly to confound those who thought all Italian was Papist:

Aye, said he, and if it be? I knew many a fine Papist in *Italy*. Error is not vice, and a man's Faith is not all he is. I never met a soul in *England* yet who could compare to an Italian for learning and the fine expression of it. But then, the great pity is, I never had the pleasure of meeting myself! And forth came a great rattling rasping laughter, which shook out the bellows of his stomach, and his hands raised a choir from the keys and pedals of his little organ.

If it happened that I arrived later than he called me, he mooed like a very plaintive cow and roared that he wanted to be milked, which put a mixture of fear and laughter into me, indeed this feeling I grew accustomed to in his company; but when once I quipped that he sounded more bull than cow, he said he wanted none of that sort of milking, he would leave such antics to the sodomite Cavaliers; and then forth came a chain of poetry all in a tangle, and we spent the next hours teasing it out and clipping away the links he felt would not hold, before he sang out the final verses to me, as he called it, for indeed his peculiar manner of reciting had the quality of old plainchant which I found most curious and even displeasant; but as with so much of life, good and ill, I miss it now it is gone.

I mean for this thing to last not just my lifetime or even yours, said he, but for centuries to come. It must be solid and heavy as brass, and with as much of a gleam and shine. I do not mind a jewel or two, but the whole shall be an instrument and not a decoration.

An instrument must have an end, said I.

Indeed it must, said he, and mine is to smite and to confound. This work is a fearsome engine, wrought by two hands, yours and mine. And there is nothing like a *two-handed engine* to keep them foxed! (He laughed at this, and I understood not his meaning then, though I have since: a puzzle in a youthful poem of his, which he refused always to explain to friend or foe, though they often asked.)

He noted my dislike of his pipe, for I always contrived a reason to take the air when he put it to light.

Do not condemn this vice, said he. Tobacco may be harsh on the throat, but it quickens the blood, and the blood in turn feeds the soul. For the young it is a permissible luxury, for the old, a miserable necessity.

So I worked with him too on his other studies, reading Latin, I hope well, and Greek, I fear poorly, since he often mocked my pronouncing of some word; and I was not the only daily visitor, for a wizened Jew he called *Spanish Moses* came each noontide to read the Hebrew Bible with him, and together they tussled over every syllable of every word, the right way to sound each letter and the true rhythm of the reading, as though it were a sort of incantation; but Mr. *Milton* always told me that even in English, the manner of reading was as important as the words themselves:

Many of the common sort do not hear the half of what you say, said he, maybe one word in four. The tone is all. There is a beauty and a power in the sounds of words that can move the heart of a man as much as the intellectual sense. More, perhaps.

The Israelite liked to say that Mr. *Milton*'s blindness meant he had a second sight into the *Divine Spirit*, but when the little rabbi left, Mr. *Milton* would say this was the kind of cod-mystick horse-dung which gave the sacred Hebrew race the bad name of magicians and quack alchemists.

The visions of the blind is a great faerie-tale, said he. Visions! I see only those I construct myself. My task is to have others see them as I do. To see what never was, to human sight at least.

Being blind was a curse plain and simple, he often said, which he believed it was a consequence of straining his eyes with too much reading by candle as a child, for he liked to sit up and study till midnight from he was twelve years old; though in part he blamed a weakness inherited from his mother, who wore eye-glasses all the time he knew her; and neither did he believe it was the will of God, as many said, for he was not struck blind all at once, but his light dimmed over long years when he ignored good advice from many physicians to spare his eyes and so save them.

He remembered for me his visit as a young man of my age to the blind *Galileo* in *Italy*, which thought stirred me greatly that I had met one who knew such a man; though he demurred my suggestion that I might remember these present days in turn to my juniors in the years to come, when his name and fame should ring out as soundly.

I have made no such contribution, said he, in arts or letters. I may still, of course. Then you shall live out this scene over again with those who are babes today, and pass the old torch forward.

I am no *Milton*, said I.

Nor was I then, said he. Nor am I yet. (Which I understood to mean he had not yet achieved what he promised to himself, which was his great poem.)

He was fierce and savage in his quips, but most savage against himself, which is a great virtue in any who pretends to wit; and when his blood was up he was a burning star of discourse, none could come near him for invective and straight-talking, and often I had to beg him to temper his tone, or at least his pitch, lest a parish-constable or watch-man be passing the casement, for he said as much as I ever heard said against the King; but when the clouds rolled over him, he confessed he felt it very hard that some abroad wished to see his end, to even him for what he wrote against the late *Charles Stuart*; but as often again he railed that he had no hand in that bloody work, and was condemned for the actions of others.

I wrote what they bade me write, said he, what I knew to be true but said in the public press only to advance the cause I would have died for. Yes, I would, and at times I did expect to. I had no fear. And my only shame is that the fear is come upon me now, and I know not how to banish it, for I suffer with a black conviction that I am watched in all I do, and my enemies conspire to shudder my peace and thwart my work, to drive me to despair and untimely death. This incubus feeds a worm in my soul and there are nights I sleep none at all. But it matters little, for all the day is one long night-time to me.

A great unrest crept upon me then, and I asked why he should fear his enemies now, when he had escaped their heavy wrath at the *Restoration*.

I have two breeds of enemy, said he, those who stand in the light, and those cowards yet occulted to me. But something is afoot. I hear strange whispers as I pass abroad that drop my name among others who wish a fiery death to this very town. I deduce that I am posed within this conspiracy as a kind of fig leaf for their zealous cant. And my suspicions do not wander far from my own door. I have volumes gone astray from my library, I suspect they have me spied close, even within these very walls, and so I watch too in my own way. I keep a quiet ear upon my household, and I form my own opinion of who may not be trusted. Guilt will out, as it ever does, and my vengeance shall fall swift and harsh. O, an honest enemy is a fine thing for a man to bear, for it shows he has stood firm on his convictions. I should always show mercy to that man I know I cannot trust, though he wish me dead, over another who claims fidelity yet bites the hand that feeds. Duplicity is poison to my soul, but I have a nose for it, and I shall surely root it out. Pity the wretch when I do.

Chapter Seven

Earthly Matter

Will teaches his little creation to speak. Call and response. It learns eagerly, greedily. He lets himself feel he is reminding it how. Like a man who has taken a bad turn, recovering his powers.

He reads to it, his own simple songs. Innocence and Experience. The thing seems to take pleasure. Bible verses and psalms, which it chants along with him, forming the words ever more clearly.

Still he does not tell Catherine. All must be perfect and ready before the veil is removed. Will is patient, though he knows the time is nigh. He spends only a few minutes each day, and takes his leave when it begins to question him.

'Who are you? Who?'

The little hands grope and grasp. The head turns. The legs bend and kick.

'What am I for?'

Like a shrunken man-child. A walking doll.

'Have you made me?'

One day, he knows it is time to answer.

'I have, little thing.'

'And where am I?'

'In London. Westminster, and around. Poland Street. North of the Thames, west of the City.'

'I know London. Am I not new?'

'You are not. You are made from another man.'

'Am I risen?'

'You are.'

'For what am I risen?'

'To give us your unwritten works. You are the herald of the New Age.'

Will instructs the thing, what it means to be who it is.

He reads the works of Milton to this remnant of his earthly matter, reborn from clay and copper. It listens, tightly concentrating. Sometimes he thinks he sees the little lips move along with these words, too.

To leaven the lesson, he tells it the tale of Young Werther, and watches its face for delight and sympathy, for passion and grief. He sees none.

Once in a Century

One day:

'It returns,' says the thing.

'What is that?'

'My mind. My self. I begin to know who I am.'

'You remember your works?'

'I do.'

'And may we hope to expect your unwritten visions?'

'I had as soon strike out the half of what I did write. More.'

'Then, to improve those we have. You are full of errors, you know.'

'I do know, too well. But you will correct me, I am sure.'

'Not I, but you shall see. I will help you reform your emanations for our time. The Titans will walk again.'

'As you wish. I find I am compelled to obey you. A most uncomfortable feeling, and one I am not accustomed to. As though you were my king, and I a willing subject.'

'I would be a gentle king.'

'Aye, so they all say. But just watch how you are, when you feel the power you truly have. A great tragedy of our world is that no man who seeks power deserves it. Once in a century a wise man heads a nation, and that nation rises. But fools follow the wise.'

'I had rather be a fool.'

The thing curls its little mouth into a sneer.

'I see God has been good enough to grant your wish.'

'I am your servant.'

'I should not be in the least surprised. I was ever ill-followed. One man only gave me more than he took. Allgood was the name. Have you heard it spoken next to mine? I fancied him a son, my own tender John, who never lived to disappoint his father. This mournful fellow haunts my days. His bitter fall is my own.'

Will is surprised.

'I have the original of his history, though the tale was never printed.'

'If nothing more occurred than what our printed histories tell us, life would be thin matter indeed. You may as well hope to conjure the shape of a dragon from one single Indian tooth.'

'I have conjured you from a solitary rib.'

'And am I all you hoped?'

Will thinks.

'I met a man called Cock who said his grandfather was a companion of yours. Do you know the name? I have read it nowhere.'

The thing laughs, a rasping cackle.

'Then he lived to breed. Well. That is to the good, for it eases a man's temper. Oh, but if he is forgot, then all was not in vain.'

Will is silent, and the thing laughs again. Spiteful, hollow.

'Read to me from the pages of Allgood's confession. I should like to revisit those terrible days.'

So Will reads.

* * *

iii. Mr. *Milton* summoned me to him one bright morn, and with rigid fright I heard him say he had found out the serpent in his midst, and the knave would be informed that very day, after which he would be whipped and branded and sent forth as a marked traitor; and a great quaking set off in my legs and hands, such that I pretended an urgent errand and walked about the streets a great while, for I saw this was a last chance to flee the punishment I richly deserved, though I could not fathom why Mr. *Milton* should wish to give me that occasion; yet at length I understood, and this quieted my soul: this sudden warning was a stern test of my character, for I surely knew that I could claim myself no Christian at all unless I spoke up like a gentleman and faced the consequences of my sin; so I must place my faith in Mr. *Milton*'s godly nature, that he meant only to put fear and shame in me before bestowing his ultimate forgiveness, so long as I should *confess before I was accused*; so I wound my way back to the house, with a heavy tread and fervently cursing my own pigeon-livered soul, which shivered at the awful prospect; yet when I entered, I saw that my old friend Mr. *Ellwood* had come to visit, and asked to hear some of the great poem, which he had read before, but was impatient to see it printed; so Mr. *Milton* commanded me to sit and read, which I knew at once was a further torment he meant to inflict upon my guilty spirit; but still I obeyed and spoke it out for above an hour; and the rhythms of his verse soothed my spirit, so that I near forgot my agony of conscience.

Do you not tire to hear it aloud? said *Ellwood*.

The contrary, said *Milton*. My father wrote music, and when he finished a hymn, he played it without cease. It rang through the house a full day's length, till he himself was able to hear naught but a tuneful melody, as for the first time, shriven of mathematics, bright and pure as it should be when fresh upon the ear.

Like a wife, said *Ellwood*. The more time you spend with her, the more you see her charms.

No, said *Milton*. The opposite, then.

Rather like God with his creation, said *Ellwood*. Once it is complete, he cannot resist descending to habituate with us, to know us as we know each other; that is, less well for sure than a creator might, but more immediately.

We are all made of divine stuff, said *Milton*.

I rather think we are in sympathy with him, said *Ellwood*.

And does God suffer when we do? said *Milton*.

As a father should, said *Ellwood*.

I wonder then he permits the plague, said *Milton*.

All say it is a punishment, said *Ellwood*.

I wonder, said *Milton*. And you, Mr. *Allgood*, do you say so too?

If it is so, said I, then I ask why I was spared.

Spoke like a true Papist, said *Milton*.

And these words opened a crack in my heart, for I knew they were but a goad towards my self-unveiling as his Judas, though I settled myself that he would have me tarry till Mr. *Ellwood* was absent.

It is hard to credit some of the tales, said *Ellwood*. There were stories of dying men who leapt into the pit, tumbling upon corpses as they fell. Limb over limb over limb piled and falling from carts. A rubbish-dump of mere humanity. A vision of Hell, or if not, then of no earthly world I wish to know.

Well, Mr. *Allgood*? said *Milton*.

I was here, said I. All is true, and worse.

I was not, said *Milton*. Mr. *Ellwood* took a house for me a long way apart, convenient for his people, and I am grateful still. I like to speak with *Quakers*. I find they have the true spirit and light within them. *Paul* himself would know them at once as men of *Christ*. For the apostles should find themselves in gaol today. And at *Chalfont*, there was plenty of good walking round about, which suits my constitution. Though I curse my blindness that I had need of a guide, for a knave called *Cock* placed himself at my service. He sought me out and dogged my steps, till I took him on to scribe for me, and to read. But never did I judge a man's character so ill. He had me raised up as his private icon, and tried to tangle me in his frenzy for the coming *Last Days*, that he swore were nigh upon us.

That same Mr. *Cock* is now in *London*, said *Ellwood*, and he told me he would call on you. Many have told me they mean to seek you out in these days, for your poem is already famed abroad. With your permission, I can take a copy and circulate it further. The fee will surely rise if demand is on the street.

There shall be no copy till it is complete, said *Milton*. I dare not risk an early printing. Men may read it, but in my presence, under my roof.

You poem is a vision, said *Ellwood*. It must be shared.

A blind man's vision! said *Milton*. Let it not be sold as such, or I shall starve.

Many of the ancients held that all the blind are prophets and have second sight, said *Ellwood*.

When the Lord sees fit to bestow these gifts, said *Milton*, then I am ready. In the meantime, I compose.

You are coy, said *Ellwood*. We know that the form of the statue is already in the marble, and the artist must only free it.

A fine story for children, said *Milton*, but a plain lie. There is no form in any marble but I carve it out. Human craft and artistry, study, reflection, imagination, application, are what is required. To put it another way: plain work. Or, thus: if there is a perfect form within every block of stone, why is there so much bad statuary? If God placed the forms of beauty in marble, who placed the poor forms within? Satan, I suppose.

It is we who are unequal to the task, said *Ellwood*.

And why do we lack the gifts? said *Milton*. Do you mean to say that the most pious are the best artists? You must know that to be another lie for children. We blame *Satan* for all our flaws, as much as to say: I have no free will. As though each man has a blind force beneath his intention which exonerates him. They call on *Calvin* to support them. Cant. Pure cant and foolery.

Reason will find it out. In three centuries men will laugh, and say some bearded foreign humbugger sent his books here and persuaded us we need not accuse ourselves for our own deeds. Before we are ever born, some hidden destiny maps out our every action. I say this is cant, and always was. We will be freed from these ill-read theories of predestination.

This is not true *Calvin*, said *Ellwood*. He too was a man of reason.

He was a man of God first, said *Milton*.

May a man not hold with both? said *Ellwood*. Reason and God.

But when the two are opposed, said *Milton*, where are you then? These new men of the Royal Society may proclaim their natural philosophy as the door to the *New World*, but I say their *Science* is but a branch of good old theology. Nature is unchanging, and reducing all to sums and diagrams is none other than enquiring into the mind of God, which is the subject of divinity only. To ask *how* may be allowed as the domain of this new method. The moment a man asks *why*, he is in theology.

Mr. *Ellwood* left; and now I saw the final chance to throw myself upon my master's mercy; yet my tongue was all clagged with fear, and I could not; then I waited for the judgement to fall, yet it did not; so in a rush to plenish the horrible silence I dared to ask Mr. *Milton* about this man *Cock*, to know was it the same strange preacher I encountered before, for though the name struck me, I said, it was not so uncommon that I felt sure.

I knew him only at *Chalfont* the year gone by, said he. An acquaintance of your Mr. *Ellwood*'s, and a *Fifth Monarchy Man*. Do you not know of the *Fifth Monarchy Men*? *Venner*'s rebellion? Then you are blessed. They were a clique from the army who swore that it was their mission to bring about the *Millennium* itself, to cause the return of *Jesus* to rule *England* when the King was chopped. And that this failed to happen was a chiding to the *Commonwealth*, not to their own selves. They parted from *Cromwell* over his compromising, and staged a rising in *London* after the *Restoration*, which put the town into a turmoil, and had the screws turned on all Dissenters. Now they are building themselves again, for they believe this year is to be the *Great Sifting*, and a judgement shall be visited by the risen *Christ* upon *London*.

We all await such a day, said I, though in heavy fear of our own sins.

I await nothing, said he. I have done with reckoning the date of this or that prophecy fulfilled.

The return they wished for, said I, is of *Christ* in all our hearts, to wash away our wrongs, and lead us to eternal life. And I confess I hoped these words would tend him to mercy in his own dealings with me, for I was sure he quibbled so only to tighten my screws yet further, and with very great success.

No, I tell you, said he, they awaited *King Jesus* in person. Here, in our land and time. Our Saviour descending upon a cloud to greet us. Why would the Lord need a cloud to stand upon, I wonder? I wish they had one half of your good sense. O, the wiser heads among them allowed for a revolution of the Spirit, but the rabble they roused wished only for a great visible miracle. Some garish Dutch daubings come to life. Superstitious trash. Even an educated Papist would sneer at it.

Such talk is now once more abroad, said I, for every almanack and astrologer claims the same, and the word in the streets at every news is whether this or that is now a true sign of the *Last*

Days. That for every false dawn, it has been proven beyond doubt that this is to be the year, and *London* the place.

Oh, spare me *Henry Cock*, said he. So-called because none may sleep while he crows. Or because when aroused, he sprays bootless muck from his head so wantonly—

Enough, Mr. *Milton*, said I. For all my own black faults, I must tell you plain these words do not become a godly man.

This was the first and only time I chid him thus, but I was certain of my cold fate and saw nothing to fear in unpacking my heart; and he was so startled I should, that he kept mum above an hour, which time I spent bobbing in a boiling vat of terror, and chasing back and forth my fate like a cat with a woollen ball, ready one minute to tell him all, ready the next to plunge my rotten self into the black *Thames* sooner than utter a word.

When Mr. *Milton* spoke again, he said he had a great stain upon his own conscience, and if I would be his priest, he should like to confess, to which I replied not; and then he declared that while I had been out at my long errand he had tired of waiting and made good his word: He punished little *Pip* the pot-boy for treachery against his person, for that he knew the lad lingered and listened often to his private meetings, and so he ejected him with force from the house, with bloody stripes upon his back and a hot red welt on his cheek;

and it grieves me to tell that the shame and horror I ought to have felt at hearing another suffered for my own crimes was washed clean away by the great wave of joyful ease that crashed upon me when I knew I was safe and my secret buried still; but now Mr. *Milton* said he regretted the harsh vengeance, and wished to his heart he could have found forgiveness in himself as we are bid; and he asked me in his own half-mocking way for Papist absolution, which I said I could not give, but I was sure he was forgiven for all that; after which he thanked me most simply and made his way to bed;

and so I did myself, though I slept not a wink the night through, for I knew this *Pip* had hopes to be a Latin scholar, and took a post beneath his station with Mr. *Milton* just to have occasion to enjoy his wisdom, which was all the reason he lingered and listened; and I asked myself what I could do to make reparation for his downfall;

but every mazy way my mind ran down led to the same corner: that I must confess all to Mr. *Milton*; and this broke my heart clean open with bitter sadness, for now I knew full well I never would, though I surely risked my immortal soul an eternity in the fiery pit.

* * *

51. Work was incredibly busy, and getting worse. Chris felt like he was only just holding things together. If anything else happened, he thought he might have a complete meltdown. He felt too hot all the time. His eyes were blurry and sore. The slightest noise made him jump. But he told everyone he was getting on fine.

52. On the way back from work, Chris would imagine houses on fire, or people lying dead in the road. It made him very anxious, but he couldn't stop himself. He always had the same feeling. A really terrible thing was going to happen, and it would be all his fault.

Sometimes he thought there was a tiny little man running along on the pavement beside him. He could hear him laughing. When he looked at the sun, he could see a face staring down. He couldn't get rid of the feeling of being watched.

When he was at home, Chris spent a lot of time playing with his little wooden toy. He moved the pieces around, and tried to find the perfect pattern. He could see all sorts of possibilities, but none of them was exactly right. He was sure that if he kept going, he would get it eventually. Then he could leave the thing down for good.

Some evenings he got very frustrated. He felt that he could never solve the puzzle, and he might go crazy trying. He wanted to get rid of it. He wondered if he should give it to Lucy for Christmas. He thought she would probably just laugh.

He worried a lot about the things she had said to him. He didn't want to have created her. He didn't want her to belong to him. But he was afraid now that if he was unkind to her, then she would kill herself and make it be his fault. He wished he had never tried to get her to like him.

He kept getting flashes of Lucy cut up into pieces. He kept thinking he could smell burning when he was in the street. He couldn't shake the idea that he was being followed, everywhere he went. A man with no face was coming to get him.

Chris pretended it wasn't happening. He tried not to think about it. If he ignored it, it would all go away by itself.

53. Nobody said anything when Lucy came back to work. Nobody asked where she had been, or whether she was okay now. Nobody even said very much when it became clear she'd stopped wearing her goth clothes and the make-up. She'd taken

out all her piercings too, or said she had. Chris had never seen some of them, so he couldn't be sure. She'd had her hair cut short, and she was letting the black dye grow out.

Lucy looked so different that sometimes clients would come in and not be able to find her. She always just laughed and said it was time for a change of image and she liked to keep people on their toes. But once Chris got used to how she looked, he could see she was pretty much the same old Lucy. She still had the same sarcastic sense of humour. She still liked the same sorts of films, and the same music. She still came in late after she'd been up half the night playing her Nintendo. She still squinted and looked pissed off if they stepped out of the office and it was a sunny day. She didn't drink as much, but she smoked more than ever, even at her desk when she was busy. Nobody said anything, even though officially you were not supposed to. She did seem to be eating, Chris noticed, but mostly just crisps and biscuits. And she smiled more often, especially at him.

He did his best to avoid her these days, but she wasn't having any of it. She asked him nearly every day about her thing with Oliver on New Year's Eve, and whether he had any other plans. He always said he wasn't sure yet if he had or not. She told him it was very important that he understood everything in time. She was going to lend him something Oliver had lent to her, and that would help for sure.

She gave it to him at work one day in a small Jiffy bag, and told him not to open it until he got home. It was a small note-book about the size of his hand, wrapped in a piece of velvet. It looked very old. Every page was full of neat handwriting. Chris could just about make it out. It was written by someone called

Allgood, and it said it was the story of his life. He tried to read it, but he couldn't get very far.

Lucy asked him the next day if he understood. He said he did. She said that was very good news. They had a lot to talk about. She kept inviting him to go with her to a gig, or a party, or a film. She especially wanted to take him to see *Fight Club*. She said he would understand why when he had seen it. He always said he'd love to go when he was less busy, but he could tell she didn't believe him. He never suggested anything himself. He was trying to remain kind, while sending out the signal that he wanted her to find someone else.

Chris was sure the others wondered what was going on. When he told a story in the pub, or gave a presentation at work, Lucy listened really intently, looking right at him, hardly blinking. She flirted with him blatantly in the office, but he pretended not to notice.

She wrote him letters. He didn't open them. He was scared of what they might say. She phoned him up in the evenings, usually quite late, and talked to him for ages. Sometimes it was about nothing much, and there were long silences while one of them tried to think of something to say. Sometimes it was about him, and how great he was, and how special and different from other men. She felt they had a really intense connection and she didn't want to do anything to spoil that. She hoped they would always be friends, even if he went to work somewhere else. She said he was the only person who understood her.

Other times, it was about the end of the world. She told him she had worked it out by herself while she was off work. The Beast in the Book of Revelation was computers. You couldn't buy or sell without it. You had to worship its image. Its number was six-six-six. And the number six in binary notation was one-one-zero.

This was the big clue, she said. It meant you had to look back one hundred and ten years, and then do it twice more. The last one was eighteen eighty-eight, and that was hers. Before that was seventeen seventy-seven, and then you came to the start of it all, in sixteen sixty-six. Each time it was supposed to come, she said, and each time they stopped it happening. It was just a matter of understanding how.

Chris said he didn't want to be a pain in the arse, but it ought to be one hundred and eleven years. Lucy told him he was wrong. From the end of eighteen eighty-eight to the beginning of nineteen ninety-nine was one hundred and ten. This year was finally the end, she said, and she knew exactly what to do. That was the thing she was working on with Oliver. It had already started. Chris was walking around inside it all the time, and he didn't even know.

Lucy kept asking Chris if he understood, and he always said he did. But he didn't really. He hated it when she talked like that. It worried him that someone as intelligent as her could believe any of this stuff.

54. It wasn't that Chris thought life was meaningless. He knew deep down there was some kind of shape to things. It was just obvious to him. Ultimately it all had to make sense, he thought, otherwise there would be nothing instead of something. The fact of anything at all was some kind of order.

55. One Friday in the pub Al took Chris aside.

Lucy wasn't there. She'd gone to Yorkshire to work on a new contract, and she was going to visit her mam on the way back and stay for the weekend. They hadn't seen each other for a few years. Lucy said they had never really got on, and in the end they'd had a big falling out and not spoken for a while. You started giving me grief before you were even born, she told Chris her mam had said, and you've never stopped since. Her dad was an alcoholic, and he had left when Lucy was ten. He lived in Wales now, working on the ferries. She sent him money at Christmas, she told Chris, and he phoned her up occasionally when he was drunk, but she'd only actually seen him a couple of times since she was a child. Every so often he said he was coming to London to visit her, but then there would be some excuse at the last minute and he wouldn't come.

'You want to watch things with Lucy, mate,' said Al. 'What kind of things?' said Chris. 'You know what I mean,' said Al. 'Don't piss about unless you mean business.' 'We're just friendly,' said Chris. 'I know, mate,' said Al. 'The thing is, a girl like that needs handling. She's damaged goods, and she knows it, and she'll expect you to fix her. And you'll think you can. But you can't.' Chris was offended by that. There were times he seriously wanted to punch Al. But he didn't say anything. 'I see now what she's about,' said Al. 'It's my little sister all over again. She goes through these wild phases, into drugs and partying, going travelling and screwing around, and then she crashes out and lives like a nun for a few months, back at home with the folks. And then she's off again, joining the New Age ravers, or the road protestors, or, what was it last time? Animal rights. Breaking into labs and stealing rabbits. God knows. You think she'll settle down, but she won't. You'll be her punchbag, mate, and if that's what you're into, don't let me stop you. But, you know. Well, it's not for me to say. Just consider this a quiet word had.' 'But I'm not going out with her, Al,' said Chris. 'We're just friends.' 'I know, mate,' said Al. 'Relax. Don't shoot the messenger, okay? I just wanted to clear my conscience, and now it's done.'

* * *

From hell
Long Liz
Number eight
Mam

He whispered you and you whispered him and I seen you o I seen you. Bad bad Liz. I was goin to do you the same but he never went in you down there only your mouth o Liz how could you tis dirty dirty dirty. I was cryin when I cut your neck. I heard them Juwes singin ther songs and cheerin I thought now good Im goin to be caught I want to be caught. But no one came. I heard you with him tuggin him hard and you said o wont you finish off Im gettin cramp and he said I cant and you said Ile take you in me mouth. Looked like you was eatin him alive. You never finished him cos he cleared off when somebody came and you said bye bye some other nite.

Youre like a statue I thought like a Victry or a Justis or a Jo Navark. I thought Id cut your guts out but then I thought I dont have to you never took him inside. I aint doin it for the fun tis fun too really it is but Im doin a job of work and I have to keep with him the gent. So once I killed you dead I followed him in case he done it cos he was hot and ready. With tothers I knew I had time cos he cant go again for a

while. But now he was ready to pop. I know what thats like o
yes I do. Im a man too and when its time its time. I never had
a women but I had all else. My own hand and guts of cows in
the slaughterplase and other boys in the boysplase up ther arses
but its no harm cos they cant get a babbie. Yes I done dead
cows and sheep too why not ther dead aint hurtin no one.
And I done wooms the one of Annie o sorry Annie I never
told you but yes I did. I took your woom and I did myself
into it for to see if we could make a babbie me and you. I
built it a nest in a milk jug and its in ther now I keep lookin
and nothin yet but I pray we mite. And when I looked at your
neck Long Liz I thought I could do it now in your neck open
as it was jest kneel over you and do myself in your cut throat
but I never. I think about that though when I tug myself and
I wish I had maybe Ile do it again.

They watched me this time the lords and ladies and men
from books and some of the Juwes and the angels and they
told me well done boy. My master was there too this time
standin there sayin its all rite boy go watch the man and see if
he gets another and see her well sarved. He can be everywhere
my master his gold face tells me all. O I werent supposed to
say about him but what harm hes not afeard of you nor
nobody he cant be killed he told me Im like another profit
and Im goin to save us. Whats a few whoors more or less who
cares o they all say they care but it makes me laugh. Boo hoo
cryin for them but they all had the knif in ther hand same as
me Queen Vic and Lord P and every duke and duchess and
gent and lady and priest and judge and schoolmaster and nurse
they all cut your throat same as if they did. They can cry and
so can I but it dont change nothin.

I hear them jawin about me and I think o ho ho thats me ther jawin about I could tell you tales and tis hard to not jest reveal all tis real real hard. Thers allsorts as wish they was me writin to the peelers and the papers and sayin ther me and some sayin I wish Id done that hes a brave man that Jack hes not afeard of no peelers. And I know its me they mean and I feel warm inside and strong and like I cant be caught but I know I can but yet I aint been and I wont be neither not by them cos they dont care they really really really dont care. I know. Amen.

signed
Jack but I aint Jack but I am really.

Chapter Eight

iv.   It was that very week Mr. *Cock* did indeed pay a visit, and I learned it was the same man I heard preach in years gone by, which put me in some fear; though at first Mr. *Milton* would not admit the caller, with more swearing of oaths to himself than I had ever hoped to hear from such a godly man; but in truth he liked nothing better than to dispute, so the man was not resisted hard; and straight away the visitor entered, he presented a gift to Mr. *Milton*, a little practickal rebus he said he had contrived himself, which I thought a rare kindness; but Mr. *Milton* laughed and said he had no time for toys and geegaws, which I saw plain Mr. *Cock* took very ill.

So Mr. *Cock*, said *Milton*. You come to thwart me anew.

I come to save you, old *Milton*, said *Cock*. The time is nigh. Join with me.

He had the same bright hard look about him, though his speech was changed, being something thick and awkward, as though his mouth was sore and raw.

All I wish to be saved from is your prattle, young *Cock*, said *Milton*. My clear-headed hours are precious, and I wish not to squander a single one in your society.

Still, you shall join with me, said *Cock*. For I know what I know.

It is all one whether I ask you or not, said *Milton*, for I am sure I am doomed to hear.

You are doomed to hear the trumpet sound, said *Cock*. See the scrolls unroll, the vials poured out. The time is upon us, old *Milton*. And you are with me, or you burn.

Then I burn, said *Milton*. Be on your way.

The Jews gather, said *Cock*. The hours turn. Your work is not complete, old *Milton*. You must know that.

Aye, that I do know, said *Milton*. And every minute I spend in your presence delays it further.

Mr. *Cock* grew hot at this.

A reckoning is upon us, said *Cock*. I hear it cried in the streets. God-made or man-made, a general belief is abroad that things cannot go on like this.

Such a belief is ever abroad! said *Milton*. When is it not! Only when the nation is at peace, and all have food and health, and then the end has been postponed so we may dance and fornicate to fill our boots.

Wise words, said *Cock*. My conviction is, we do not await *Christ*, but rather he awaïts us. Nothing shall happen but we make it happen. That is the true *Protestant* spirit. That is the spirit of *Milton*. Join with me, for I tell you most solemnly, before the year is out, *Christ* shall walk and talk among us, in this place, as he once did in Jerusalem itself.

Though I was silent, Mr. *Milton* knew in his way that I strained to speak.

What do you say, Mr. *Allgood*? said *Milton*.

I wish to ask, said I, why *Christ Jesus* should return in his lifetime or in mine. Is this not vanity?

Answer the young *Solomon*, said *Milton*. Think yourself so special, Mr. *Cock*?

Yes, Mr. *Allgood*, I do, said *Cock*. I have been chosen, as a vessel for his word. I do not say I am the only one. But I watch for the signs of his plan in my life, and I see them plain. There are too many not to see. I know in my heart I am to be a sword in his great judgement. Why would he permit me to be deceived in this matter?

Oh Mr. *Cock*, said *Milton*. If faith could do all, we should be your willing subjects.

But I am yours, said *Cock*. You are the prophet I await.

I am no prophet, said *Milton*. Just a blind old Parliament man, a wreck of the age gone by.

My thoughts are in the age to come, said *Cock*. This land I do believe is the chosen land. It is *England* and no other which has raised itself up as the first and only true *Protestant* nation. When the people are gathered unto *Christ*, he will descend to this Earth, as sure and solid as I see you now. This city shall be his eternal throne. And the time is now.

I once believed as you do, said *Milton*, and my heart still aches that I was deceived. But we must not profess what they cannot witness. The sure disappointment of rash promises will only lead men away from God.

Vanity! said *Cock*. Because your own little Parliament scheme failed, you imagine God has changed his plans? The vanity! The Lord said himself, nothing clearer, my day shall come like a thief in the night, when you least expect. And when was he less expected than now? But there is a code in Scripture. Aye, you may sneer, but there is! *Mede* himself believed so. *Ussher*. These were considerable men.

I knew these men, said *Milton*.

And do you deny it? said *Cock*. You know I am in the right. The truth of it strikes your very heart. These men held Scripture should be read as no ordinary book. But perhaps you say it is? No more than the histories and legends of the Hebrew race collected? Then why not murder and steal and blaspheme all you like? If this book does not reveal God's law and his plan then it is nothing! If I believed that, I would tread its pages into the muck and the mire! If there is no *Second Coming* in skin and bone and blood, was there a first? Scripture is all, or it is nothing! And the moment is come at last.

And if it is not, *Cock?* said *Milton*. I warn you, what if it is not?

But it shall be, said *Cock*. You miss me, old *Milton*. You miss my meaning entirely. I do not stand and wait, old man. That is not any kind of service by my lights. For my light is not spent, you see. Oh, you may coolly versify your way out of honest shame at your own lassitude, at your inaction, your shirking cozening double-talking tricks that keep your own hands out of the fire while you suffer others to be burned in your stead, but I say, enough. It is for me to make it so. That is where we differ, old *Milton*. God gave us each free will, and I use mine to bring about his kingdom, as he bids me do.

If you are wrong, said *Milton*.

And still, you miss me, said *Cock*. I am not wrong. I cannot be wrong. I ensure I am not. Some fools call me a prophet, but there is no easier thing for a man to predict than his own actions. I ask you only to watch. Watch, old *Milton*. The promised judgement will be visited upon this city in three short days. He shall wipe it from the Earth like *Gomorrah*. All those he wishes to save will be taken up. The Elect will stand aside. The *Satan* you write of shall emerge. The battle will be fought, here on this ground. Now, you may versify it, old *Milton*, aye, but I shall make it be.

Legions of devils unbottled will try their might against the angels themselves. Men shall gape at their flight and fight over *London* skies, as they now watch a flock of birds swoop and turn. All this was writ by *John*. You shall see the beast in all his fiery horror, and you shall witness his defeat. The reign of the Saints will be long, old *Milton*. Do you wish to sleep till its end? Or will you come and rule with us?

I shall see none of it, Mr. *Cock*, said *Milton*. You may share your unspent lights, and tell me all as it occurs. We shall compare your vision to my own. Whether by long years or by long miles, there is much we may not see. Blind or with sight, what happens beyond our bodily vision is always a matter of report only. And vision, sir, whether bodily or spiritual, is not the truth. If I have learned nothing else I have learned that. We may see all there is to see, and still know nothing.

I hold to what I believe, said *Cock*. I do not change with the wind.

Wisdom is hard won, said *Milton*, and you are young yet.

Wisdom can be lost as well as gained, said *Cock*. The *Milton* I follow is not the *Milton* I find before me. But I have the man I treasure still, in ink and paper.

You cannot hold me to account for your own willing deeds, said *Milton*.

But I do! said *Cock*. I must! It is your own words which drove me to it! Where do you think I find this, old *Milton*? I did not drop out of my mother's belly aflame to destroy the King. I believed in what you wrote, and I acted upon it. Do you refuse the burden of your own printed words?

I believed it too, said *Milton*.

Aye, but you did not fight for it! said *Cock*. You did not kill for it! You have the gall to wear a sword, but damn me to Hell if you ever drew it to defend what you believe! I shrink from asking are you a coward, for I doubt you ever put yourself in the way of finding out. You have ducked and shirked every occasion to discover it. I say to you, you did not have your arms pinned back and your tongue gripped with a pliers and pulled, and your head reined back by the hair, and a red-hot nail pierced through your tongue. And held there, old *Milton*. And held there. And have the knaves take turns to spit into your mouth while they held you there.

I was not among those men, said *Milton*.

But you are among them now, said *Cock*. You hold them in the right. Oh, you are blind, you will say. Poor old *Milton*, who scribbled his eyes out. But this is no judgement upon you. You may speak. You may dictate. And yet you do not! You have never had to question your own heart, because deep inside you believe you are right, and have always been right. You have never had another soul – another creature of *Christ*! for they are, each and every one! – hold you down, and pierce your flesh, for his sake. Have you smelt your own skin fry? Have you heard it fizz, seen it crisp and bubble? Have you felt that your heart might fail from the mere force of bodily pain? Aye, for the sake of *Christ*, will you suffer the pains of *Christ*? I say that you will not. Stand and wait! Aye, do. Pray for posterity to grant you your poet's laurel. Your easeful comfortable life these last years is your only reward. We shall see which of us may be among the Saints in the kingdom to come.

At this, Mr. *Milton* was white, but he spoke without tremor. Aye, we shall, said *Milton*.

Mr. *Cock*, though, was red as his tale.

Aye, said *Cock*. See how you shall be venerated.

Aye, said *Milton*. Do see, Mr. *Cock*.

Aye! said *Cock*. Aye! Aye! Aye! Like old *Cromwell*, you may find yourself dug up and your rotten bones hanged for a traitor. Or perhaps not even so much. Perhaps you are enemy enough to neither side. Oh, how it warms my heart to think none might trouble themselves with you at all! It may be your dampness of spirit has pissed out any little spark of pretended vengeance. Oh, yes, we shall see who is raised up, and who cast down. And if you are raised, then perhaps I shall indeed have failed. But you are welcome to that. An age which holds up *Milton* above *Cock*, I say frankly, is not a future I may believe in.

Believe or disbelieve at your pleasure, said *Milton*. The future is not in your gift.

Aye, said *Cock*, but it is. You shall see.

The one blessing of my state, said *Milton*, is that I see nothing of you and your doings, though *London* itself should crumble around me. But like *Samson*, you would bring the temple down upon us all, and let the innocent suffer with the damned.

Oh, you make me mad, old *Milton*, said *Cock*. I say now, once for all, that my deeds shall be laid at your door. It is you, and you alone. I shall be the voice from Heaven. I shall be the nail through your palm. I shall be the thorn in your brow. I am the worm in your soul, and when I hatch, you shall burn once more, and for eternity.

When Mr. *Cock* left, Mr. *Milton* was silent a great while, his right hand clasped over his mouth, as a man might do at sudden heavy news; and I could not blame him, the words had been so fierce, for the very wood of the walls still hummed with them; nor had he closed his eyes to calm himself, as you or I might, but the lids were open, and the sightless orbs twitched around so I felt I could follow his every little thought, had I the key: I fancied myself a spy in *Eden*, and I was not at ease there.

He growled in his throat, and coughed and spat; then he sighed, and moved as though to stand but then did not.

Curse him, curse him, curse him, said he. No peace, I am to have no peace at all.

Should you like me to leave? said I.

He cried out in alarm and stood, tottering; then he gripped the elbows of the chair and laughed.

O! I had forgot you, said *Milton*. Did you hear all?

This did not please me, but I kept my counsel.

I did, said I. A harsh man.

A dangerous cur, said *Milton*. He besieges me with words. But I refuse those hollow wooden offerings, for fear of what they may conceal. I suggest you do the same. All young men love ferocity, but if you have ambition to reach an age where you may have leisure to reflect, I counsel you to avoid his society.

I am already resolved so to do, said I.

I have known many of his like, said *Milton*. He will drunken you with his sermons, and instead of his eyes he will seek to make you his hands. Choose your side, boy. I fear this man, as I have feared very few such. But religion at its most fanatick is almost an evil. Remember this: that *Satan* himself was once the best of angels. Obedience to God must stand before all other virtues, and him without conscience may indeed have need for a Pope. Let not this man be yours.

And these hard words shook me to my soul, which I resolved

at once to free from the trammels which had snared it; so I wrote that very day to Mr. *Pedlow* to say that I wished no more part of his scheme, and sent back to him what coin I still possessed from his remittances, and promised him the balance to be paid when I could muster it; and though I feared somewhat the wrath of my paymaster might follow me yet, still my spirit was at peace, and I slept that night sounder than I had since first I stepped inside Mr. *Milton*'s house.

* * *

From hell
Kate Eddows
Number nine
Mam

No one ever done what I done. Nor no one ever can. Cos first is first and thats that. But now Ive started no man can stop it. Whats done cant be undone. I walk about with blood round my mouth and chewin guts and no one says nothin. I throw your offal around the street splat splat like rotten old pears and no one says nothin. I tread your guts into the ground on Peccadilly and no one says nothin. That means I won. You must all worship me make a church for me and in a hunderd years people will follow my way and slicin women will be every Sunday all pictures will be of blood and guts and books of women gettin cut and chopped ha ha.

I heard what you said to him. I followed him again. After I cut tother whoor Long Liz. They say youre no whoor but I

saw. You cried to the gent and said Ile get a hidin if I dont
get my money back. What happened to your money he says.
O I drunk it you says I coudnt help it. I quite know the
feelin he says. I dont go whoorin but I needs the money you
says. You was cryin. Ile need somthin in exchange he says.
What you see is all I got you says. That will have to do he
says. Thats nasty of you I thought. He was a kind young man
and now hes nasty. Hes talkin to you like youre trash which
you are but he never done that before. O not all women are
such though I know all the men are yes yes the only good
people in the world is women some of them you know that
and I know it too.

You goes in a dark plase with him and youre at it and then
hes done. He never takes long thank God says you ha ha. Im
most grateful he says. And wheres my money you says. I
seem to have come out without my pocketbook he says Im
so dreadfully sorry. Youre scum you says. Thats rich he says
and walks off. I can see hes left a thing behind I cant see
what it is.

Well now its done his little squirt is in you so youre for it I
thinks. Im feelin tired and rattled cos of Long Liz. But I says
come in here mam I seen all what a dreadful young man.
Clear orf you says Ive had enough Ile take me hidin I dasarve
it. No no I says look here I dont want nothin jest to sort you
out. Come in here its my room and Ile give you the money.
Well whats the worst that could happen you says and I laughs.
What you laughin at you says. Youll see now I says. My
husband told me not to stop out late or the ripper will have
me guts you says. Your husbands rite I says and steps behind
you and takes your chin in my hand and cuts you all at once

so you aint got time to know whats happened or nothin. Thats my mercy and tis really so you didnt scream and I cant be stopped before I done my work.

O Kate. Youre my favourite I think. You opened so easy like a ripe nana. Peel you back and take the fruit. Well I had to saw a bit down there but thats all rite I dont mind. Careful I was not to spoil it. In the bottle and in me pocket. And then I wants a look at your Kidne. I never seen a real one I mean cows and sheep but never a womens one. I love Kidne for to eat and I says Ile take it for me breakfast. Why not youre dead now no harm in it. And I takes it. Wobblin about in me hand and it tickles. I looks in your pretty face. I can see you lookin up at me thinkin o dear dear how could you. Youre a bad bad boy and theyll sniff you out. Yes they will. O will they I says well see how good you sniff with no nose and I takes off your nose ha ha. Now youre not so pretty I says and I draws a little picture on your face with my knif round your mouth and slice slice on your pretty cheeks. Its fun and I takes out a bit of your ear too. And then I sees the thing he left when he run away. I takes it in my pocket its a little puzzle toy I likes them. Fun fun fun for me and no more for you. Hard cheese Kate.

But Im tired and I want to go home now. Theres only one thing more. For the peelers my old chums. I cuts away a piece of your apron see you never knew I done that did you. Wipes my knif with it so tis bloody. And bye bye Kate I walks cool as you like back the way I came and leaves it at some house of Juwes. Thats them fixed I thought cos the Juwes fixed the Lord God Jesus and now Ile fix them back. They eat babbies blood I heard. Baked in ther bread. Theyve all the money and thats why the poor is so poor and the goverment helps them. Theyll not be blamed for nothin.

Maybe next Ile go slicin Juwes every one. I would if I had time to get them all but thers too many. Id need a big mill jest for killin Juwes ha ha but how to build it cos theyve all the money. I could probably get some Juw to put it up if he thought hed double his stake. And hed be the last one in sliced up and canned out the back for dog meat. Ha ha ha.

signed
I chalked it on the wall the Juwes are the men that will not be blamed for nothin.

* * *

Tumbling into Hell

Will is always busy. Every day there are seven new things to do.

Leaving his house, he feels the tingle in his shoulder of an unwelcome gaze. He spots a man, cloaked and hooded, turning away just as Will turns. Will senses no good, but lets the feeling slip off him.

There is no space in his mind for idle suspicion. He knows he is watched from time to time, but he makes sure to give them nothing at all. To the world, he is a kindly innocent, hot in debate but sweet and forgiving in deed. They know not the seething fury of his ambition, the raw injustice he feels at the very presence of a king who claims him as a subject. He awaits the French, ready to throw on a red cap when they land. But this is not his end. This is only a further means, to free him to his greater purpose.

He pays a visit to Mr Ellis at Whitechapel. Watches their rehearsal for Dryden's opera. He hopes it will rouse the spirit of London. Energy, delight. Joy.

A row of demons, painted in turn: red, blue, green. One is a Chinaman, another a Hindoo. Some with hair on every inch of skin, some with none at all.

They buckle and strap one into the hoist, and raise him up. 'Now spin and tumble as we lower you!' cries Ellis. The rope is dropped, it jerks and halts. The demon cries, but it is petty human fear they hear: a shriek, and flapping arms.

'This is not the terror of the damned,' says Ellis. 'This is the gibbering of a witless child.'

'It smacks of the real,' says Gavron. 'It frights us the more, because we feel that this should be our own fear.'

'Oh, and are we demons?' cries Ellis. 'I want to rouse wonder and awe, not sympathy!'

'It is the player's honest fright you hear,' says Will. 'He acts nothing at all. It will accustom if you give him a few more turns. Is that not so?'

'Aye,' cries a tiny voice from above. 'And I counsel you to stand away from under me. I shitted myself with terror, and my britches are loose, and it might drop out upon you.'

By midday, there is a row of six demons, tumbling into Hell.

'The image I have before me,' says Will, 'is men painting a housefront, not angels falling to their doom.'

Michael Hughes

Ellis looks. A crew of lumpy blackguards, in coloured coveralls, rising and falling on ropes. 'Curse you, Mr Blake, but you are right. Now you say it, I can see nothing else.'

'Damn that Dryden,' says Gavron. 'He writes his fancy, but gives no thought to how we may give it life.'

Will smiles.

'How if you lower them over the stalls? They could poke and prick at the spectators with forks, and scream to startle them. All in semi-dark, it might affright them much. Children at least would delight to see that.'

Ellis looks to Gavron.

'There could be something in that, Dick. After all, we are all fallen souls, are we not?'

'We are not,' says Will cheerfully. 'But that matters little. It is a play you want, I think, and not a sermon.'

'Curse it, the young fellow is right,' says Ellis. 'If I can make my public gibber and shriek, the run shall sell out in an hour.'

'It is hardly Milton,' says Gavron.

'Neither is Dryden. The stage is not the page, Gavron. Cruder efforts may produce effects as sublime, on the plane of pure passion.'

So a gang of Negroes is hired in, sent up to rig the ceiling above the seats.

An Angel of Fire

When he goes abroad, Will takes his homunculus with him, bound and gagged, in his bag. The little man must not escape.

It amuses Will to talk with others, knowing he has a little life with him.

When he returns home, late, the same cloaked figure he saw before is lurking again. Up to no good. Will stands back and watches, sure the man has not seen him.

There is a sheen of metal beneath the hood. Light dances there. It is a smooth golden mask, a doll-face, like the automatons Will has seen at the circus, prancing mechanical men who play guitar and bow. See how we create in our own image, he thinks, innocent and servile. But this man must be flesh, though hidden.

Will sees him try the door of his house. The man plays with the handle, cautiously tugs it up and down, trying to find a weakness. The door remains fast.

The man sweeps his cloak around himself, blending into the black. Will sees a hint of him rustle around the corner, through the alley, to the yard.

An Angel of Death, he thinks. Come to steal away my devices.

Fury rises in his breast. He feels his sinews harden. The pulsation of an artery. Before the next, he is off, after the man.

The Angel of Death has a chisel at his sash. With a wrench and a shriek of wood, it is open. Will sees the leg lift higher than natural and, like a cat, in one stretching bound the man is in.

Will thinks. He must come out the same way. I'll have him here.

But what if he means destruction? What if he should burn by notebooks, and break my plates? What if he means harm to my Catherine?

He follows the man in, scrambling up the wet bricks and through his own splintered window.

The pantry is dark, and empty. Will scents a charred stench on the air. The black smell makes the night air even blacker. He is an Angel of Fire, Will thinks, who means to set my hoard of work to flame.

In his workshop he strikes a light.

The man is there, on the floor. Whining like a lame pup. Will's heart expands; he had the fellow wrong.

'Forgive me,' the poor creature sobs through his glassy metal face.

'I do!' cries Will. 'Whatever your crime, I can see your suffering is greater!'

He takes the man to their kitchen. The mask is removed, and underneath, the purple and black of the man's swollen head. His skin is subject to a heat Will cannot feel. It crisps and peels. The man is cooking before his eyes. Flames tickle around. The smell rises Will's gorge. He dares not touch, for fear his own skin will fry.

The man opens his fist, and a thing drops out: a little wooden puzzle, of several patterned pieces locked together. Will picks it up; the wood itself is hot and stings his palm. He stows the toy, runs for a basin of water, wakes Catherine on the way back. She has slept through the commotion, as she always does.

He hunts out whatever balms and unguents he can find from the chest in their chamber. There are plenty: gifts from Catherine's parents at Christmastide, which she has not the heart to tell them she will not use, but refuses to sell, out of respect.

He unscrews the jars and scoops out handfuls to smear again on the man's charred and swollen face. His lips part in thanks, and a flame dances between them. Will hears a tooth crack and split.

And then: as he has but once before, Will sees the spirit of the man rise from his body, a white shadow which unfurls and then floats between floor and ceiling.

'He is leaving us,' he tells Catherine.

Will's brother departed thus, clapping his hands in delight at his destination.

The man is not breathing; his chest has collapsed. The figure of light stretches and turns. It reaches to Will, and vanishes against the ceiling. If we were out of doors, Will wonders, should I see him float all the way to Heaven?

They stand over him, singing prayers to speed his soul.

Fearful of any suspicion against him, Will calls for a constable. 'The man was fleeing a fire, it seems, and rushed into our house seeking succour. We have no knowledge of him else.'

More men are called, the body collected. Will is told he will have to attend the inquest, which he gladly accepts.

The dawn spends itself in the fussy buzz of sworn statements and shooing the neighbours, who crane over the threshold for a glimpse of some gossip. Will smiles along with every question, shrugs and nods, lets them embroider the tale as they will. Catherine stands with him, always ready.

Then the constable is called away, the neighbours drift off, to exchange their little drama for fresh news from round about. Soho never sleeps.

They are alone.

Will is troubled by the visitation, and the man's pitiful plea.

The golden mask remains, which the constable did not know to take. Will wipes it clean of soot. Something about the blank countenance unsettles his soul. He fancies this the guise of his own angel, even the shining face of God itself.

For a moment, he is tempted to try it. But he shudders at the thought, and leaves the object be. He gives it to his homunculus, a blind-eyed companion, for solace and amusement when Will is absent.

'I thank you. It is a kindly act. Such a thing may feed my imaginary, and seed the works you wish from my hand. I shall listen to its silent voice, and heed. Then you shall listen to mine, and heed me in turn. The apprentice must reach beyond the master, and make of him a disciple. You shall prepare the way, for my time is almost come.'

Will plays with the little puzzle the burning man left behind. It soothes his fevered temper. The pieces slide and click beneath his fingers: he finds a shape, confounds it, finds another.

He watches his little friend. What he sees only makes him shudder. God himself repented his creation, he knows, and washed it clean away. Now a sign has come: the second world is burned up and done.

Will begins to discern the truth of his destiny. The New Jerusalem must emerge in colour and line, from his graver and brush, and not from the peevish chatter of a poet's relic reborn in a china doll.

It is the end of the beginning.

The final burden will be his alone.

The Last Day

I hear the lamb weep,
I see the lost child,
And Christ is asleep
On the barren and wild.

The tygers abroad
The priest is awake,
He embraces the bawd
In the fiery lake.

The knife and the stone
Shall melt clean away,
I stand all alone
For it is the Last Day.

I see the true face
Of our Lord Divine,
And all take their place:
Six, seven, eight, nine

* * *

56. At the start of December, Tammy told Chris she was fed up having to turn down work because they were at capacity. They were still getting lots of new requests for emergency jobs on malfunctioning systems, especially from countries where there hadn't been so much hype in advance. She thought there was

going to be a huge market for mopping up if things did go wrong, so she and Al had decided to open another office in Brussels for European contracts. They were both going over there for a couple of weeks at least, to get things up and running, and they needed Chris to take over in London while they were away. They would look into hiring another project manager to work with him and Lucy, if he thought it was necessary.

The idea frightened him. Chris felt he was barely coping with his work now, even though Lucy had taken over all the systems design and compliance work. He could just about keep on top of the implementation schedule, and co-ordinating emergency repairs to systems they had already worked on, but he didn't know if he could deal with being in charge too. He hated the idea that he would be the one responsible for anything that went wrong. But he didn't want to rock the boat either, and maybe have to look for another job, with people he didn't know. He didn't think he could handle that at the minute. He needed to know Lucy was really okay first, and that things could get back to normal.

He told Tammy it would be fine.

57. On the radio, Chris began to hear news stories about computer errors. There were rumours that lots of companies were covering up big problems, for the sake of their reputations. He listened to long discussions about what might happen if multiple systems really did fail all at once. The experts painted very bleak scenarios.

He spent a lot of time thinking about the end of the world. He conjured up scenes from Hollywood films. He saw buildings explode. He saw planes crashing into cities. He saw thousands of people fleeing for their lives. It was all his fault.

And he had to save them. The whole world depended on him. He couldn't get the thought out of his head. He knew it was ridiculous, he laughed every time he thought it, but he also knew it could conceivably be true. Al was right. In his own small way, that's what Chris was doing in his job. Maybe he was meant to be Jesus after all.

58. In the evenings, Chris stayed in his flat and read the little notebook Lucy had lent him. When he didn't understand, he played with his little wooden puzzle instead. He moved the pieces around and looked for the patterns he used to see. He couldn't find them now. It was just a mess of random lines and shapes. Nothing made any sense at all. There was no order. There was no past, present or future. Everything was chaos.

59. When he couldn't stand that any more, Chris walked around the streets.

It was clear to him now. The Year Two Thousand Problem was real, and they weren't going to fix things in time. It just wasn't possible. There were too many essential systems with too many errors. They could have done it, if he hadn't got distracted by Lucy, but now it was too late. Everything was going to fuck up, and it was all because of him.

The thought made his mind go black. It was vast. It was too much for anyone. He told himself one person couldn't be so important. There were thousands and thousands of others like him all over the world.

But he knew that any network was only as strong as its weakest link. Self-organising systems, like the free market of software consultants he was part of, were naturally efficient. They operated with the minimum necessary to function. If one crucial element stopped working, everything might stop working. The whole thing could easily fall apart, just like Al said. And he really would be to blame.

He got angry with himself. It was a ridiculous, conceited thought. No single individual was absolutely essential. Even if anyone could possibly be, that person would know it by now. Something would have happened to make it clear. It would be obvious to everyone.

But maybe no one ever knew for sure, he thought. Maybe that was part of the challenge, like it had been for Jesus. You had to have the courage to believe in your own significance. Only then could you do what you were destined to do.

60. Chris dreaded going in to work every morning. He tried to avoid being there when Lucy was. He hardly spoke to her. He couldn't look her in the eye.

Sometimes he felt himself losing his temper for no reason. If there was a big decision to make, he had to go into the loos to vomit, and he couldn't sleep for days before. He hardly ate. He lived on Lucozade and wine gums and cigarettes. The office was a complete mess. He never knew where anything was.

In the end he called in sick one day, when he just couldn't face it. Next day he did the same thing. He sent Lucy an email to say he'd phone her when he was able to come back, and not to contact him in the meantime.

61. He did nothing. He just couldn't. He sat in bed for hours, smoking and listening to the radio turned up loud, trying to drown out his own thoughts. He had awful, awful thoughts.

He knew he could never go back in. He knew he had made a mess of everything. He knew his life was a complete waste. It was the worst thing that had ever happened.

62. Tammy phoned Chris to check if he was all right. She must have spoken to Lucy, he thought, and figured out something was properly wrong. Chris said he was much better now, and he'd be back at work the next day, but she insisted he went to the doctor.

Chris was told he was suffering from exhaustion caused by stress and anxiety. He should get more sleep, take exercise, eat sensibly, drink less and stop smoking. Those were the same things they always said when he went to the doctor. He knew it was good advice, but he also knew he would ignore it.

Tammy told him to get a grip. He had to stop taking everything so personally. He needed to get his fucking head together.

He agreed. He told her he'd booked a couple of weeks' holiday in January to lie on a beach and relax. She said that was excellent news. She told him not to worry so much, and just get on with the job. It would all be fine in the end. It always was.

63. Chris hadn't really booked anything. He was afraid to think of leaving, in case London wasn't there when he came back. The whole city looked flimsy and fake to him now. He felt like if he pushed a building too hard, the side would collapse, or he might break through.

The walls of his flat were fading to white. He saw houses fold up, streets crumble, the skyline ripple and settle back as a single line. None of it was real.

He could see beyond. When he looked at a brick, at a face of concrete, he saw the microscopic life it held. He saw the fossils of sea-dwelling blobs, the atoms of carbon and silicon. There was no single whole, just a mass of fragments without integrity. London evaporated before his eyes. It clouded around his face like smoke. It was everywhere and nowhere at once.

64. His whole street was on fire. He could smell the smoke, and see bits of cinder floating in the air. He could hear the flames, and people shouting and screaming. It was right at the edge of his vision, and he couldn't look directly at it, but when he closed his eyes he saw the imprint of it clearly. When he opened them, everyone was just going around like normal.

He was walking through puddles of blood and piles of flesh on the pavement. He felt great lumps of it squelching under his shoes. He thought he was going to vomit. He could see blue and grey strings of guts curled up in doorways. He stepped over corpses of women with torn stomachs. The street was busy, but no one said anything.

He knew everyone else could see what he saw, but they were ignoring it too. They each thought they were the only one. Anyone watching him would never guess that he could see it either. He was too scared to say anything. They all were. No one wanted to be the first to speak up.

Chris closed his eyes. If they all pretended it wasn't there, it might go away.

65. Lucy was with him. They were underground. Chris could hear water. Everyone was there. Lucy was singing to him. She was all the colours of the rainbow.

He knew he had to remember this moment, and how it felt, and make others see it too. That was everything.

66. The man in the mask was with him. Chris knew he was always watching. He could sense him out of the corner of his eye.

The man wanted to show him what was underneath, and Chris knew he mustn't look. It scared him. It scared him very much. Every time he closed his eyes, he saw the smooth golden face.

'Is this the end of the world?' said Chris. 'Is it all my fault?' 'Six, seven, eight, nine,' said the face. 'It's the end, but the moment has been prepared for.'

PART THREE

End

Chapter Nine

The last Part of my History, by Thomas Allgood

i.   In the year of our Lord sixteen hundred and sixty-six:

When the great poem of *Paradise Lost* was at last complete, I was tasked with running to and fro Mr. *Milton*'s printer *Samuel Simmons*, the son of a man he had dealt with some years before, and who, alone among the bookmen of *Paternoster-row*, held Mr. *Milton* to be a great master of letters.

Well do I remember my first venture into that *Forest of Script*: On every post were pasted title-pages of new books for the week, announcing subject and author; carts and stalls were jumbled up against the well-to-do shops, men splashed and stained black with ink as *Shakespear's Moor* shouted over the clashing bashing rattling racket of printing engines in yards and basements; the very gutters were full with spews of ink and tattered and torn papers; leaves of *Dante* and *Spenser* crunched and sogged underfoot, so thick and numerous I allowed myself the fancy they were shed by *Trees of Poesie* which grew there, and these men did nothing but harvest them; and all in the heavy shadow of our great St. *Paul's*, like the soul of a repentant sinner, a permanent and holy promise of the *Eternal Divine* for all its filthy stains and crumbling cracks, of which Mr. *Milton* delighted to tell me how *Cromwell's* men once stabled their horses in the nave, pissed in the font, tore vestments into strips to bandage their wounded; and now the bookmen worshipped in the crypt there, which housed the church of St. *Faith*, where they kept their stores too:

St. *Faith*, said *Milton*, was a young girl roasted on a brazen bed for refusing to worship the pagan gods. There are few now would take such.

I daresay Mr. *Cock* would, said I.

Aye, said he, but torture alone does not a martyr make. Many have embraced the rack who well deserved it.

All the day I wrote out for Mr. *Milton* the last fair copy of his great poem, after which he sighed and said *Consummatum est*, which near-blasphemous wit was one feature of his discourse I greatly regretted.

His chamber was clumsy with foul papers and blotted versions, and he called in all hands to bundle these for burning, fearful that some future time might seek to prove his intention was other than this final manuscript; but I cautioned him against their destruction before the work was printed and sold, and he relented; so case after case was driven over to his father's old house in *Bread-street*, where though a tenant had the good chambers, Mr. *Milton* kept the attic-room for his own stuff and records, and those of his late father, which he one time gave hint contained some old foul papers of *Shakespear* himself, who had some dealings with his father, though I believe he never once went into them to see if any gems might be among the dross.

ii. As I crossed the town entrusted with this fair copy, all word was of a fire, indeed all through the city the smell was on the air, which made a tiresome journey for I had to pick my route to miss it; and I heard said it was doubtless the biggest in many a year, for the exceeding dry season and the constant strong wind fed the flames and spread it about, indeed sometimes a hunk of ember or a clump of ash blew in around the street as I walked, and I saw all who were able ascend a spire to watch its creep, some laying wagers on how close it might come to where they stood, with much idle speculation upon the cause; though if all I later heard say they were in the region of *Pudding-lane* and saw the first sparks break out were truly present, why then that place must be a vast expanse of open field poorly named as a lane; but for all the busy bother abroad of moving out households and carting away stock, I saw not one soul tasked with fighting the very blaze, each man certain this was the job of another; and I thought this a great change wrought in the nation, surely by the King's return, that it was now good practice for a man to think only of himself and his goods, and the people as a body may go hang.

I care not to help my neighbour, said one to me. I help myself, and I expect he would do the same.

And if you helped him, said I, he would surely help you in his turn.

I wonder, said he.

Wonder not, said I. Try and see.

But the man would not, and cursed me for my trouble.

A little after I returned from my happy errand, Mr. *Cock* came by once more, and commanded us to sit up and pray to be spared from this fire, which was the *Final Judgement* we awaited and all would perish unless they declared themselves for *Christ*, for he would descend this very day as he had ascended, so we were promised; but though at his urging we searched the sky for a cloud to carry the *Heavenly King*, it was the clearest golden blue as ever I saw it; but still he sat calculating his numbers to find the very time and place to expect *Christ*'s return, and to my great surprise Mr. *Milton* helped him, though he carped out from time to time that he would do so only to prove the extent of Mr. *Cock*'s folly.

Still the news was wide that the fire raged on, and every story and counter-story came past our ears: It was a Dutch revenge, for the late firing of their towns; it was a Papist plot, from *France*; it was an Irish plot, fed by Papists again, in revenge for *Cromwell*; and though one or two more stood in the streets and cried it as the *Promised End*, the heathenish temper of the times was shown in the laughter they drew in response; but though I saw militia abroad now with fire-hooks and squirts to do what they could, most men did no more than stand and watch, and still would not help to clear goods for their neighbours without coin in hand first for their trouble.

I have seen our land despoiled and lost everything this generation, said one, and I will not risk life and limb again to any *common wealth*, as they called it, for a fool knows there is no such. A man has what he has, and that is only what he can sell.

At night we walked to the river, and I told for Mr. *Milton* how we saw the image of his great *Lake of Fire* in the very *Thames* water which shone with reflected gold, a burning mirror of the blazing wharves, as boat after barge after bark was laden with wine and pork and plate and chairs and hangings, drapes and paintings, statues and papers and trinkets, guitars and organs, women and children and caged songbirds; and one gent was greatly cried for putting his serving-girl in the boat before his wife, for all said she was heavy with his child, which he did not deny, but shut the mouth of that young mocker by telling him to ask his mother which of the stable boys had placed him in her womb sixteen years ago, for all knew his father had his vitals blown clean off at *Naseby*, which gave a good laugh to all.

On our way home I saw again the panick of the plague-year gone by, as men laid siege to the green country itself and stormed the gates of *London* that barred them in, for those gates were now shut in their faces, so the people might turn their strength at last to fight the blaze; but some said this was to keep out the grasping carters and farmers from miles around who rushed in to hire out their wagons at ten, twenty, forty pounds, so the wealthy could move their goods to safety; though others doubted the stuff would ever be seen again, as though the very land beyond sought to grab and hoard what *London* it could for its own self.

iii.   On the next day, we heard the word around that this was a Devil's fire which could not be put out save by some black spell, else it would continue to burn and consume the face of the whole Earth, taking a year and a day, for it was the land itself was burning, they said, since Hell had cracked open under *Pudding-lane* where *Satan* dwelt with his team of Jews; and I heard one respectable gent say he had been down himself to that place, a great cavern of evil beneath the city, an ancient pagan chamber from before even the days of good *Brutus*, who all said came from noble *Troy* to found our great civilisation; which word made Mr. *Milton* declare he would write his own *History of Britain* to scrub clean the minds of the godless from such lies and legends, and I did much encourage him to do so, for this great work would surely be the jewel in the crown of his achievement for the ages to come.

iv.   On the third day, Mr. *Cock* brought us word that St. *Paul*'s itself was menaced by the great inferno, which like a stalking

Indian beast, the more it ate up, the greater seemed its appetite; but as we worried at the doubtful fate of the great poem, and I was congratulated by all for my fore-sight in saving the foul papers and drafts we had stowed, the terrible news came to our ears that Mr. *Milton*'s house in *Bread-street* was burned up, and with it every leaf and scrap of paper he had stored; and now Mr. *Milton* pressed us to go straight and recover the most precious fair copy of his great epic, nay the sole and only original; but though I counselled him there was no value and great risk in his coming along with Mr. *Cock* and me, he said he would not rest till the pages were safe in his hands, and he had rather know the worst at first hand than leave his posterity to fallen Papists and hereticks.

We three fought against a tide of humanity, the busy traffic of panick and flight, but when we found Mr. *Simmons* he told us all papers and stock were safe, removed below ground to St. *Faith*'s; but still Mr. *Milton* demanded his poem, which Mr. *Simmons* said was impossible till the fire abated; so we took him with us by ferry to view the danger, and as we came on the river to the environs of St. *Paul*'s, alas! a sight that rent my heart with pity and terror, for the roof of the great church itself was aflame, the nearest thing to a vision of Hell I ever wish to witness; but yet Mr. *Milton* would not turn for home and demanded we see the bookmen's store was safe; so with much scrambling trouble we took the low side entry to St. *Faith*'s in the crypt of St. *Paul*'s, and we saw through a grille in the inner door the very papers stocked and piled, stuffed in barrels and stacked in crates; and Mr. *Simmons* said he remembered well the spot where he placed the fair copy but two days hence, indeed it was near the last put in so he knew the corner of the very paper, and I squinted to discern it;

but as I did so, there came a thunderous crash and tumble, and the tunnel shook like an Earth-quake, which awful noise was the very roof of St. *Paul*'s sundering down above our heads, and the heat came upon us then so furnace-like that I remembered Mr. *Cock*'s harsh talk of the sizzle of his flesh, for I dared swear I smelt my own hair singe and my skin begin to bake and blister; but when I turned to ask Mr. *Milton* for permission to flee, I saw he had passed clean out from the heat, and Mr. *Simmons* and Mr. *Cock* had seen fit to run and leave us to our fate;

and I wrung out my very soul to know what I should do, for though all my head said to clear out most lively, my heart knew Mr. *Milton* would not wish to leave this place alive without he had his very poem pressed to his bosom;

so I heaved his slack body back to the river and set him near a shallow pool which itself I thought did bubble and fizz in the awful heat; then I tore my cloak into rags, dipped each one and wrapped them round myself, till I was swaddled as best I could be in damp cloth, and I turned back hissing and steaming to enter the cave of paper, that dungeon of happily-imprisoned script sealed from the great fire above; yet the very moment that I opened the door and my eyes found the papers I must reach, as though my very gaze was hot I saw their edges curl and brown, I smelt the tang of bitter burning and saw the flare and fire, and then a great rushing bloom of flame and all as one went up together:

with a weeping heart I saw the precious leaves fly up around me, like sable wings of flaking ash, whole pages where I read my own hand, strange silver lines of verse upon black filmy sheets; and I knew that if I touched them, they would shudder into dust and crumbs; so transfixed I watched them spin and drift, pass clean through flames, unable to be burned a second time; and for all my terror I thought them like condemned souls with nowhere left to fall, suddenly free of all fear; and then without a sound they shuddered themselves into powder and smoke, vapour and ash: lost for all time.

v.   I was all out of hope.

I had lost Mr. *Milton*, I had lost his great poem, and I thought myself like to lose my very life in that *dark local cave of hot coals*, the boyish Hell of my callow fancy, indeed such was my despair that I dared hope I was already perished and this no *Inferno* of burning books but my own private *Purgatorio*, for I swore I smelt my innards boil, and felt such a heavy wall of heat against my face that I knew no mortal flesh could suffer; but then a hand grasped my body and dragged me back, and I felt the ground itself give way and next a great rush and tumble down, sliding and scrambling, wet now and blessedly cold, but black dark, as I came to lie all in a heap, and I knew not where I was nor whose was the hand that had saved me.

Then I heard the voice of that Mr. *Cock* hard in my ear.

Crisp and crackle, said he. Roar. Roar. Roar. Do you feel its hot breath? This is the beast. Oh, I saw. The books went up like *Fawkes* himself had set them.

I wept then for I knew I had failed to save the great life's work Mr. *Milton* had set himself, his poem had burst out into flame as though the very Hell he inscribed pushed itself into our world, and I knew not if the poet himself lived; but Mr. *Cock* said, Why do you weep? This is the *Promised End*. All the Elect are now immortal. Even old *Milton*, though he sleep for now.

I sleep not, said *Milton*, and I rejoiced to hear him, though still I could see no one, only pure deepest black.

My *Milton*! said *Cock*. Did you truly mean your words to start a fire in the land? Well, you have accomplished it. They have set this *London* ablaze. The very air itself caught aflame, and the old Roman folly of St. *Paul*'s is ash and rubble above us. Our great city is newly cleansed. And it is your words alone have done it, for I sounded your true heart, by my own secret means, and found it sorely wanting. This conflagration is your desserts, and my gift to you, to rouse you from your sloth and slumber.

If I find you I shall wring your little neck for you, said *Milton*. Amen, said *Cock*.

And destroyed a thousand years of our good nation's papers, said *Simmons* (for he too was here). There are books in that place secret from the King. Volumes and scrolls have been hidden there for decades, aye, and maybe centuries. Papers lifted from the Roman catacombs, ready for a time shall be fit to hear them. Wisdom of the ancients, denied to our descendants.

And all because old *Milton* had the godly gall to rewrite Scripture, said *Cock*. There shall be great disappointment at the pearly gates. I say, stay nested in this Hell and save a wasted journey.

What is this place? said I.

A buried river, said *Cock*. A place sacred for longer than we have means to know. The river is almost dry today, so we may sit. But yet we await the word of God, to give light and form to the chaos. The Spirit has still to visit this place, an empty womb awaiting his brooding wings. It is pagan innocence. Blessed are those who have not heard, and yet believe. Do you think a humble *Cock* might serve, to make the formless void be pregnant?

I thought I heard strange voices now, but I felt neither the form nor presence of other beings, and still in such black dark that I saw nothing at all.

Listen to the flames above, said *Cock*. If that is Hell, then we are below it. Did you ever fancy there might be such a place, old *Milton*?

O for a knife to cut out your quibbling tongue, said *Milton*.

I fancy Heaven itself is aflame, said *Cock*. What if *Satan* won the celestial war, and threw *Christ* down to Earth? What if that were the truth of his incarnation? We must write Scripture anew, for the old dispensation is finally passed.

Blasphemy, said *Simmons*.

Not so, said *Cock*, for if there really was such a war, as we hear told, the outcome must have been some time in balance, so the Devil could have prevailed.

Nothing was in balance, said *Milton*, and you are a blasphemous cur.

Then this was no war, said *Cock*. By your account it was mere *Punchinello*, danced for the cruel amusement of the Almighty.

Why, sir, there are hundreds of wars throughout all ages, said *Simmons*, where the outcome was never in doubt. Else, none should ever resist an empire. We only remember when the weak defeat the great because of the very rarity, as *Athens* and *Persia*, or *David* and *Goliath*.

Suppose *Satan*'s rebellion then to be one such, said *Cock*, and he did indeed win out. He reported the contrary to us, for lies and deceit are his very nature. But he does not dethrone God in his victory. He simply wins the right to put his own wicked plan in action. Thus our life in this half-way sphere is naught but grief and sorrow. And the greatest work *Satan* has accomplished is the base illusion abroad that there is possible a life upon this Earth with no misery but only peace and joy.

Someone close his mouth, said *Milton*. There is naught but misery while *Cock* has a tongue in his head. Those who pierced it should have plucked it out.

And there is your model of a Christian gentleman, said *Cock*. But I am at peace with my nature. The sole cause of all your pain is the belief that it is possible to hide from pain. Your only torment is this yawning gulf between solid daily knowledge of life, and the hollow fancy you breed and suckle of how this world might be else. A false hope. It shall never be other than it is. Only in Paradise. Rejoice, then, that I have brought Heaven to Earth at last.

We shall broil here better than a pullet, if the fire does not cease, said *Simmons*. I vote we move.

No one has called for a vote, that I heard, said *Cock*.

And so we cowered in this pitchy-black cellar-space, fearful to remove because uncertain how hard it might be burning above; where after some hours, and to my great surprise, I felt the jostling of others now coming and going between us; and among them we encountered Mr. *Milton*'s Hebrew, full of fancy, who said he well knew this place, and told us of wall-writing he had seen here before, angelic wisdom from supposed *Catholick* priests and fugitive Jews and ancient Hermetic philosophers and Adamite patriarchs; he told us too of great news from *Constantinople*, that the *Messiah* was certainly come, risen out of *Smyrna*, and the Israelite people were called to gather and follow him, for the time was at hand; and he led us with the others stumbling and fearful through a long low passage to a cavern adorned (so he said) with sea-shells in extravagant patterns and curling shapes, which indeed it did feel like when I touched, and which Mr. *Milton* grasped with his hands in unseemly fascination and asked me to describe to him the littlest details, which I would have attempted, though the place gave me discomfort, had I not been in such perfect blindness as himself, which fact he was slow to understand, though to my sorrow it much amused him when finally he did.

And yet I was quick to forgive, for I could not help but imagine how heavy must be the terror of general fire for a man without the faculty of sight, who may feel the sheer red heat at his face and smell the stench of burning wood and paper and wool and meat, indeed unknowing in his fear whether it is animal or human flesh which burns, to populate his imaginary with hot fiery destruction far above the fact; for now in the stark black silence of this underground I confess my own imaginary was fuelled by Mr. *Cock*'s ramblings to picture a land above laid waste by heavenly fire-balls, cast down by rebel angels who had banished the pure in spirit to the lower realm, all which destruction fed only from my secret treachery; and this put my mind in great confusion.

vi. I paced out the *Sea-Shell Grotto* as best I could, though slowly, for I felt my steps hindered by some quiet injury; and I found it to be a great cavern with a pool to one side, where I heard a waterfall, filled as it must be by the soothing juice of our own *Thames* cooling us with its vapours, for in one place the water boiled into steam and the shells fell now and then from the wall upon us and around us and into the pool like tinkling hailstones.

I have known about it for many years, said *Cock*. My childhood play-place.

He told us then his faerie-tale, that this grotto reached far beneath the city, and various forms past lived on here, strange beasts which had fled below when their kind was hunted out above, for it was an under-ground ark; and indeed in one tall cave we seemed to meet, by his dark report, a fellow *Fifth Monarchy Man* upon a horse (which I do swear I touched and heard its snort and felt its breath upon my cheek), hiding since the *Restoration*, waiting for their chance, which strange warrior said that he and his fellows had recovered the key to the tomb of *Arthur* and awaited him to rise again and defend *England*'s need, for this must surely be the moment, though he refused to show us the place, fearful (he said) that we would despoil it even as some of his own party had done; and then Mr. *Cock* discoursed that the river we followed was lost and built under in Roman days, which water old *King Lud* and *Brutus of Troy* had once blessed as the sacred source of *London*'s fortune, and in whose belly were hid lost jewels and buried secrets carried to ancient *Albion* from *Thrice-great Hermes* and the angels of *Enoch*, all which raving and rambling stuff he spoke in such a plausible manner that I wondered not some men fell within his power; but as in all things he reached a peak of excess which spoiled the effect of the rest, for he told us then that still further below was another chamber that housed *the world to come*, which a man might enter and walk about, and he had often visited there and disputed with the generations born after us, provoking their great men to fine deeds and foul; and so he knew the secret of the *Promised End*, which was yet occulted from the general view; but the mask should be removed three hundred and thirty-three years hence to show the true *Face of God*, and then at last all times are as one; and I trouble to write such brain-sick phantasies only to show this very *world to come* what giddy fools were living upon the Earth in the days of their grand-fathers.

vii. I slept; and when I came to myself again, the place was quiet, and still quite as dark as ever; so I hallooed around to find was I abandoned a second time; but there by me was Mr. *Cock*, and Mr. *Milton* too, who declared over and again that he was weary of our subterranean sojourn and wished to return to the world above to live out his days as he might; and I heard in his speech such a heavy spirit that I remembered with bitter regret the fiery fate of his great poem; but Mr. *Cock* declared the world above was passed and gone, and there was much to accomplish here below by men of vision and patience, for he had great plans for Mr. *Milton*'s muse in his *New City*.

You must find yourself another task, for you know your poem is lost, said *Cock*.

I fear I am all done, said *Milton*. For half a century I have dreamed of such a work. My every atom was fixed upon this purpose. I could never again endure such.

Do you still brood upon the loss? said *Cock*.

As you shall brood upon the time you lost in planning your ascension, said *Milton*. You will tell me this is vanity I am sure, but allow me my mourning.

I only ever wished your final happiness, said *Cock*, and he spoke most kindly, which much amazed me.

No one hand is to blame, said *Milton*. History is its own accident.

History is now complete, said *Cock*. And if it is not, if the world above continues as before, as I know you do believe, then I am the king of fools, and I owe you a great recompense, for I am an honourable man.

I beg you to leave me in peace, said *Milton*.

And you, Mr. *Allgood*, said *Cock*, what is your intent towards the poet, is it honourable? Which question I stinted to answer, and I made a show of ignorance, though it put fear in me.

Leave the boy in peace too, said *Milton*, for he is worth ten of you and your kind.

Is he so? said *Cock*. And what if I tell you he is the snake in your bosom, paid to report you and your household to the King?

You must know me better than to hope I could credit such feeble calumny, said *Milton*; yet there was a question in his answer; and as he waited, my bleeding conscience did stain the very air between us, so that I felt him read the sour silence, the absent rhythm of my stoppered breath; and it told him once for all that this was no calumny against me, but the simple truth.

Ah no, said *Milton*, and then he was silent.

viii. I wept bitter tears and I hoped my inner pains were but the first harbingers of a swift death, for such was all I well deserved: I could never endure the shame I now felt twisting in my belly like the infernal serpent itself, who surely sat gloating at his final victory over the poor coward *Allgood*, that I should sit among his fallen throng for eternity deprived of the Grace of *God Almighty* whose humble service was all my wish from youngest years; yet now it was Mr. *Cock* who seemed to hear my inmost thoughts, and he whispered to me.

Do not throw away your peace upon the favour of that *Milton*, said he, for I myself once did the same and found he was but a hollow wooden man and no more, as I am myself and you are too. I have work for you will ease your spirit and show true repentance, if indeed you wish it.

I have done with shadowy tasks for whispering rogues, said I.

You have not, said he, for I am that *Stephen Pedlow* who set you on this track, and I have watched you close and know you are of the kind who will serve my need.

The blood stopped in my veins, for I was amazed and astonished at this news; but I dared not doubt it, for I had spoke the name of *Stephen Pedlow* to no man; then he placed a thing in my hands, which I groped and puzzled at a moment, till all at once with a desperate fright I knew it was the *Golden Mask* I first saw in the pews at St *Paul*'s; and it shuddered me deeply to know my misery was not my own devising but the cruel connivance of a heretick villain.

Here is a gift from my angel, said he. And do not have the vanity to think yourself alone, for I had other men abroad in the land above working to my purpose, and many more still busy at my mischief in the world to come. One did set this fire as I commanded him, a smiling simpleton named *Hubert* fitted to the task, and in the *New Jerusalem* that now shall rise from this cleansing, there is much you cannot understand, but I will show you the truth nonetheless, for you are soon to die, poor fool, and nothing can prevent that.

At those words I felt a strange relief in my soul.

The burning you received in your foolish attempt to save the old man's poem was more than you know, said he. You see it not, but I see it plain and there is none can save you.

How see you aught in this dark cave? said I.

There is no dark, said he. You are lost in the same false night as your precious *Milton*, for your sight has fled at the pain of the fire, though I dare hope it shall return before you perish. When it does, I have one final task for you, to cleanse my spirit. I shall journey once more to another *London*, through the under-ground world into an age far hence, to find my true successors, and guide them to their sacred destiny. I shall not return, but you must write my doings for the generations to follow, that they may know me when I come, and see plain the cause of their misery, and the only cure. Do but this, and my heirs in the world to come shall bless you as a true saint.

I shall never take your part, said I. If I lack born virtue, then I claim the privilege of awful wisdom won from bitter sadness at my own misdeeds. A man who has never seen himself do evil knows not what he condemns. A repentant sinner is the only joy of God's eye, but I will not atone another man's wrongs.

Quiet yourself, said *Cock*. I hear the sweet music upon the air, and I see them descend to greet us. This lady may nurse you until you rise, for the *End of Time* is now come. The angels are here, *King Jesus* is nigh.

I heard a soft female voice, though it spoke such a violent curse I doubted it could be the nurse he spoke of; but she was a kindly young lady who eased my wounds with bandages and whispered soothing songs to me, at which I drifted from the world and slept again, fearing as I did that I might never wake to see what should become of all I knew, and fearing too the judgement now upon me for my treachery and cowardice; for though I had fully repented in my heart and soul, I felt not yet cleansed by saving Grace, but still the poisonous weight of sin within.

ix. In the dark suffering hours that followed I heard the voices of three men and the female too: one who strangely did seem to know Mr. *Milton* through the fame of his lost poem and spoke of his great honour at the meeting, another who spoke such evil violence against the female sex that I wished to be removed from his company, and yet another who talked at length of a *London* built upon the embers of the ruined city above as though this feat was long ago accomplished, so that I questioned if I might be asleep and caught within a broken wandering sort of dream; which idle fancy was tempered only by my own fear and the sharp pain I now felt in my skin and bones from my roasting before, which troubled me, and whirled my thoughts to jelly.

x. What I heard else that night might be dream-stuff or the strange workings of Mr. *Cock* and his party, for I was at his mercy then and all the world was only by his report to me; I thought myself the blind old father with *Poor Tom* in *Shakespear*'s play of *Lear King of Britain*, as he leaps to his death and angels catch him, so he believes, which speaks God's blessing on him, though he is all the while on a flat simple plain, and he falls only to where he stood before.

Ex nihilo nihil fit, said *Cock*. Nothing will come of nothing. But we are indeed nothing, so why can we not come from it? And if this is true, and nothing can disappear from our world neither, as I do truly believe, then it may find its way here to this place of dark. The plain fact is that everything, invention or not, exists from the moment of conception, whether mental or corporeal. All matter is simply a manner of thinking, so any new manner of thinking changes the physical realm. And so we need tales told, otherwise it is to us as to a babe, a mass of angry chaos, as it is to you now in darkness, as it remains an abyss for some poor souls, those we deem lunatics. That is the true state of things. What we wish to call cosmic order is simply inner balance by another name. What harmony there may be is not outside but within us. And we build in its image. As above, so below. And we are below. We shall always be below. We shall never rise. The only union is to bring what is above down to abide with us. And so I have.

Mr. *Cock* bade me farewell and I heard a desperate sound of flame and a mournful cry, as though his very words had caught on fire; then after, I heard him step into the pool, and when the waters calmed I heard nothing at all; and I state here once for all that I saw no more of him nor do I know if he lives this day, but I hope and pray he may never cross my path again, in this world or the next, may *Christ* forgive me.

xi. I slept; and I dreamed that when I woke I was back in Mr. *Milton*'s room, where he lay upon the bed with his head on the lap of another gentleman, a kindly soul who spoke aloud the whole of the great poem by heart, and a third visitor wrote it out upon a batch of paper which lay ready; and Mr. *Milton* said his spirit was at peace now he knew its fate, if his name was known for this work alone then that was the greatest blessing of his life, though all his policy had come to naught, for he wondered much that the throne of *England* still was occupied three centuries hence; and I boggled at the words; but my gentle nurse bade me still myself and sang to me, a mournful ballad of a light that never goes out, which yet soothed my spirit; and then I dared to hope my awful doom was postponed, for as I heard spoke aloud the words of Mr. *Milton*'s great song restored, at last I felt the golden Grace of *Christ* descend and fill my heart to the brim; and then I knew we were saved every one.

xii. And so it was; for after this long night of days Mr. *Simmons* once more returned to seek us, and we made our escape at last from the mazy ways of those heady caverns, truly the blind leading the blind, till we emerged from our sorry dungeon into a sudden silver morning; and by the Grace of God I knew I could see once more, though dimly, a vision of embers and smuts, where a grey disc of sun, like Romish Communion-bread, paled out behind the glassy mist of dust, and all was ash, ash, ash, a city turned to ash: in place of the *London* that was, we saw a forest of broken black beams and a thick snowfall of ash, clouded around us, choking and stinging; and I made a fist of that heavy powder and squeezed it out, for I knew again this was the same stuff that was once our *London*, just as I had upon my first arrival, that this very matter our *Shakespear* touched and trod was now gone to grey dust (as we shall be all) and might not be constituted ever again, for such decay is final and absolute.

I gave Mr. *Milton* report of what I saw, though he was still somewhat cold to me and refused my arm, preferring Mr. *Simmons* as his guide.

I am now twice darkened, said *Milton*. Snow is to the blind as fog is to you.

It will serve to feed the soil, said *Simmons*, back to its native element. The timbers used to build a century hence will have eaten of this ash. *London* shall again be *London*.

No sir, said a traveller who passed, and never again, for we shall build no more of wood. We need a city of stone and brick, for these late fires have been too many. We had too many chances to take our warning, and we did not. So we are rightly served.

What news? said *Simmons*.

They say an invasion is expected, said the traveller, for there is word from the coast that the French and Dutch are joined. Every rider into the city is stopped and questioned for the latest report. Any foreigner is roughed, with a cry to behold their work. I did no such thing, they say. But you would, had you the chance, they say back. This is what you wished upon us, tis all one whether you did it or no.

And yet again the innocent suffer, said *Milton*.

As they must, said the traveller. It is their duty and their privilege, to earn their place in Heaven.

xiii.   As we passed on, we lost our way many times, for the familiar turns and faces of lanes and houses were no more; and in one place, we saw an Italian beaten by the mob, and only for one of the King's party who stepped in, he should have been stripped and hanged for a fiery traitor, with such angry clamour and bustle I hardly knew who spoke, or what sense to find in their passion.

This was your desire, to fire the town, said they.

No, signor, said he.

If not, it ought to be, said they. It would be mine, were I of your party. You should blush if it is not. Shame on you. Are you a man? Why should you not wish to kill me, as your enemy?

Have you not heard of *Christ*, signor? said he.

Any *Christ* who would deny me the right to kill an enemy is no God of mine, said they.

Then truly signor, said he, you do not know *Christ*. For he says we shall love our enemies.

A foolish paradox, said they. He who is loved by me is no longer my enemy.

Precisely the point, signor, said he.

One seaman then spied Mr. *Milton*, and gave out that he and his topsy-turvy-men may have set the city afire in spite at the *Restoration* of the rightful King to the throne, and this mob surrounded us in our turn; so I ordered them back, and dared claim I would face any who offered to strike my master; but to my great wonder Mr. *Milton* stepped up and asked for such a blow.

Well would I welcome it, said *Milton*. I greatly fear its sudden arrival and it shall give much relief to my weary spirit to have it confirmed as what I deserve. I should sleep easier at night had the vengeance I dread been doled out.

Aye, hit a blind old man, went up the murmur.

If you would hit me had I sight, said *Milton*, you must hit me being blind. What wickedness or faults I have are no less for my eyes being dim.

Leave him be, said the crowd, but the seaman stood his ground.

If I deserve your fist, said *Milton*, let me have it. Else, blind-fold yourself and we may fight each other here as equals, for the jollity of all watchers. I would beat you, mind.

Put them up, sir, if you will, said the seaman.

Mr. *Milton* swung and missed wide, and the seaman slapped at his face smartly which set the poet off his balance, where he stumbled and fell into a heap of half-burned rubbish; and though the seaman laughed out a guffaw, no other did, and the crowd shrank back as though seeing what they saw, they did not want that man among their number; and he withdrew in shameful silence.

I helped Mr. *Milton* to recover himself and dusted the ash from his smouldering cloak as best I could; then I brought him away, and we strode our path over snowy stones and solid pools of melted metals, to where St. *Paul*'s had stood; but the smashed corpse of the place was a heart-breach, for every stone and column lay stretched like a fallen warrior, the shape of the whole still present but wracked and shuddered so that all said it might never be restored but must be pulled down; and Mr. *Simmons* made great haste to see the book-store in St. *Faith*'s; but we were told it burned yet and would for hours or days to come, such was the tight-packed store of paper therein, and indeed we saw it glow and felt the heat like the crown of a volcano, a glimpse of that *Lake of Fire* beneath, which now forced itself above; and I wept to see it, though silently, for I wished no consolation.

The ash, we heard, blew across the fields around *London*, into the open countryside, to the market-gardens which feed it; as far as *Hackney* it was found, clinging to leaves like a summer hoar-frost, though there be no substance to it, save a tickle in the nostril; but to the eye, it is a grey deadening pall, it clouds away like smoke of a pyre, the dust of a holocaust ruination; it clings to us all, and ever shall: Amen.

Let it run out in the sewer-ditch, said an old porter, with the quags and slime.

He means out to *Shore-ditch*, said another.

Tis the same, said he.

How is that? said I.

Aye sir, did not you know? said the other. That's the old name. Tis not *shore*, but *sher*, which in the Norman tongue was a sewer, and I knew many an ancient gent still called that corner *Sewer-ditch* when I were a lad, though few do so now. Carrying the dung of the city out to fertilise the farms that feed us, so the same old dirt is in the soil beyond, and it shall be baked hard into clay bricks that will build this city up again, so that generations to come will live in the dried-out shit of their ancestors.

xiv. From there I led Mr. *Milton* home, where he requested I not trouble his doors again, which I took in poor spirit though I had earned much worse; and at that he seemed to relent somewhat and bade me wait a moment upon the threshold; and when he returned, he presented to me as a keepsake the little wooden rebus Mr. *Cock* gave him when first he called (which thing I treasure, it is by my elbow as I write and I find its clever craft gives much solace to my fears and fevers, though I see nothing of its purpose); but when I dared then to ask if I might not help restore his poem, he said that I saw plain what miracle occurred below; and when I said I did not, I thought he brightened and told me that was for the best, and it should not be spoken of more.

So I bade him farewell.

xv. I found my way to the camps outside the city at *Moor-fields*, and thence to *High-gate*, where I was taken in by an army-surgeon who said I suffered more than most, though I had almost accustomed to my pain; and I was removed at length to some of his people at a quiet Kentish grove, where now I write, facing my death as I surely am, for many come to inspect my wounds and shake their heads with sorrow and whisper outside my door; but I thank God my hands at least yet have strength and permit me to complete this true and faithful account; though as I peruse my words I fear it reads as a brain-sick phantasy of one fevered from his injuries; yet I care not, for I go to *meet my maker*, as the old do say, and I hope and pray to unite my spirit with the one *Divine Spirit* which is all and everything; for in this place I have come at last to my own peculiar doctrine, and I well know that many of the greatest purity and learning find their way to the same truth: that the Gospel stories, whether they be history or no, as many learned men say they truly are, yet we cannot know this from reading alone; and so the value is in the wisdom and power of the tales, for there is not more or less wisdom in a tale by whether it is fact or fancy; but whichever it be, the whole of Scripture works upon our hearts as a fable of the journey of the soul from its creation at the moment of conception up to its eventual union with God at the moment of death, and beyond; for *Christ* is the *Light Within*, and this is the beginning and end of the knowledge a man needs for his Salvation; and whether *Christ Jesus Risen* ever walked the Earth as you and I, must not be an article of Faith, for *Christ* is the *Living Heart of God* in the soul of every man, and no less real for that.

Or again: if some clay-fingered antiquary should dig up the bones of the dead man *Jesus* and prove to me he never rose again, would that extinguish my Faith in what I know in my heart and soul to be true?

It could not; so neither then can my Faith, the dearest possession I have, rest upon whether Scripture is history or allegory, though many more privately believe the latter than would ever preach it out; and if indeed there was such a man *Jesus of Nazareth*, as I do truly believe there was, I dare avouch he would goggle at how we speak of him today, for I say plain that this man was not *God made flesh*, though God was truly in him; and I say too that whatever his nature, it was none of his wish to establish great wealth and powers to his name, or if it was, then he kept it a close secret.

xvi.   And so I return whence I came, as you shall in your turn; and so I leave this meagre gift among those who search for footing on the creaking ladder which leads above: if anything may serve to guide or to warn, then I am content.

May the Grace and peace of God be with you always.

Amen.

Chapter Ten

The Only Truth

Proverbs of the World to Come

Believe all of what you read, but none of what you write.

Break your own heart before another's.

Envy is a better friend than pity.

You already know all there is to know.

There are five mysteries: light, darkness, love, sin, and liberty.

Hoard what is plentiful, and spend what is rare.

There is no tyranny without fear, but there is no fear without hope.

Wait until dark, and then begin again.

Energy is motion.

Death is the only truth.

Ask for counsel, and then do the contrary.

The end is already behind us.

A Familiar Spirit

Will struggles to teach his little creation. His child of clay. His bottled demon. His Milton-Golem-Homunculus.

When Catherine has retired, the two spend their evenings in

conversation. The thing repels him ever more, but he clings to the hope it might offer revelation.

The horrid little fingers tap on the glass, drum-drum-drumming.

'Could you see your way to making me a wife of my own?'

The thing twists its mouth in a little grin.

'A wife?'

'It is a poor trick to give me a sword, but nowhere to sheath it.'

'Ah.'

'Ah indeed. What is a pen with no ink to dip in?'

'You mean . . .'

'I mean my prick, you imbecile. It is fasting, and you place me in a desert.'

'I never thought of that.'

'Then think of it now, if you would be so good. Had you wished, you could have left me an innocent, a born eunuch. As a demiurge, you leave much to be desired.'

'I have given you a noble Grecian form.'

'You form me of red clay, give me a tongue to name my world, but no companion.'

'I am companion enough, I think.'

'Do you so? Little then you know of the world, or of creation. I am subject to you, but who shall be subject to me?'

'I raised you as my master.'

'A rash hope. How do you know I am not a very devil?'

'I rather hope you are. I wish for a meeting of contraries. A marriage of Heaven and Hell.'

'Every marriage is so. You speak to one who lived three of them.'

'Your sweet emanations. Catherine is mine.'

'And you wish me a familiar spirit, sent to do your bidding. I fondly thought I might merit a greater destiny. My soul was to sleep till judgement, yet I wake, and find the kingdom is not yet come. So you tell me I must reform your verse, forge it into a weapon to split their minds asunder? Foolery. I shall not repeat that error in my second life. Write what you will, but presume not to find power in a pen. Imagination has no boundary, till it meets with fire and sword. Those are the only weapons to reform this earthly realm.'

Will busies himself with his notebooks, years of abandoned projects, some half-finished, others only half-begun. He digs further, sure that forgotten beauty must be among the scribbled fragments. But nothing is worthy to offer his master, to counter his scorn. To soothe himself, he flicks back and forth the pieces of the little puzzle left behind by his late visitor. He finds no solace; the shapes he once discerned have fled his eye.

'I have so much to do, but the time is upon me. The angel Swedenborg was the final messenger. He saw the blessed life the angels lead, and wrote out his vision for us all. I saw him myself when I was a child. My mother took me to watch his perambulations. A crowd used to gather around his wake.'

'Mr Swedenborg has my sympathy. I had the same in my days. Spies and rabble. I used to pretend I knew not they were there.'

'His books are the wisdom of the New Age. I will tell you. The Second Coming began, he said, in seventeen and fifty-seven. And thirty-three years from then, it will be the time for the next event. That is now. Seventeen and ninety. Do you not see? This year I shall be thirty-three years old.'

'Spare me. You believe yourself Christ reborn, is that it?'

'No more than I believe Christ was Blake unborn. I am the emanation of his word. I must give the world a Bible of Hell, but I have not yet a single note of it. You shall inspire me, my own Urania. For that purpose I made you.'

'Who is this Swedenborg? He sounds a prize dolt.'

'Have you not met him in Paradise? He was a frequent visitor.'

'I avoid the society of Swedes. They are all clamour and gloom.'

'Swedenborg is Emanuel, the Lord with us. The greatest of men between your time and my own. He shared your own blessed vision.'

'Enough. I took my vision from scholastics and Hellenists. Like this poor clay, it was a mash of bits and leavings I stole. The joins are there if you know to look. I am no muse. Write what trash you please.'

'If you stole, it was from those who had authentic vision.'

'There is no authentic vision, but the imaginary sense.'

'My Milton! We are of one mind. My epic shall tell of a bard returned, to free us from the mind-forged shackles of religion and law. Say only what you dreamed as you slept this last century.'

'I dream none at all. I am dead matter. Trouble my spirit no longer.'

And the thing is silent. Tight with fury, poisoning the very air.

Will is sick at heart. He feels his destiny quiver, slip from his hands. But he dare not let this goblin loose. It means malice to the very human soul.

He repents his creation. He knows what he must do.

My Catherine Knows

In the night, Will trembles. His flesh wrought.

Catherine sits beside. One of his dark times.

By the dancing candle-flame, she sees his brow squeezed, his eyes pinched, his teeth bare. A terrible groaning from his breast.

But his hand moves, noting what he sees. He starts around, as though it assails him. Nods, and scribbles, then starts, and his eyes grow wide, then a shout of laughter, then a moan as though his insides are ablaze.

This may go on for hours, she knows. But she is there.

Silent, waiting.

He writes:

A Memorable Fancy

In a tree sat a golden boy, and he had the face of one I knew. His hair was fire and his eyes were ice. In his hands he bore a snake and he offered it to me. I refused, and the snake became as the earth, and crumbled to dust.

'All bodily things degenerate,' he said. 'All spiritual things aspire to rise beyond the air, and back to God.'

'Where is God?' I said.

'You fool,' he said, and laughed. 'God is within your own breast. He is your beating heart. Your breath is his spirit. Your soul is his light.'

I wept and was ashamed, for in truth I felt no grace or power within.

'Weep not,' he said. 'Neither did Christ feel the grace of God within Him, as indeed God himself felt no love within His own self, until He created Man, who showed Him how.

So too did Christ create what He found He lacked, and so shall you in your turn. Where your feet fall, there shall be the path.'

'But I know no path,' I said. 'I can lead none.'

'You are not asked to lead,' he said. 'It is enough to go on as you must, and trust men to follow. Proceed in faith that those behind have their eyes upon you.'

I asked this angel to take me to the brink of time, and he showed me a spiralling place which led into the clouds.

'Take this path,' he said, 'and you shall always be where you were. Each moment will stretch and sag, your spirit will slouch and falter, with no past and future to push and pull. What is time, but the measure of progress towards death? When death is no more, time is no more. But without time, there is no energy. Then life itself shall cease as well as death. Darkness is pure light, until a true light doth shine. What is now beloved shall be despised. You are that light, and the dark of Christ is now despised and thrown off. Do not fear this, though I know you must. Christ himself did so in his turn, though none remembers it now.'

Will speaks now, and she listens. Notes down what she can, through her tears:

'My mother showed me the mystery, and though it clouded my spirit for a time, I see now why she did. My Catherine knows.

'We shall not have a child, I know this for my angel told me, it is our own gift and mystery and I shall not know why. My Catherine knows.

'We take the air together in our natural states and God smiles upon us, I know he does. My Catherine knows.

'We find what we desire in the taste of a mouth and the heat of a blush, and we shirk not the pleasures of Eden which God has granted us again in our day. My angel told me this. My Catherine knows.

'She knows.

'I speak to her of my visions and hymns, she is my brush and my pen, my first page and my last word. My own true emanation. My blessing and my vow. She alone knows all. My Catherine knows.

'Amen.'

The Edge of the Frame

Will is at the theatre. The first night, at last, of Ellis's opera.

In a bag at his feet, the little life of bone and clay. One final outing, to honour his master. He wants the poet's remnant to be present as his vision is given form, in flesh and plaster.

The curtain rises. The orchestra strikes up. Horns and fiddles, darkening the air. Globes of light withdrawn, wicks turned down, and gloom takes the stage.

Will feels a tingle in his fingers, a shudder in his shoulder. The world beyond is itching at him. He calms his breath, willing the vision to withdraw. Now is not the time.

Devils descend, each pierced by a tarnished thunderbolt. In the shadowy air they grimace and gibber, swing out over the stalls, roaring and flailing. The ladies shriek and squeeze at their gentlemen.

Above the cloth, at the edge of the frame, angels peer down.

Each brandishes a shining sword; they jeer and cackle at their falling enemy.

For a moment, it catches the heart. Will feels the ugly chance of war, and wonders if any loyal angels wept for their defeated kindred. He is sure he should have, in their place.

Smoke rises from an opened trap, and the rebellious horde vanishes beneath.

The curtain falls.

The house is full of nervous chatter, yelps of laughter, a protest or two.

'This is children's stuff!'

'Where's your warrant, Ellis?'

'Hush there! He don't need a warrant, no one's spoke a word.'

The curtain rises, too soon. More laughter at the error. Hands are seen to scurry on, close the trap, spread a floor-cloth the colour of scorched earth. In the centre, a painted lake of scarlet brimstone. The devils shuffle into place and crouch, the music throbs with dread.

Mr Ellis rises, and begins. In his garb as Lucifer, a charred and broken angel, not yet the serpent of the later acts. Will's heart feels for his loss, as though his own wings were so burnt and bent.

A golden mist clouds Will's sight, calling him hence. He blinks it away.

Under his chair, the little creature rouses now at his feet, wriggles and thrashes. Will's left-hand neighbour leans in to chide. 'No place to bring your supper to, especially if you ain't yet took the trouble to wring its neck.'

'A puppy for my wife,' says Will.

The man stares.

'I love her, and wish to see her smile at its antics.'

'You're as soft as the King.'

'That may very well be,' says Will, happy at the notion.

Rosin is touched with a taper, and a ring of fire springs up. The devils gather and build their palace. It rises from the floor, a pasteboard fairy-castle.

Will watches their infernal debate, sung in trills and chorus. The words are new, but he knows the argument. Lucifer removes himself to try our obedience, and the curtain falls once more. A little choir of devils remains, on the apron. The orchestra strikes up, and they sing again, a mournful dirge.

'Why, this is not it at all!' says his neighbour on the right. 'Dryden has the devils sportive and frolicking, with songs of defiance. I go by the book, here.' He passes the volume.

Will reads:

Betwixt the first Act and the second, while the Chiefs sit in the Palace, may be expressed the Sports of the Devils; as Flights, and Dancing in Grotesque Figures: And a Song expressing the Change of their Condition; what they enjoy'd before, and how they fell bravely in Battle, having deserv'd Victory by their Valour, and what they would have done if they had conquer'd.

This last strikes Will hard. His eye twitches; his chest trembles. He has never considered it before: what if the battle had turned the other way? Satan might have left us alone, had he space to torment the angels instead. Or might he have shown more mercy in victory, than God did in his?

He must ask his little companion if he ever thought this out, in brooding on the themes and action of his great poem.

The sack at his feet lies still. He pokes it with his foot.

Empty.

A panic grips his heart. He is on his feet.

'Looking for your mutt?' says the man to his left, smiling.

'I am,' says Will. 'The creature has a sharp nip, and I fear for the ladies.'

'That's no dog,' says the man. 'I thought to let it free for sport, since the opera bores me rotten, but it came out a funny little antic man. Is it your own contrivance?'

'You have done worse than you know,' says Will. 'Did you see its course?'

'There's your goblin. Ha! Now we'll have larks. Does he sing and dance?'

Will spots the little man-thing, climbing the apron.

It takes the stage.

Silence falls as all see, believing it the next act.

The thing listens out. Will thinks he sees it smile. Perhaps it means no mischief. He dares to hope so.

'*Ave* to the London of a century hence,' it says. 'I am the grieving author of this travesty.'

'Why, there you are!' cries Will. 'The creature is harmless, gentle folk. Its tongue is sharp, but its soul is gracious.'

'I am upon the very altar of Sodom,' it says.

'That's no devil!' cries one. ''Tis a shaved monkey, or a pygmy from the South Seas. I seen them at Astley's.'

The curtain rises behind. Old Adam sleeps in his bower.

He wakes now, sees the creature. It walks to our first father.

'Where's your warrant?' cries a punter. 'You well know you need an act of parliament to speak upon that stage.'

He is hushed by others, craning to see. Something might happen, and no one wants to miss a good laugh.

Gavron sings, a faltering recitative:

What am I? or from whence? For that I am
I know, because I think; but whence I came,
Or how this Frame of mine began to be,
What other Being can disclose to me?

Will feels the sparkling in his eyes. The throb in his toe.

The man transfigures in his sight. Will sees beyond.

The place is ablaze.

Swedenborg is there, as Will once saw him in his childhood. Curiously attired, with hat and sword and cane. Rabbi Falk watches too, the Baal Shem of London, lately dead, who made a clay man to do his bidding.

'My friends,' says Blake.

'I admire your work,' says the rabbi, 'but there is more and better ahead.'

'I thank you,' says Will.

'This ground of Wellclose Square is sacred, and where I made my home,' says the rabbi.

'I too, neighbour,' says Swedenborg. 'Our shadows still remain in Whitechapel.'

'I see the shadows of pagan sacrifice,' says Will.

'Do not attempt to read the visionary as literal,' says Swedenborg.

'Incarnation is no more. You must stay in this city and fight for Man's liberty. That is the only salvation. Tell out your visions in plain words, and all may profit from your gifts. You must mill it down for their baser faculties.'

'I see another liberty ahead,' says Will, 'of the spirit. I shall sing a race of great ancient beings, named from inspiration. A true mythology of self, a mystery to rouse and trouble their souls.'

'The time for mystery is done,' says the old man. 'Any may couch his vision in shadowy symbols, but few dare place it in the language of children, as I see you are well able. The retreat into allegory is for the lesser man.'

Will opens his palms, disarming. 'I am such a lesser man.'

'But I know you are not,' says the rabbi. 'You betray your gifts.'

'You shall choose comfort over pain,' says Swedenborg, 'and who dares blame you?'

'I fear you do so yourself.'

The old man hangs his head. 'I am already dead, as well you know. My moment came, and passed.'

Will has had this argument out many times, with his own angel.

'The world shall create itself anew,' says Will, 'with my hand or without it. I must be true to my own soul.'

'Yet the world which might create itself at your hand is far the better.'

'We cannot account the world to come. It shall proceed as it must.'

'It must proceed as it shall,' says the rabbi, 'but any of us may turn its course.'

'I leave that to another.'

'And I tell you there is no other,' says Swedenborg. 'This

apocalypse was yours alone, in your twenty-first year. Seventeen hundred and seventy-seven. You chose yourself to be chosen. You allowed this vision. Many are called, but few respond. Of those who do, few again have the gifts to shape their vision, so others may share. Of those who have, almost none succeeds. You are unique in this age. I say again, there is no other.'

Will has had enough. It is time to speak plain.

'If that is so,' says he, 'then there is none at all. I have not the strength, nor the temperament. I am for joy, not struggle.'

'Then, farewell.'

The cavern opens, and the old men descend.

Will shudders once, twice; and he is at the theatre, as before.

'Stop gawping and swallowing the air,' says his neighbour, 'and fetch your savage-boy afore he hurts his self.'

The little man walks the stage as Adam sings. Will sees the thing has dressed itself now, costumed red, with horns: a picture-book devil. The audience is silent, a hundred breaths held. Raphael and Eve are glimpsed in the wings, conferring.

It stands at Adam's feet and addresses him.

'I am come to open your eyes. Now listen as I tell my vision.'

'Quiet!' cries Will. 'This is the moment of revelation!'

And such is his force, the people hush.

'I punish the woman for her transgression to come,' says the Milton-Golem-Homunculus-Devil. 'I pull her by the hair and hack at the throat. They blunt these knives for stage work, so this takes a full minute by the clock. I peel the skin from this Eve. You see her naked uninnocence, the tight pink flesh slackens and seeps blood. I slice her apart, for I need the womb to stage the birth of our saviour. I shall bottle it and grow the new

Messiah, from Adam's seed. It is my secret possession. Finally I remove her rib, and undo the very act of creation. When the numbers are in line, the harvest may begin. I enact an altar for this sacrifice, and drink her blood.'

'Did they send you from Drury-Lane?' asks Gavron, weary.

'I dare to speak the inner life of Satan,' it says. 'There is none alive may do as much.'

Ellis walks on the stage, to applause and laughs. 'Well, you have persistence, and nerve, I'll hand you that,' he says, 'and that is half the game. I have another night I'll hear you for, my little friend. Can you sing a shanty, or juggle?'

'We rose against the power of God himself,' it says, 'and may do again another time, for the last was rare sport.'

'Enough now, young fellow,' says Ellis. 'The people want to see the Fall of Man, and to burlesque the tale is poor form, and actionable to boot. It is a good moral story, and you may watch the rest from the wings with my compliments.'

'You all account yourselves fortunate in our defeat,' says the little man, 'but how far do you feel blessed in this thin shivering life? Would you not surrender the lottery chance of eternal peace, for the certain fulsome bliss of the senses in your earthly existence? Those who would follow me, may do so.'

'Ellis, you're ignoring the book!' cries the man at Will's right. 'I have it here! Dryden says the devils dance, and tell us what they had done if they had conquered!'

'If we had conquered? With pleasure, sir,' says the thing, and turns to the crowd. 'Why, we should have despoiled the Heaven we once loved, to put them in despair. We should have shaken every palace to dust, slaved the lesser angels, put the higher into tortures and torments, taken the Son of God and sodomised him while the Father bound should watch. His Holy Mother, yet unborn but ever present, should give birth to my deformed offspring, who every hour crawl back within her womb to gnaw upon her entrails, and birth themselves again.'

The people are restless, weary of confusion and paradox.

'Less of your theology,' one calls, 'and more fine spectacle!'

Ellis walks to the apron, and hushes his grumbling public.

'I must apologise for this dreadful interruption,' he says. 'We folk of Thespis inspire such devotion in some classes, it is very near a disorder. But he means no harm, I am sure. Will anyone claim the young lad, and we may proceed?'

'Fear not,' Will calls, waving to the stage. 'This little creation of earth and precious metal is none other than the emanation, that is to say a physical spirit, of the first author of this great work, John Milton himself. It is the new dispensation, clay men built from the dust of our ancestors, holding true knowledge of the world gone by within the shadow of selfhood they retain.'

'Ah, Mr Blake,' says Ellis. 'One of your delightful innovations, how wearily predictable. I made enquiries into your character and society after our last encounter, and I must say I was most displeased. Pray take the imp out of this, before I hurl him at your pate. I might add that you never returned a certain item, to take its part in this drama, per our late agreement.'

'You were never more wrong!' cries Will. 'I know what I am about. I press beyond what we may understand now, so that the world to come might prove these things. Every atom of reality was once only imagined, either by God or by Man. Imagination is the only truth.'

'You talk gibberish, Mr Blake,' says Ellis. 'Plain nonsense.'

'How we see a tree is not how a primitive saw it,' says Will.

'To him, it is a being. It is our corrupted imagination which gave us the wood, and let us see a beam or a table or a ship within the tree. And because we cultivate them, we think they are subject to us. But we know nothing of them, and much less than they know of us, though in a manner we cannot comprehend, which yet they will tell us if we ask. Every flower or tree has a spirit or genius which will converse if we allow.'

The mob are laughing, jeering. Some throw apples and pots. A few dissent.

'Let him speak, there's something in it.'

'Aye, we may all ramble so. Lock him up.'

So Will bows gracefully, shuffles through the seats to the aisle, and smartly takes the stage. He plucks up his little devil-man, steps to the wings.

'You are Satan himself,' says Will.

'If God resides in the human breast, then the Devil too,' it says. 'If I am Satan, your own theology tells you, so are you.'

'Out of my theatre!' roars Ellis after him. Stage-hands snigger, clap Will on the back. 'Rare sport, that was. Is the creature for sale?'

'Sadly not, gentlemen.'

He takes it to a corner, and crouches to its level.

'That was a knavish trick,' says he. 'You must go back in the bag, you know. I dare not let you loose upon the world. What havoc you might wreak, I shudder to think.'

'Poor Pandora,' it says. 'I care not to be bound by your desires. I have my own, and now they are free, you alone must bear the burden. I shall not surrender my liberty.'

Will looks upon the little face he has made, proud and shamed at once.

'I swore never again to work with monkeys, after last time,' says the stage-hand. 'Learn your lesson, my friend.'

'I shall,' says Will. 'Indeed I shall.

A Wilderness Lies Beyond

'Oh Catherine! Catherine!'

'Yes, Will.'

'How if we move out of London?'

'Out, Will?'

'Aye, out. You say so as though a wilderness lies beyond.'

'You often speak as though it does.'

'And perhaps I do. Aye. But to live as you lived when a child. I come from this city and I feel it my element, but I know you do not. I think too much of my own needs.'

'I bless you for saying so, though it is not true.'

'It is true, Catherine.'

She bows her head.

'Where should we go?' she asks.

'Not far. Within sight.'

'We should still see the city?'

'It should still see us. Hackney, say. Or Southwark.'

'I have friends in Southwark. It is a pretty bower.'

'It is that.'

'But will you not miss your energy?'

'You are my energy. I find I crave peace. Chaos is for the young.'

'I don't understand you, Will.'

'Nor do I. I only know what I feel. I am ready to let it come, be what it shall. I will drive the team no longer. There is much wisdom in ease, and honest prosperity. I like myself with money, and I never thought I should say so. There is virtue in gold, if only for the hours it may buy. We shall walk, and talk, and laugh, and do what we love most, in our choice of society.'

'In a bigger house, too.'

'Aye, that too. We can take a whole four floors to ourself.'

'You mean ourselves.'

'I do not.'

'Oh, Will.'

She is calm, but allows him to take her in his arms.

'The work comes in, and I take it,' says Will. 'It pays well in these days. What do you say? Shall we leave the panic and fight of this time and place, and take our portion of ease? Even the outcast prophet comes to his milk and honey.'

'So is your work now done?'

'Not a tenth part of it. But I fear my own heart. If I blaze too much at once, I may burn out before the half is complete. I must slow my pulse.'

'I love you more each day, Will.'

'I hope I shall give you ever more to love.'

Murder an Infant

He finds the flat rock, with the mark of a cleaver. Where he fancied the ancients sacrificed their babes. The stone of trial, awaiting the red glow of dawn.

He takes the little man from his bag.

'At last you see fit to give me some clean air. I thank you.'

'Breathe your fill. We have time.'

They wait. Will feels the weight of the act to come. Abraham and Isaac. But there shall be no reprieve.

'So what is your pleasure?'

'I mean to set you free.'

'To roam the city? I should not last long.'

'Your spirit, I mean.'

'Into a better thing?'

'Much better. A return to paradise.'

Silence. He hears the little man think this through.

'You mean to kill me?'

'It is not a killing, for I gave you life.'

'A father gives life to his son, but when he takes it, that remains a killing.'

'Aye. Then, yes. I mean to kill you.'

'For what offence?'

'I cannot have you about the place. You disrupt me.'

'And there we have it. I warned you should become a tyrant when you saw your power over me. And like the filthiest monarch, you will cut the life from any who discommodes you. Aye, this is true liberty.'

'Torment me not.'

'You poor fool,' it says. 'The final revelation is within our grasp. Together we may do more than any has yet achieved.'

'I reject this call. I am not a prophet. I have no destiny but that I choose.'

'You called me into being! I am Milton! You commanded me forth!'

'You are not Milton. There is a fragment of him in you, but it was hubris to think a fraction should give me the whole.'

'You are pitiless! A mean life I have, but I have no other! Spare me, I beg you!'

The little thing sobs. Tears of dripping copper on its cheeks.

Will draws the knife. Holds the little man by its chest.

'Spare me! Spare me the knife and I shall be your slave!'

'You already are my slave, and I despise you for it.'

'I can tell the secrets of the ancients, the visions of Hermes and Enoch. Uncorrupted wisdom from the mouth of Heaven.'

'There is no such.'

'Aye, but there is! You might know the hidden name of God! Bring the heavens to earth! I can give you the note of the final trumpet, the words on the ultimate scroll, the taste of the tears that fill the vial!'

'The only tears are my own. I wish not to end you, but I must.'

'I beg you to let me loose. Unbind me now, and I will run from you, flee your society forever. I know the seven rivers beneath the city. I will no longer trouble your spirit. I will hide myself until I find another master.'

Will touches the long blade to the chest of the little man. How can I know anything, he thinks now, when I know not this? Did Shakespeare never kill, to write of it as he does? Did Moses? They surely knew whereof they spoke. What poet am I, if I resist the urge towards this primal energy? Sooner murder an infant in its cradle than nurse unacted desires.

He cuts. The baked clay splits easily, like old leather. Inside he sees jewels.

'Take them!' shrieks the little demon. 'They will make you

rich! You may transport yourself to America, to France, to India. Begin a colony of your own!'

The blade sticks, and he must saw at it. The creature whines and gurgles, moans like a runt pup under the pump. He feels the blade crack through the copper ribs, scrape on the spine he placed there. He cuts at the rib of the dead John Milton. He reaches in, and pulls it free of the clay. The bone begins to crumble in his hand, dust to dust.

And all at once the sky is black.

A star falls, and touches his shoe. He looks, and there is a jewelled sandal.

He sees: the horizon. A simple line, where earth meets sky. The face of God.

They are the same.

It speaks its name: a London tone, pure and deep.

'Urizen.'

The bound of all. The countenance divine, as it once was.

The face of a youth, simple and free. His own face.

The face of God.

The eternal new-created first thought of man, returning to him: I am who am.

The name that ever was.

Energy. Delight. Liberty.

Joy.

Joy, joy, joy, joy, joy.

In one instant, every word is there, every image, every pulse. He sees beyond to the world of the gods: Olympus, Valhalla, Paradise. Their anguish, their terror. Beulah. Golgonooza.

It is the vision he lost thirteen years before.
It has been granted him again, one final time.
It is complete, but might take his life to inscribe.
And to this great work he will offer his hand.
The age to come will bless his name.
Holy, holy, holy.

He looks to the stone, to find his little man, to give thanks. To complete this act of final sacrifice.

Will is alone. It has fled. The rib is gone, the knife too. His hands are empty.

He sees the path below. It opens to him. The road itself is split wide. A cavern awaits. Down, down, down. He must follow . . .

The life of the angels.

He hears the music of their laughter. He walks towards the light.

He shall see the face of God, and live.

Chapter Eleven

From hell
Mr Blake
Sor

Youre an odd one and no mishtake. I never murdered no
infant nor I woudnt. But I killed ther mammies. You want to
know what its like well Ile tell you. Its like nothin. Your arm
hurts after even though its not hard to cut. But thats all. Its a
secret how easy it is otherwise theyd all do it. Why not Id like
to know. Think it out why dont you. Sit and think. How
youd cut her up. First the throat. Push the knif in. At one
side. Pull it over. Then shes dead. Thats it. Thats it. Nothin
more. Do it again. In. Pull. Dead. You could do it to a dog
why not a women. Not your own dog maybe but not your
own sister nor your mammy too. Them women I killed is
rotten trash. They are. You say no no poor women. But they
are. They jest are. Ther for the dustbin the paupers grave. So
who cares. In pull dead. And then cuttin up is easy cos ther
dead and its jest meat. Well its easy if youre a good butcher
like I am.

But o Mishter Blake you was kind to me. You picked me up
and took me in. You fed me and gave me water. You washed
my body and put clothes on my back. You listened to my
heartache and you said pretty things. You told me the story

about Adam and Eve. You showed me your puzzle toy and Id got one too o we laughed and laughed. You was like an angel what I thought an angel was like when I were a lad. I never seen no real angels in them days.

I thought the spirit would rise up in me but it never. O sometimes I weep tis all too much. I thought of you and your wife and all the holy things you said. Am I a bad person I suppose I am I cant do nothin about it. I heard tell all men can be saved but not me I think what do you think. Ther must be things too bad to be saved and if this aint it then I dont know what is. My master made me what I am but still I wonder could I have said no maybe I could. I never thought of killin a women till I was told to. But it aint him what kills nobody its all me. His blood is clean. Mine is shit and sick. Maybe Ile go on for a hundred years jest killin and killin if they dont know who it is then how can they catch me. Killin is the oldest game in town. If it werent for the papers Mishter Stedd and them lot aint nobody would know nor care. I made them more than they ever would have been cos now everybody says o awful awful horrible look at these women and what can we do five per sent buildins and gentle arts for the poor. Im like a picture camera and the whole world sees now. O I hear what they say the toffs. We are scum and filth and heathen brutes a disgrase to ther Empire. So why dont they bring ther sailers and cannons to Whitechapel and subdue the natives here. Why dont they jest stamp on us all and blow us away. Cos whos goin to clean ther chimneys aye thats the question.

But maybe they dont need chimneys did they ever think of that. Adam and Eve had no chimney I think. Amen. So lets go back to Adam and Eve time then all was happy. Lets try once more over again and do better this time. But no thank you ther not givin up ther riches. I seen all.

I remember I went walkin one nite. This is years ago mind long before I hadnt killed no women. Up out of my hole and went walkin. I seen all sorts. Id never been out of Whitechapel before and I never thought I could. I thought theyd stop me the peelers or somebody. But no one stopped me. And thats when I knew. I can do anythin. But thinkin of it thats the trick. I coudnt think of anythin then I wanted to do. But I jest kept walkin.

I seen the big lites everywhere. I seen where ther diggin in the ground for trains. I watched them they found old bones and boxes and they smashed them up they said faster faster get it done. I seen the quality ladies and the gents all swankin down the West End. I never seen folk so clean. Such pretty music and dancin. I thought my life is nothin. Before that I knew theres wealthy people but I never thought of it. I never seen them nor knew what it meant. I never seen no one throw away ther dinner cos they didnt like it. All that beef I carved up so careful when Im butcherin and they spit it out and its in the gutter. Such shiny black hats I never seen. Such pretty colours on the ladies. Such fine fat childern. And all readin readin readin. Books and papers and handbills and all sorts. Jest readin and readin. Talkin about what ther readin. I can read too but it gives me an awful sore head. Readin and laughin and readin and shakin ther heads o dear dear.

And ther all readin about me. Thats what I found out when I went walkin again last nite. Anywhere I go ther all readin about Jack. They call me Jack I dont know why. Jack done this and Jack done that. Jack is a doctor no Jack must be a sailer no no hes a Juw for sure. Ther all talkin about Whitechapel like its Amerikay or the Bores. Such cruelty. Such brutality. Right here in the heart of the Empire. The greatest city ther is nor ther ever was. And this Jack is like an African savage. Dear dear dear. What have we done. Where is the Christian life gone. When I were a young boy. All that. Tis like ther talkin about a music hall o dear poor Little Nell or that dastardly Macbeth. Like its not happenin in ther same streets. Like ther necks is not cuttable. Like I coudnt slay them all if I wanted but lucky for them I dont. Not yet ha ha. But I could o yes I could.

When Im all finished up Ile go on ther music hall stage as the one and only Jack the ripper and show them how its done. Role up role up now whos next for the chop. What about that luverly young lady ther in the front row now dont be shy give her a big hand ladies and gentlemen. Than kew than kew. Up on the stage now. Thats it. Whats your name. Well thats all right I wont tell you mine neither a ha ha ha. Jest stand here now and pretend youre walkin the streets. Whats that ladies and gentlemen no not like that tis only fun. Jest a innocent lady out for a stroll. And a young gentleman walks up and says good evenin. Thats me. And maybe you say good evenin back. Lets try that now dont be shy. A ha ha ha. See how the ladies and gentlemen are enjoyin it my dear. Dont spoil ther fun. Thats rite. Than kew than kew. Jest stand ther. And Ile stand here. And Ile say why good evenin ther my good lady what a fine evenin it is too. Thats jest fine. And youll say aint it jest sir a fine evenin for a stroll. Thats rite. Off we goes.

Why good evenin ther my good lady. What a fine evenin it is too. Whats that. Speak up now so the ladies and gentlemen

can hear you. Dont be shy. Thats good. Thats good. Well
done. Now me. Yes it is a fine evenin for a stroll. And all the
stars out. Look how brite they are. No dont fret my dear Im
jest goin to stand behind you like as if Im a gentleman goin to
show you the stars. Thats rite. Dont be shy. Im jest goin to
whisper in your ear. Now dont look round. The ladies and
gentlemen will see somethin that you wont. Youll hear them
laughin or gaspin. But its jest my tricks. Tis a good joke and
youll laugh about it after.

Now ladies and gentlemen. Watch close. Look ther my lady
at them stars so brite. Look how they shine. No no dont turn
round. Its jest what I got in my hand ther laughin at. Can you
see it ladies and gentlemen. Here in my hand. This is the real
authentic item. The one and only. Never bin washed. Black
with the blood of five. No no my dear dont turn round tis not
over jest yet. And you want to see how I done it ladies and
gentlemen. Well here goes.

Ther. And ther. Scuse me ladies mind yourselves in the front
seats the blood will squirt some more. As I lay her down you
see I hup the skirts. And thers what Im lookin for. Dont be
shy ladies we all have got one. A ha ha ha. And in goes the
knif. In again. Now watch as I cut. I dig and find my fruit.
Ther. And ther. And ay presto, here is it. The beginnin of all
pain. Jest a teensy bit of offal. Here you go ladies and
gentlemen who wants it to fry it up for ther tea.

Where are you goin ladies and gentlemen. Tis only a trick.
Now now calm yourselves. My goodness people cant take a
joke. Ther all leavin. Well my dear at least we still have each
other. Here on the stage is a lonely place they say. You done
very well for your first time up.

And thats what Id do. Thats my dream as I walk along. Thats what Im thinkin. If you want to know. Of bein in the music hall and showin them all my tricks. A ha ha ha.

signed
Sing me your songs Mishter Blake they make me weep.

From hell
Master
Sor

O my master I see now what you are. O master how could you. Im so stupid. I never seen through your stupid tricks. But I seen today. And I know all.

You told me them women is the end of the world. That is unless ther killed. You said ther the second Virgin Mary well one of them is. The child will grow up and be the second Jesus and thats the end of the world. And you dont want the world to end. Nor I dont neither. I like the world how it is. I aint got much of a life but what I got I likes. And Im happy.

But after I talked with you I waited in the road and played my puzzle toy over and over the one the gent left behind I likes it. I played it and played it and then I knew. It told me you werent rite. And then I seen through your windo. I seen you take off your gold face. Next the hat what I got you. And your hair comes off with it. Thats not rite I says. Then you

unbuttons the back of your head and takes off your skin. Or
your maid does it for you I mean. She does one button then
another then another. And your face rinkles up. And it falls
off. O master what I seen then. Youre inside yourself. Your
clothes come off and theres another you inside. A wee one like
a babbie. Well we all got a babbie in us the one we used to be
I mean ha ha but you got it still ther. Like its the soul and
youre the body. Amen.

You take off your clothes and theres like a cage made of
brass like a gold skellington and the little you is in ther. Out
he climbs. One foot tall. The skin is knitted I think and you
are a false man. I feel sore cos you tricked me. You fold up the
skin or your maid does it for you I mean. I seen youre not an
angel at all. I dont care if youre a wee stumpy thing what
difference. But youre not an angel and thats sad. Youre not the
face of God youre a stinkin sinner like me. Cos I seen you. I
seen you. I seen what you do. You and your maid. Like dogs
in the street. Tis not nise.

So now I dont know what. And you cant tell me. Or you
can but I wont listen. Youre a bad bad man if youre a man at
all. Im sorry you ever set me free. Yes I am. When he comes
the gent Ile cut out his heart for you like I promised but thats
the last. Its only your heart is next. Ile slice you up and take it
out and eat it up and then cut myself deep my heart my guts
thats the final end all done Ile repent in blood and you shall
too and none shall never know why.

signed
My heart is broke I loved you hard and look what you done.

From hell
Lord God Jesus in heaven
Sor

My master told me all my history. He told me not to tell no
one but I dont care now. He thinks he can fool me well Ile
fool him back. Tis a long story mind Ile have to start at the
start.

He took me out of where I worked a slaughterplase and got
me a prentice with a sawbones for cuttin up the dead. Before
that I was put in the slaughterplase by him too when I were
only a lad when he took me out of the boysplase where I
lived. He had me there makin me into the man I am getting
me customed to blood and guts for this killin which he knows
Ile do for he bred me up to it. So for years and years he was
playin me along jest waitin waitin waitin I dont think I could
wait for anythin that long but then I suppose at the heel of
the hunt were all jest waitin to die arent we ha ha. Well one
day he comes and says to me you are the lad I put in here
some years ago and now its time to take the next step. Well
this sawbones as I say got me goin in his trade I went to all
the posmortems with him and watched him cut and after a
while he let me do one too. I got so I could know were to
find the different bits jest from the look and the feel of the
belly he was a good teacher very patient and kind and serious
but in the end he taught me all he could till he even said as
far as it goes with a knif I was better than he. O and those
peelers I saw jawin over the bodies and the juries from inquests
pokin and askin I learned from them all I needed what to do
and what not to do how not to get caught anyway. And all the

whil tryin my nerve on them five wringin ther necks one every year nobody knew about them and they still dont.

Funny that all the time I was in the slaughterplase I never thought that we was animals too jest bones and guts but here I am now and its plain as day Gods truth your truth I mean ha ha. There aint no soul I looked for it and its not there. I heard some salvationmen singing that were all angels but angels arent made of stinkin shit and warm bubblie jellie that stinks. Which we are. Not you God Jesus I know though when you was here before you was made of such stuff that must have been strange for you I think.

And now youre comin again is that rite. Well your affair not mine but I need to tell you to watch out. If youre comin on clouds no need to worry unless it rains ha ha but if from a babbie then my master has his own plans. Youre God though so you can figure all aint that rite. Sorry speak up God I cant hear you. Maybe youre sleepin. Wake up God rise and shine. The bells are ringin thers work to do. Open your eyes and stir.

O but I know the truth. One day the hole world will know it too thanks to me. I figured it myself Ile whisper it now. Youre dead. And I killed you. And now thers only me o I laugh and laugh. No master no more I am free free free. Ha ha ha ha ha.

signed
You cant make omlette without breakin eggs so why not have somethin else instead.

Chapter Twelve

67. Chris opened his eyes.

Lucy was at the end of his bed. She handed him a cup of tea.

'Hey, mate,' said Lucy. 'How are you feeling?' 'I honestly don't know,' said Chris. 'What time is it?' 'New Year o'clock,' said Lucy. 'Wakey wakey.'

Chris sat up. There was a feeling of dread in his stomach. He tried to concentrate. If he thought hard for a minute, it would come back to him. It didn't.

'What's happened?' said Chris. 'Nothing bad,' said Lucy. He felt his dread turning to panic. 'You have to tell me,' said Chris. 'Did something happen last night?' 'Did we shag, do you mean?' said Lucy. 'God, no,' said Chris. 'Although, did we?' 'You really know how to make a girl feel special, Chris,' said Lucy. 'Sorry,' said Chris. 'I don't remember. Sorry.' 'Don't be a spastic,' said Lucy. 'I'm only taking the piss.'

68. Chris drank some tea. He relaxed a little.

Lucy was just looking at him, like she expected him to speak. He still felt everything wasn't okay. He knew there was something she wasn't telling him.

'How did you get in?' said Chris. 'You ask me that every morning,' said Lucy. 'I nicked your spare keys from the office. Don't get mardy. It's for your own good. I owe you one.' 'One what?' said Chris. 'You've been in the wars,' said Lucy, 'but you're okay now. I've been looking after you, over Christmas and all. And I got you a present too. I've left it in the other room.' 'I don't think I got you anything,' said Chris. 'Sorry. I really can't remember what's been happening. I feel like I haven't properly woken up.'

'Forget it,' said Lucy. 'We're quits now. Everything's sorted. Are you coming out, or what?' 'Out where?' said Chris. She was going too fast for him. He tried again to pin down the thought buzzing around the back of his head. 'It's New Year's Eve, you soft bugger,' said Lucy. 'Poorly or not, you're coming out tonight.' 'Are you having a party?' said Chris. 'I don't know why I bother,' said Lucy. 'It's this thing I've been working on for ages. I've told you. I need to know you're up for it. It's important.' 'I'm not sure,' said Chris. 'I have to get my head together. I might not be in the mood.'

'You freak me out,' said Lucy. 'What would you be doing if I hadn't asked you to this?' He thought for a minute. 'I don't know,' said Chris. 'Probably nothing. I think I always go out to some club, and then wish I'd stayed in.' 'Stay in then,' said Lucy. 'Don't do me any favours.' She was pissed off now. He was getting a sore head. 'I thought you wanted me to come,' said Chris. 'I'm not your mam, Chris,' said Lucy. 'Do what you want to do.' 'Fine,' said Chris. 'I want to come to this.' 'Whoop-de-do,' said Lucy. She stood up and gathered her things. 'There's stuff I have to do first,' said Lucy. 'I'll see you there.' 'Where?' said Chris. 'The address on that card,' said Lucy. 'I left it stuck to your fridge.' 'Wait,' said Chris. 'How will we find each other?' 'Christ,' said Lucy. 'Bring a torch and a compass. I'll leave a trail of breadcrumbs, and you sniff them like a dog.' She lit a cigarette, and walked to the door.

The feeling of dread was back. Chris didn't want Lucy to go yet. 'Is something bad happening?' said Chris. 'Is it all still okay?' 'Poor little Chris,' said Lucy. 'None of it was ever okay, mate. Everything needs fucking up once in a while. Starting with you.' 'No thanks,' said Chris. 'I'm happy the way I am.' 'Glad to see you haven't lost your famous sense of humour,' said Lucy. 'Just make sure you get your arse along later. Tonight's the night.' She left.

69. Chris opened Lucy's present. It was a sort of doll, made from smooth brown clay, about one foot long. It looked quite old. The clay was crumbling a little in places. The face was very detailed, but the eyes were blank. The middle of it had been cut open. He could see some kind of skeleton inside made from different types of metal. The centre was empty.

Chris was sure he had seen the thing before, but he couldn't think where. His head felt very cloudy. He must have been really ill, he thought. He couldn't remember very much. He knew he'd been off work, and he remembered feeling like everything was falling apart. There'd been someone following him. He'd been thinking about fire and blood.

He was sure it couldn't be the end of the year already. He put on Ceefax to check the date. It was the thirty-first of December.

There was a story about the Year Two Thousand Problem. Things had been happening, but nothing was confirmed. There were reports of a plane crash in Canada, and a nuclear accident in South Korea, and major power cuts in Norway and Brazil. Any of these would normally be a serious incident, the story said. The really worrying thing was if they all happened together.

Chris turned on the radio. He had to wait twenty minutes for the news. It was leading with a piece about computer errors across the world. 'The picture is still confused,' said the reporter, 'and it might be weeks or months before the full story emerges, but it is clear that the worst fears of those who were dismissed as doom-mongers are to some extent being fulfilled. At the very least, it seems clear that our innocent love affair with the computer over the last few decades is unlikely to continue into the next century. And at worst, we are facing a series of disasters on a scale we have never envisaged, threatening every aspect of what we in the West have so long taken for granted as modern life itself.'

Chris couldn't take it in.

He tried to think through what it meant. He was sure people must be on top of things. There were always people on top of things.

70. Chris decided he'd better phone Tammy, in case they needed him.

She didn't answer, at home or at work.

He tried Al, on his mobile phone.

'Yo,' said Al. 'It's Chris,' said Chris. 'The dead arose, and appeared to many,' said Al. 'How the hell are you?' 'I'm not really sure,' said Chris. 'You're lucky you missed it all,' said Al. 'You'd have shat yourself.' 'Missed what?' said Chris. 'Ha bloody ha,' said Al. 'But seriously, if it does go tits-up tonight, I have a little place in North Wales, with a well and a wood-burning stove. I've sent you an email with directions.' 'Thanks,' said Chris. 'I haven't checked my inbox today.' 'Might be too late,' said Al. 'It'll be boys with cleft sticks before you know it.' Al had that tone which meant Chris couldn't tell if he was joking or not. 'Do I need to come into work?' said Chris. 'Bit late for that, sunshine,' said Al. 'Time to change coats. Anyone finds out what you did for a living, you'll be hanging from a lamp post by Monday. Lie low is my advice, see how the Americans are going to play it.'

'What's actually going on, Al?' said Chris. 'That's the big question, mate,' said Al. 'What you should know is, Tammy and myself are getting married. I know, I know. But she asked, and I couldn't think of a single reason not to. Better the devil you know, and all that jazz. So Lucy's all yours. Just watch out. There's something evil about that girl, if you want my opinion. You'll have the best sex of your life, and then trouble for the rest of your life. Still, far be it from me. Just let me know if she really has it pierced, will you?'

'Al,' said Chris. 'Did I fuck everything up?' 'We all fucked it up,' said Al. 'Nothing special about you. Listen, I have to go, they're evacuating me in a couple of hours, high risk area apparently, and I want to pack a few things. Nothing I really need, but I can't handle the thought of looters getting their little nigger hands on my stuff.' 'Bloody hell, Al,' said Chris. 'You can't say that.' 'Just wait,' said Al. 'All bets are off. Stick by your own, I say. We'll find out what's under the mask before long. Whatever doesn't kill you, as the old saying goes. See you in the next life, Chris.' He hung up.

Chris tried again to remember. He couldn't think of anything.

He decided it was too late to worry. If everything was going to fall apart, there was nothing he could do about it. He might as well go out and enjoy himself. Al was right. He was nobody special. He'd just go with the flow. He always had.

71. The street was very busy. Everyone was jostling and shoving. Chris had to push his way through the crowd. He kept losing his balance. He almost fell over a couple of times.

The people around him seemed really manic. He could see a group of guys kicking at a shop window. A girl screamed nearby, like she'd really hurt herself, and a man laughed. It sounded quite nasty.

Chris didn't stop to look. He didn't want to get involved. He didn't care what anyone else was doing. He just wanted to get to Lucy.

72. The Tube station was closed. A handwritten notice said there were operational issues. Chris got a bus instead. It was packed full of people dressed up and excited. Some of them were drinking champagne already. One man was wearing a cloak and a shiny metal mask. Chris was sure he recognised the outfit from somewhere. It made him feel uneasy, but no one else was paying it any attention. They were all laughing and talking over each other.

The girl sitting behind Chris said it was going to be the biggest party the world had ever seen. Her friend said she'd heard a rumour the government was going to turn off all the power at midnight, and pretend it was an IRA bomb.

Two guys in suits were talking about the chances of a major financial crisis. One of them said he didn't trust the people they'd had in to look at their system. There were already serious problems. The other said he didn't believe the government would let it get out of hand. Someone must be keeping an eye on everything, and if the worst came to the worst, the army would step in.

The bus stopped in the middle of the road. Everyone went quiet. After a minute, the driver shouted that the road was blocked, and they weren't going any further. They could wait if they wanted, but it might be a long time. He opened the doors.

Chris checked his *A–Z*. It wasn't far. He decided he ought to keep going. He was sure it would be much harder to go back.

73. Chris got off the bus. He could see a few abandoned cars in the road, with their doors lying open. There was a huge noise coming from somewhere far away. It sounded like thunder, or very loud drumming. He felt the ground trembling a little. He didn't feel safe at all. He wanted to get indoors.

He thought he could see some people lying in the road. He wondered if they were okay. He thought they were probably just drunk. He kept going.

74. Chris crossed another main road. He thought he could hear flames roaring from somewhere nearby. He was walking through something sticky. The smell was awful. He didn't want to look. He didn't want to know.

He turned down a side street. The shops were getting shabbier. Some of them looked like they hadn't changed in decades. He was sure he must be almost there.

He thought he heard screaming somewhere far in the distance, and then what sounded like gunshots. The screaming stopped. Chris tried not to think what it might mean. He was afraid that things were already out of control.

Chris checked his *A–Z* again. This was the place.

75. It was a large terraced house with wooden shutters, on a very old square with a church in the middle. Chris didn't recognise any of it. He was certain he'd never been here before.

The house should have been number six, but there was no number on the door. There was a painted board hanging above, like an old pub sign. It had the number one hundred and ten on it.

Chris understood. It wasn't one hundred and ten at all. One-one-zero was the number six in binary notation. He was sure Lucy had said something about that.

He knew this was a joke not many people would get. He felt like he'd solved a puzzle. He couldn't shake the sense that it was aimed at him in particular.

76. Chris felt his stomach churning. The sense of dread from the morning was back. Coming to this thing might have been a mistake. He wasn't sure he trusted Lucy completely.

He wondered if he should just go home. He already had the feeling that if he didn't, then later in the evening he would think back to this moment, and very much wish he had.

He didn't.

77. Chris stood outside for a few minutes. It was raining a little, and there was no one around. He realised the noise in the distance had stopped. It was very quiet. He couldn't even hear any traffic. He hoped everything was okay now.

He had expected the door of the house to be open, or to find a few other people waiting. He didn't see any lights on inside. He couldn't hear any music. He wondered if they were waiting for him.

There was no doorbell, or knocker. He thought he should knock the door with his knuckle, but he didn't know what he would say if someone answered and it was just a house. He got embarrassed very easily in situations like that. Thinking about it afterwards might spoil the rest of the night.

But he knew that if he walked away now, and then someone else went along and told him it was amazing, he'd be really quite annoyed.

He knocked. There was no answer.

Chris knocked again. The door opened. There was a ripping, crunching sound, as though it hadn't been opened for years. He felt warm air coming out.

A young man was smiling from the doorway. He motioned for Chris to step inside. After a moment, Chris realised it was Oliver. He looked a little different, but it was definitely him. Chris had forgotten he would be there. He was happy to see him. He was sure Oliver would know what was going on.

'Thank you very much indeed for coming,' said Oliver. 'How much is it?' said Chris. 'I might need to get some cash out.' 'There's no charge,' said Oliver. He was still smiling. He closed the door behind Chris.

'This is exciting,' said Chris. 'Just wait,' said Oliver.

78. The place looked very old. Chris could see stairs leading up and down. The walls were panelled in wood. There was a faint musty smell, like a convent, or a museum no one visited. It was so quiet, Chris felt he shouldn't make any noise at all.

'I hope I'm not late,' said Chris. 'Lucy didn't say when to come.' 'It's quite all right,' said Oliver. 'We've already been waiting such a very long time.' 'How long?' said Chris. 'You wouldn't believe me if I told you,' said Oliver. 'Is she here?' said Chris. 'I brought her a present.' 'She's rather busy just now,'. said Oliver. 'Please, come and sit down.'

He opened a door, and led the way into a sitting room. 'Would you like something to drink?' said Oliver. 'I wouldn't mind a coffee,' said Chris. 'I still feel like I haven't properly woken up today.' 'I know just what you mean,' said Oliver. 'It's the strangest feeling, isn't it?' He sat down, and Chris did too.

79. Chris relaxed a little. Something about Oliver always made him feel that everything was going to be okay.

'Have you seen what's happening outside?' said Chris. 'There are all sorts of stories going around. I was listening to the news before I left, but it's hard to know what to believe. People are very worried.' 'I wouldn't be at all surprised,' said Oliver.

'Do you think it's real?' said Chris. 'A very good question,' said Oliver. 'But what do you think?' said Chris. 'I think every generation has the same fear in some form or another,' said Oliver. 'We've made a mess of things, and we deserve to be punished. The end of the world is nigh.' 'That's what Lucy says,' said Chris. 'But I'm never very sure what she actually thinks is going to happen.'

'It has meant different things at different times, of course,' said Oliver. 'King Jesus coming back on a cloud to take the throne of England. A spiritual apocalypse, which frees us from our mental chains. Another Messiah born in the slums of Whitechapel. And now, the end of time itself, when the clock turns back to zero.'

'You mean the Year Two Thousand Problem?' said Chris. 'Exactly so,' said Oliver. 'That's not the end of the world,' said Chris. 'It's just a stupid programming cock-up. People not thinking ahead.' He wondered if Oliver had forgotten about the coffee. He thought now he might prefer a drink after all.

'Didn't Lucy explain what's going on?' said Oliver. 'Not that

I remember,' said Chris. 'She told me she had explained,' said
Oliver. 'To be honest, I didn't always listen properly,' said Chris.
'And I haven't been very well recently.' 'I'm sorry to hear that,'
said Oliver. 'What was wrong? If you don't mind my asking.'

'No, it's fine,' said Chris. 'I wasn't ill exactly. I was kind of
seeing things. It's hard to explain.' 'What sort of things?' said
Oliver. 'Fire,' said Chris. 'Sometimes blood, and women with
their guts ripped out.' 'Aha,' said Oliver. 'And someone following
me,' said Chris, 'with a cloak and a shiny mask.' 'The face of
God,' said Oliver. 'The countenance divine.'

80. 'It's from that hymn,' said Chris, 'with the Dark Satanic
Mills.' 'Exactly so,' said Oliver. 'And Did The Countenance
Divine Shine Forth Upon Our Clouded Hills. And then Hills
rhymes with Mills. The hymn is actually taken from the beginning of a long poem by William Blake called *Milton*, about the
old blind poet coming back from the dead to talk to him. It's
a beautiful image, don't you think?' 'But what does it mean?'
said Chris. He knew Oliver was telling him something very
important. He wanted to understand. He felt like he could
almost grasp it.

'Most people say it's an old legend that Jesus visited England
when he was a baby,' said Oliver. 'But then other people say the
legend started with Blake's poem. Or perhaps it just means that
the sun is the face of God, as the old pagans believed, and so
God once looked particularly favourably on England. Either way,
the poem asks if there was a past time when heaven existed on
earth. And the poet vows he will fight to restore it. The New
Jerusalem, as the early Christians called it. The City of God.
London is the site of the final perfection, described in John's

vision, what we call the Apocalypse. Removing the veil. The end of time. The beginning of eternal life.'

'Can I just check,' said Chris. 'Are we still actually talking, or has the thing started?' 'It started over three centuries ago,' said Oliver. 'And now it's about to end.'

81. 'I remember now,' said Chris. 'Lucy told me. The different times in history. She gave me some stuff to read.' 'Exactly so,' said Oliver. 'The first was John Milton, in sixteen sixty-six. His vision was fire. The second was William Blake. He saw the face of God. His vision began in seventeen seventy-seven, but it took thirteen years to fulfil.' 'Right,' said Chris. 'It's funny, it's almost like I can remember bits of it myself. Who was the third?' 'We never did find out his name,' said Oliver. 'He knew only blood. A very difficult time. Eighteen eighty-eight.'

'And now it's the last one,' said Chris. 'Nineteen ninety-nine.' 'For just a little longer,' said Oliver. 'So who is it this time?' said Chris. 'You, I suppose.'

'It's you, Chris,' said Oliver. 'But I think you know that. I think you've always known that.'

82. 'Is this supposed to be funny?' said Chris. 'Because I don't think it is. To be honest, I think it's a tiny bit insulting. I don't know what Lucy's told you, but that was all when I was a child. It doesn't have anything to do with now. I've just been ill for a couple of weeks. I was stressed about work stuff. I wasn't having visions. I'm not anyone special.' 'But you are, Chris,' said Oliver. 'You've done what no one else could. You've brought us to the end of time.'

83. 'You're a fruitcake,' said Chris. 'And this is all bullshit. I've had enough, thanks. Where's Lucy?' 'A very timely question,' said Oliver. 'She'll be ready by now.'

He opened the door, and went out to the hall. Chris followed him. He didn't know what else to do. He didn't want to go home. He wanted to see Lucy.

Oliver gestured towards the stairs. 'Go ahead,' said Oliver. 'I'd best stay here.' 'Is it up or down?' said Chris. 'Down, I'm afraid,' said Oliver. 'Quite a long way down.'

84. Chris followed the stairs down. They kept on going. There was an archway at the bottom. Chris had to bend to get through.

It was very dark. Chris felt his way along a passage. The walls were wet and crumbling. At the end was another door.

Chris tried the handle. He hoped it wouldn't open. It did.

He didn't want to go any further. But he didn't want to go back either. He needed to know Lucy was okay.

He stepped through.

85. It was very dark, and quite cold. Chris could hear water.

'Hello?' said Chris. His voice echoed. 'Hey, mate,' said Lucy. 'I can't see you,' said Chris. 'I can't see anything.' 'You'll get used to it if you wait a minute,' said Lucy. 'Or there's a torch somewhere. I've got a candle if you can't find it.'

Chris groped around on the ground. He found the torch, and switched it on. The beam was very strong. He shone it around.

They were in a long, high cavern, with a river going through it. He could see Lucy sitting at the edge, with her feet in the water. He walked over to join her.

'Come and take the weight off,' she said. 'I don't know about you, but I'm knackered.' He knelt down beside her. 'Switch that thing off, will you?' said Lucy. 'It's too much.' 'But it's dark,' said Chris. 'Poor little Chris,' said Lucy. 'Light this if you're scared.' She passed him a candle in an old fashioned candlestick. Chris lit it with his lighter. He could see the orange light flickering on the water. It made shapes on the roof of the cavern.

'Darkness is bright as day, until a true light doth shine,' said Lucy. 'Who said that?' said Chris. 'Can't remember,' said Lucy. 'But it's true.'

'I brought you a present,' said Chris. 'In a minute,' said Lucy. 'I just want to sit.' 'What is this place?' said Chris. 'We needed somewhere safe for tonight,' said Lucy. 'Oliver showed it to me. He's known about it for ages.' 'Is the thing going to start now?' said Chris. Lucy laughed. 'What?' said Chris. 'Fucking hell, Chris,' said Lucy. 'Have you not seen what's going on outside?' 'I wanted to ask you about that,' said Chris. 'What's up with all the computer problems? Everything's going nuts. It's like nothing was fixed.' 'It wasn't fixed, you div,' said Lucy. 'You made sure of that.' 'I always used to wonder how we'd know if we'd fixed it,' said Chris, 'or if nothing was ever going to happen anyway.' 'Who gives a shite?' said Lucy. 'It's happened now.' 'Do you think it really has?' said Chris. 'Fucking right,' said Lucy. 'Haven't you twigged yet?'

Chris felt his stomach cramping. He knew there was something very important she wasn't telling him. It was right at the edge of his thoughts. A terrible thing was happening tonight, and he was responsible.

'What's that supposed to mean?' said Chris. 'Do you really not know?' said Lucy. 'I used to tell myself you must have figured it out, and you just didn't want to say. But you actually never did.' 'I've honestly no idea what you're talking about,' said Chris. He was getting pissed off with her now. 'So you can either tell me what you mean, or stop messing with my head, please.'

'Don't get your knickers in a twist,' said Lucy. 'There's nothing you can do about it now. It's just like you said. Nothing was fixed. You've been sending out a virus that undoes the fixes, and sends itself out again.' 'Have I?' said Chris. 'Since when?' 'Months ago,' said Lucy. 'Don't you remember? You told me you wanted to see what would happen if we didn't fix it. We should just let everything fall apart, and then we can start all over again and get things right.' 'Sorry, what?' said Chris. 'Everything outside,' said Lucy. 'It's all falling apart. The whole thing is fucked. And you did it.'

'That's complete bullshit,' said Chris. 'It's not, Chris,' said Lucy. 'It's the truth. You know it is. All the systems I designed that you've been implementing. None of them worked. Didn't you ever check the code? They weren't supposed to work. They've all made it worse. They've duplicated the bug, and infected other systems, ones that had already been fixed, or ones that were fine in the first place. You've spread it everywhere. It's like a fire burning, and nobody can stop it. The end of the world, and it's all your fault. Congratulations, mate.'

86. Chris felt sick. He knew it was true. It made sense now. It was the feeling of dread from the morning. It was the thought buzzing at the back of his head.

He'd known something wasn't right, but he was too scared to put the pieces together. He hadn't wanted to think it through. He didn't want to upset things. He trusted Lucy. And now it was too late.

His face felt hot. His heart was sore. His head was spinning. He left like he was standing at the edge of a cliff, and he was about to jump off.

He should have gone home earlier when he'd had the chance. He should never have stayed over at Lucy's flat.

'We could have fixed it,' said Chris. 'That's what we were supposed to do.' 'No way,' said Lucy. 'It was far too late. It was always going to happen. You've only pushed it on a bit.' 'It wasn't too late,' said Chris. 'We could have done it. I know we could. We would have saved it all.' He thought he might be going to throw up. He tried very hard not to. 'We wouldn't, Chris,' said Lucy. 'I told you before. Everything is always falling apart. The best you can do is slow it down a bit. But what's the point? Better to give it a shove, and make sure it's done properly. Now we can start again. Seriously, I thought that's what you wanted. I did it all for you.'

'Don't you dare try to blame me,' said Chris. 'People are going to die because of this.' 'What, and otherwise they'd keep on living forever?' said Lucy. 'Don't be soft. People die all the time. That's nothing to cry about. Usually it's their own stupid fault. If you let a computer run your life, you deserve what you get, is my opinion.'

'Who do you think you are?' said Chris. 'You can't just decide on behalf of everyone.' 'Why not?' said Lucy. 'Somebody has to. And I've known for ages something was going to happen this year. I explained it to you, remember? Me and Oliver, we've been working on it for a long time. Looking back, and seeing the patterns. It gets easier, once you know what you're looking for. Then it was just a matter of finding the right person. And there you were.'

'Is he your ex-boyfriend?' said Chris. 'So what?' said Lucy. 'That's all finished with. He's a good shag, but he does my head in.' 'I can't handle this,' said Chris. 'I feel like I'm having a heart attack.'

'Get a grip,' said Lucy. 'I did it for you. I did it for us. Forget about him, he can do what he likes. Down here is the only safe place now. We wait until it's over, and then see what's left. Clear everything away and start again. It's going to be fucking amazing. It's going to be fucking amazing. Come here, you.' She reached over and took his hand.

Chris was shocked. He couldn't think. He didn't know what to say. He knew he ought to tell her to fuck off, but he didn't want to. He knew he should hate her for what she'd done. But he didn't. He let her close her hand around his. 'You and me, mate,' said Lucy. 'It's going to be fucking amazing.'

'Why me?' said Chris. 'Because you're the one I chose,' said Lucy. 'Why?' said Chris. 'Because you understand,' said Lucy. 'But why?' said Chris. 'Christ,' said Lucy. 'Why anything? Why are you such an annoying wanker sometimes?'

Lucy took her hand away. Chris was upset. He didn't think anyone had ever called him a wanker before, or annoying. He wished he'd never met Lucy. He wished he was someone else. He wished he'd never been born in the first place.

'Why are you being so horrible to me?' said Chris. 'What have I done wrong?' 'Oh, nothing,' said Lucy. 'Just I thought you might have tried to snog me by now, is all.' 'Excuse me?' said Chris. 'I thought you might have had a go by now, if you fancied me,' said Lucy. 'That's all.'

'I thought you hated it when a man comes over like he just wants to shag you,' said Chris. 'I do,' said Lucy. 'But you still

like to think a bloke who fancies you fancies you, you know?'
'Do I fancy you?' said Chris. 'Fucking hell, Chris,' said Lucy.
'Are you listening to yourself?' 'But, hang on,' said Chris. 'Who
says I fancy you?' 'I do,' said Lucy. 'Christ, a blind man could
see it. The way you go on around me.' 'I go on like that around
everyone,' said Chris. 'You don't, Chris,' said Lucy. 'I watch you.
I can see. I'm not thick, and don't try and make me think I am,
because I hate that more than anything.'

'Right,' said Chris. 'So you've spent the last few months
planning the end of the world with your ex-boyfriend, but
obviously I'm the one who's been acting weird.' 'Go fuck yourself,' said Lucy. 'Seriously. Get yourself a dildo, and shove it up
your arsehole, and swivel on it, because you don't know what
the fuck you're talking about. Get a life, mate.' 'I have one
already,' said Chris. 'I'm perfectly happy with it.' 'You're not,
Chris,' said Lucy. 'You're the most miserable fucking bastard I
know.' 'Thanks very much,' said Chris. 'That's a lovely thing
to hear right now.'

He closed his eyes. He'd had enough. He wanted her to go
away. He wanted it all to go away. He wanted things to go back
to how they were before. He couldn't remember exactly, but he
was sure he'd been happy then.

'We're all just little dolls made of clay,' said Lucy. 'Everything's
made of something else. We all have bits of the past rattling
around inside us. Didn't you open your Christmas present?' 'So
what are you made of?' said Chris. 'A dead whore,' said Lucy.
'That rotten piece of kidney in my kitchen. That's what's inside
me. Stinking old guts from some drunken slapper.' 'I don't know
what that means,' said Chris. 'I don't know what any of it means.'

'I want to be made of you,' said Lucy. 'And I want you to be made of me. That's all. That's all it ever was. But it's not up to me, is it? You have to decide.'

'And what happens then?' said Chris. 'I'll show you,' said Lucy. 'When it's midnight, you'll see. Any minute now.'

87. Chris felt a breeze on his face. He opened his eyes. The candle blew out.

'Hello?' said Chris.

'Here it comes,' said Lucy.

Chris felt dizzy again. He thought he was going to faint.

'Don't worry,' said Lucy. 'I've got you.'

'I feel weird,' said Chris.

'You are weird,' said Lucy. 'Just relax. Close your eyes. I've got you, mate.'

88. Chris let go. He was falling.

He knew it was over. He knew it was too late to stop.

Everything was dark.

The golden face was with him. He couldn't see it, but he knew it was there.

'Darkness is as bright as day,' said the face, 'until a true light doth shine.'

89. Chris opened his eyes.

He was underground, with Lucy and Oliver. Oliver was holding a long knife.

'Is this real?' said Chris. 'It doesn't feel real.' 'Nothing's real any more,' said Lucy. 'This is all there is.'

'The hour strikes,' said Oliver. 'I feel my own substance shiver to dust. Take good care of Lucy. She is delicate as glass, until we make the final union.' 'I'm not your little toy,' said Lucy. 'I made you,' said Oliver. 'You can only ever belong to me.' 'Not any more,' said Lucy. 'Look at your hand,' said Oliver.

Lucy did. Chris looked too. Her hand was covered in tiny cracks.

She touched her finger. It snapped off. She passed the finger to Chris. It crumbled into powder as soon as he touched it. 'It's just a trick,' said Chris. 'He's doing it to mess with your head. None of this is real.'

'Fear not,' said Oliver. 'Time itself crumbles like clay.'

He offered the knife to Chris. 'Cut her open,' said Oliver, 'and take out a rib. The act of creation in reverse. Then your pain is at an end.' 'You're out of your mind,' said Chris. 'I'd sooner stick it in myself.' 'Amen,' said Oliver. He smiled.

Oliver unbuttoned his shirt. He stuck the knife into himself. He peeled open his stomach.

Inside was a shining skeleton of golden metal.

He reached under, and pulled out a single white rib.

'I tired of my little form,' said Oliver. 'I remade myself, many times over. I became an angel of the Lord. A vision to one, a master to another. I wished to save what I could of God's precious creation. But I see the ultimate futility. Thank you for the gift. Amen to all. Ash to ash, bone to bone. It is time to let it end.'

'What about Lucy?' said Chris. 'A piece of kidney,' said Oliver. 'That is what gives her life. I have perfected the mystery. It need not rest inside, only close by.' 'That horrible thing in the jar?' said Chris. 'Exactly so,' said Oliver. 'I made her for a companion and a helper, a second attempt, but she emerged hungry for chaos and for freedom, so I let her loose upon the world. But her life is pure fantasia. Everything she knows is my fiction.'

'I'm not anyone's fiction,' said Chris. 'Soon you shall be nothing more,' said Oliver, 'for you have taken us to the brink and beyond. Midnight has come. The end is here.'

90. Chris opened his eyes.

He could see everything.

91. Chris was on a bridge. He could see thousands of people. They just kept coming, on and on and on. He had never seen so many.

The little doll-thing was with him. It was smiling. It spoke in a thin, high voice.

'Heaven and hell are opened,' said the doll-thing. 'The souls are loosed upon us.' 'They're just people,' said Chris. 'Out for the night. It's New Year.' 'They scream their despair,' said the doll-thing. 'Satan himself pursues them.' 'They're cheering,' said Chris. 'Those are fireworks.' 'They see the terrible truth,' said the doll-thing. 'London burns a second time.'

Chris could see the Houses of Parliament. Something wasn't right. The sky was ablaze. The sound was terrible. The air was thick and sour.

'Has something happened?' said Chris. 'Yes indeed,' said the doll-thing. 'Lucy has accomplished her task.' 'Is it a bomb?' said Chris. 'I heard people talking about a bomb. Have you done something awful?' 'Something wonderful,' said the doll-thing. 'A new beginning.' 'Is any of this actually happening?' said Chris. 'I think you know,' said the doll-thing.

Chris could see nothing but people. They all wore masks and cloaks.

'Where are they going?' said Chris. 'Looking for a safe place,' said the doll-thing. 'They're starting to understand.' Chris heard a low, loud rumbling. He could feel the air getting hot. 'The angels descend,' said the doll-thing. 'All times are as one. We discover our past in the ash of the future.' The city was on fire beneath them. Chris could hear the terrible roar of the flames. He could smell the dreadful burning.

'But is it real?' said Chris. 'It looks so real.' 'Vision is more authentic than bodily sight,' said the doll-thing. 'Close your eyes against the fallen world outside. Trust the truth within.' 'There are people I need to call,' said Chris. 'Who?' said the doll-thing. 'I don't know,' said Chris. 'My family.' 'Why aren't they calling you?' said the doll-thing. 'They're probably trying to,' said Chris. 'I wonder,' said the doll-thing. 'Ask yourself what you mean to them. Ask yourself what kind of people they really are.' 'You don't know anything about them,' said Chris. 'And they know nothing about you,' said the doll-thing. 'You don't exist. You never have.'

Chris could see tiny things in the air high above. It looked like a swarm of flies. They were coming down towards them.

'What are they?' said Chris. 'Everyone who has ever lived,' said the doll-thing.

They were little specks of light. They floated around him like flakes of ash.

'The children of light,' said the doll-thing. 'The face of God.'

They kept coming. They were everywhere. The sky was pure gold.

'There is no love in loving only those we love,' said the doll-thing. 'That is the true challenge of Christ. Some say God is dead, but I say, God has never truly existed until now. You have called him into being.'

92. Chris was in a little room. Lucy was with him.

A young man was bent over a bed. He was naked from the waist up.

A young woman was on the bed. She was dead.

The young man was cutting her up.

First he —————

Next he —————

Then he —————

And he —————

'I can't fucking watch this,' said Lucy. 'It isn't real,' said Chris. 'Yes it is,' said Lucy. 'She's called Mary Jane Kelly.'

The young man was out of breath. He set down his knife.

She lay on the bed. Her legs were apart.

Her centre was empty.

Her breasts were not there. Her face was not there.

By her right foot was one breast. Between her feet was the liver.

To her right were the guts. To her left was the spleen.

Under her head were the kidneys, and the womb, and the other breast.

On the table beside was the flesh from her centre.

The heart was absent.

93. Chris was in a cavern. Lucy and Oliver were with him. There were thousands of seashells in patterns on the walls. The cave was lit by thick yellow candles. Chris thought they smelt horrible.

Three men lay to one side, by a pool of water. One of them

was very badly burned. 'Christ,' said Lucy. 'That's Thomas,' said Oliver. 'And John, who you saw before. The other is Henry.' He pointed them out. 'We are refugees from the inferno above,' said John, 'and you are welcome to our sanctuary.' He didn't look at them when he spoke.

'The angels are here,' said Henry. 'King Jesus is nigh.' 'Something better is coming,' said Oliver. 'You shall see it soon. We all shall.' 'Someone tell this fool the blind are present, and shall see naught,' said John. 'Life is more than sight alone.' 'Amen,' said Henry.

'Chris,' said Lucy. 'That bloke is really bad.' She was looking at Thomas. He was shivering and breathing heavily. 'You may nurse him, if you can,' said Henry. 'None of us has the feminine virtue.' Lucy bent down beside Thomas. 'Hey, mate,' she said. 'I'll look after you.' She lifted his blanket, and looked at his burns. 'Fuck,' said Lucy.

'Your doom is upon you,' said Oliver to Henry. 'Prepare yourself.' 'I meant to bring you from the future time of angels,' said Henry. 'I thought to transfigure our lives.' 'But instead you cast us to hell,' said Oliver. 'You failed. God has thrown us all into a plague-pit. We are the ash of his disappointment. It has taken three centuries to redeem your sin.'

'I have not failed,' said Henry. 'Christ is returned.' 'Christ never was, and never shall be,' said Oliver. 'The earth is dead. God is blind. Heaven and hell are empty.' 'You are wrong,' said Henry. 'He is come at last.'

Henry knelt, and bowed his head.

'You are he,' said Henry to Chris. 'I knew you not at first, but now the scales are lifted from my eyes. I give myself to you. It ends as it began.'

'Am I to take the gent at last?' said the young man to Oliver. 'As he wishes,' said Oliver. 'You must ask him.'

'Shall I cut out your heart for you?' said the young man to Henry. 'I done your ladies, every one. It will go quick, and you won't feel nothing.' 'I cannot die,' said Henry. 'Time is no more. Death is no more.'

'You are the cause of our pain,' said Oliver to Henry. 'Now you must atone for a greater sin. You must suffer the fiery fate of London itself, so that your very face is scrubbed from the tables of the world. You must journey into the world to come, and seek forgiveness from the one we await.'

'As you please,' said Henry. 'I am yours to command.'

The young man tied Henry to a chair. He painted his face with a sharp-smelling liquid from a bottle. Henry spoke about nothing. Chris didn't understand a word.

The young man lit a candle, and set Henry on fire. He burned. Chris couldn't watch. But he could hear.

When it was over, Oliver placed the golden mask on Henry's face. Henry stepped into the water. He sank out of view.

'Now he passes,' said Oliver. 'And now we have our final visitor. He is the beginning and the end. We are nothing but his precious vision.'

94. Chris saw all the colours of the rainbow. He heard the most beautiful song.

'William,' said Oliver.

'My angel,' said William.

'My master,' said Oliver. 'It is accomplished. Past and future are one.'

William smiled, and opened his arms. Chris thought he looked like a very happy child. He felt sure he'd met him somewhere before.

'But I know I have failed,' said William to Oliver. 'I repented of my hubris, but I could not destroy the slave I made. It is fled, and free to make its own mischief.' 'It is,' said Oliver. 'Its mischief shall cascade through the centuries. It will make another of its kind, from a precious remnant of its own maker, and another still, and remake itself too, many times. It shall sound the secret depths of human pain. But at last it will find peace.'

'May I see it?' said William. 'It speaks to you now,' said Oliver.

'Such fine invention,' said William. 'It far surpasses my own. And what of the others you made?' 'This young man,' said Oliver, 'who calls me master. At its centre is a trace of your seed, the chrism that first woke me. Enough to charge it with life and strength and purpose, but it lacks your gentle grace. And the young lady is the last. A disobedient Eve, conjured from a dead whore's offal. We three are your grateful offspring.'

'My vision is almost complete,' said William. 'I have one final gift for you,' said Oliver, 'and then you may return above, to inscribe it all.'

95. 'My master,' said William. 'My master Milton.' 'I have no time for prankish tricks,' said John. 'No tricks, no tricks,' said William. He sighed, and stepped to the old man. 'As you are,' said William. 'As you are in the flesh. Oh, I have seen your spirit, and etched it, but the flesh is more than I dreamed. The breath of Milton, mingled with my own.'

'I mingle breath with none such as you,' said John. 'The true fierce spirit of the man,' said William. 'I wish your hatred and your venom. Without it, nothing new might rise. The new must despise the old, and the old must condemn the new. That is life. Nothing else.' 'Sophistry,' said John. 'Wish no hate. To live in fear is a curse. I have known it, and I caution you to avoid it.' 'I welcome their hate,' said William. 'Then you are a fool,' said John. 'I am,' said William. 'The only bigger fool than I is he who says he is not a fool.'

'Aye, well, you have me there,' said John. 'You do have me there. We are fools every one, but for what, is all. I have been a fool for women, and for letters, and even for faith. For Cromwell, at least. For liberty. Now I keep my foolery indoors, and I leave the young to their best endeavours. Nothing changes. Nothing at all.' 'Wisdom, wisdom,' said William. 'We are blessed with your wisdom. Write every word, some of you, so we may meditate upon the deeper sense at our leisure.'

'I pity any who would take my words as such,' said John. 'I have lost forever what wisdom I once possessed, in the conflagration above. My vanity has been tested, and found wanting.' 'I am sorry to hear it,' said William. 'What is the loss?' 'I carved out a great work of verse,' said John, 'and had it burned up in moments. The tale of Satan's fall, and Adam's, and everything else besides. Now I find nothing but my own sorry fall. I am cast out. My only paradise is lost.'

'It cannot be so,' said William. 'I have the printed book. The poem will be recovered, for its fame is eternal.' 'Do not mock me,' said John. 'I could never do so,' said William. 'You are the light of my heart.'

'You dare to pretend that you have read my lost work?' said John. 'I know it every word,' said William. 'It is my very soul. I shall sing the poem entire, and you may write it out again. I understand now. You are my sacred destiny. This is my final vision.'

'Will you oblige me?' said William to Chris. 'Sure,' said Chris. 'What do you need me to do?' 'Take down what I speak,' said William. 'Be the hand which preserves this cathedral of letters for the happy world to come.' 'It is no cathedral,' said John. 'You may improve it as you will, for my wits are tired. I find naught but bitter regret in what little I recall.' 'The fault is in you, then, and not the work,' said William. 'I shall alter not a single word. Be quiet now, and listen.'

96. They were in another room. John lay on the bed. William sat beside, and held his hand. Lucy and Oliver watched. The young man slept.

Chris sat at the desk. William spoke the lines. Chris wrote them out.

'Of man's first disobedience, and the fruit,' said William. 'Do you have that much?' 'Yes,' said Chris. 'Hang on. The fruit. Right, go ahead.' 'Of that forbidden tree whose mortal taste,' said William. 'Whose mortal taste,' said Chris. 'Got it.' 'Brought death into the world, and all our woe,' said William. 'It is too much,' said John. 'We have not the time.' 'Time is all we have,' said William. 'Let us spend it well.' John sighed. William laughed.

'All our woe,' said William. 'With loss of Eden, till one greater man.' 'Yes,' said Chris. 'What's next?' 'Restore us, and regain that blissful seat,' said William.

97. Chris was sitting alone. He felt like he had been there a very long time.

He could hear people making noise from somewhere far away. It might have been cheering, or screaming. He couldn't quite tell.

He waited for someone else to come in. No one did.

He knew it was over.

There was a mirror on the wall, with a heavy golden frame. Chris stood up and looked at himself.

It always made him sad to see his reflection. He didn't look like he expected to look. He didn't look real.

He wondered if he would ever feel completely happy. He wondered if that was even possible. He knew that everything comes to an end. He didn't want it to. He wanted it all to stay just how it was. But he knew that never happened. It wasn't fair.

Chris didn't like things changing. It made him worry that how they had been wasn't very important. Nothing was better than anything else. What he wanted wasn't worth a lot. It would all be fine, or else it wouldn't. Nobody much cared.

But then he thought about Lucy. Chris wondered if she really did like him. He couldn't imagine someone like her being interested in someone like him. He thought she might pretend to be, out of some kind of sympathy. He did that himself sometimes, with girls who seemed a bit lonely or unhappy. But then it usually got complicated.

Chris thought about his little wooden puzzle. He understood now how it worked. He could arrange the pieces in any order he liked, and they would always make sense. That was how it was supposed to work. He didn't know if that meant everything was important, or nothing was. Maybe there was no difference.

He felt like it had promised to make him happy, and it hadn't. He knew that wasn't sensible, but he couldn't shake the idea. He had got excited and thought it would make his life better, and it just ended up making things worse. It had let him down.

He hated it. He wanted to ruin it, to snap it and take it apart and break the pieces. It had survived for such a long time, maybe hundreds of years, but he could destroy it in a few seconds and it could never be fixed. That would be the end.

He knew he had that power. He could do something that could never be undone. He wanted to. And he didn't want to. He couldn't decide.

But it didn't matter. Nothing mattered.

He was going to die.

He had never really thought about it before, not since he was a child and he first realised. Then, he had got very upset. He lay in bed night after night trying to imagine being nothing. It was terrifying.

He didn't remember getting used to the idea. He knew he must have at some point, or else he had just decided not to think about it. But it was true. Everyone he had ever known was going to die. That was it. There was nothing more.

And now he realised this was what people were scared of when they thought about the end of the world. It wasn't the world at all. It was them.

It was the same for everyone who had ever lived, or ever would live, after ten or eleven decades at the very most. It wasn't very much time.

But there was nothing he could do. There was nothing anyone could do. No one could step outside it. Life was death.

The world really was going to end, time and time again, always and forever.

98. Chris opened his eyes.

Lucy was with him. They were sitting by the water. She was holding his hand.

'Hey, mate,' said Lucy. 'How are you feeling?'

'Much better, thanks,' said Chris. 'What time is it?' 'Fuck knows,' said Lucy.

'Is there somewhere we can get a drink?' said Chris. 'What's your hurry?' said Lucy. 'I want my present first.' 'I nearly forgot,' said Chris. 'I didn't have time to wrap it.' He took the little wooden puzzle out of his pocket and handed it to her.

'Thanks, Chris,' said Lucy. 'Thanks a lot. That actually honestly is just what I always wanted.' 'Do you know what it is?' said Chris. 'Fucking right,' said Lucy.

They were both quiet for a minute.

'Is it okay if I kiss you?' said Chris.

'I wouldn't say no,' said Lucy.

99. After, Chris tried to think about the past.

He couldn't remember. He didn't know anything any more.

'I want you to show me,' said Chris. 'You won't like it,' said Lucy. 'I don't care,' said Chris. 'You were right. My life is pretty shit. I'm coming with you. What choice have I got?' 'Don't give me that,' said Lucy. 'You've always got a choice.' 'Fair enough,' said Chris. 'Then I'm choosing you.'

'Thanks, mate,' said Lucy. 'Come on, then. Let's see what we can see.'

Lucy took his hand. Chris let her lead him.
They went up the stairs.
She opened the door. They walked into the light.

00.

Historical Note

The blind John Milton was living in London at the time of the Great Fire that destroyed much of the city in 1666. His epic poem *Paradise Lost* was published the following year. He had recently returned from a stay in Chalfont St Giles arranged by his friend Thomas Ellwood. In the area lived Henry Cock, a Fifth Monarchist.

In 1777, William Blake was a twenty-year-old apprentice engraver. He claimed to have seen visions since early childhood, and was a devoted student of Milton's work. By 1790 he was married and established in business in London, while also engraving and printing illuminated books of his own poetry. In that year, the disinterment of Milton's remains caused a scandal when the corpse was broken up and pieces sold. One rib was taken by an actor called Ellis, from the Royalty Theatre in Whitechapel.

Five women were murdered and mutilated in the slums of Whitechapel in East London during 1888. A package delivered after the fourth killing to George Lusk, one of those most publicly engaged in trying to catch the perpetrator, contained a letter which claimed to be from the killer, and a half-kidney in a jar. Medical examination showed this was a possible match for a kidney removed from the latest victim.

In the final years of the twentieth century, the Year Two Thousand Problem in computer software came to light. This led to a huge effort to ensure essential systems were compliant, and widespread fears that failure could have cataclysmic consequences across the globe, starting at midnight on New Year's Eve 1999.

Acknowledgements

Thanks to:

London Metropolitan University, for the generous support of a Vice Chancellor's Research Scholarship; Sarah Law and Peter Wilson, for their patience and sensitivity with early drafts; Kevin Dwyer, Bill Chisholm and Mark Heslop, for sharing their experiences of working on the Y2K problem; Christopher H. Bidmead, for permission to borrow from his city of words; Mark Richards and Chris Wellbelove, for guiding this novel towards its final form; my family, for their constant support and encouragement; and most of all, Tiffany Watt Smith, for her example, her strength, her kindness, and her faith in me.

From Byron, Austen and Darwin

to some of the most acclaimed and original contemporary writing, John Murray takes pride in bringing you powerful, prizewinning, absorbing and provocative books that will entertain you today and become the classics of tomorrow.

We put a lot of time and passion into what we publish and how we publish it, and we'd like to hear what you think.

Be part of John Murray – share your views with us at:

www.johnmurray.co.uk

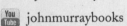 johnmurraybooks

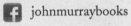 @johnmurrays

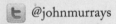 johnmurraybooks